T0129181

Pink Lips

STREBOR ON THE Streetz

ANDRE D. JONES

SBI

STREBOR BOOKS

NEW YORK LONDON TORONTO SYDNEY

Strebor Books
P.O. Box 6505
Largo, MD 20792
http://www.streborbooks.com

ISBN 978-1-59309-562-8
ISBN 978-1-4767-5662-2 (ebook)
LCCN 2013950694

First Strebor Books trade paperback edition May 2014

Cover design: www.mariondesigns.com
Cover photograph: © Keith Saunders Photos

10 9 8 7 6 5 4 3 2

Manufactured in the United States of America

For information regarding special discounts for bulk purchases,
please contact Simon & Schuster Special Sales at 1-866-506-1949
or business@simonandschuster.com

The Simon & Schuster Speakers Bureau can bring authors to your live event.
For more information or to book an event, contact the Simon & Schuster Speakers
Bureau at 1-866-248-3049 or visit our website at www.simonspeakers.com.

I dedicate this novel to my grandparents, Walter & Elizabeth Jones.
I know you two would be here if Heaven wasn't so far away.
Thank for you for everything you've ever done for me.
Keep watching as I make you proud.

Acknowledgments

First, I would like to thank God. Without him, I would be nothing.

To my agent, Joy, thank you for believing in me. Thank you for your knowledge on this business and your tips. You have helped me out with my writing skills tremendously.

To Zane, Charmaine, and the rest of the Strebor family, I would like to thank you for the opportunity. I promise I will not let you down.

To my mom, Evelyn, and my brother, Corey, I did this for you two. Nobody believes we're capable of anything but something that's mediocre or below. Every word I write is with you in mind. I'll do something for all three of us.

To my nieces, Mykalah & Jasmin, and to my nephew, Corey Jr. I love y'all with everything in me. I write for you as well to let you know that dreams can come true. Never become a victim of your environment and make sure to chase every dream you dream.

To my cousins, Lamon, Shanice, Taneisha, Sherika, Sharetta, I love y'all unconditionally. Thank you for the bonds and the encouraging words.

Keisha Yantine. My best friend. My ace. My boo thang. My ear and my shoulder. I love you, girl, and blood couldn't make us any closer. You and Khai mean so much to me. Thank you for being there.

The Past

You cannot understand who someone is
unless you get a glimpse of who they were

*S*weat poured profusely from the doctor's face as the barrel of an ice-cold 9mm pressed against his temporal bone. His nostrils flared as the smell of gunpowder danced around, lingering in the air surrounding him. The room was so silent that only the ticking from the Audemar watch snugging his wrist could be heard.

He had wished that he had gone straight home after work. He had no idea that a late-night movie to get away from his problems at home with his nagging wife and kids would be the death of him. The moment he was dragged away from the movie theater in broad daylight at gunpoint let him know that he was going to die. And the fact that no one helped him assured him of such.

"It's a girl," the doctor huffed as healthy cries boomed throughout the spacious bedroom. His heart stopped playing hopscotch as he cut the umbilical cord and laid the baby on her mother's chest. "Can I leave now?"

"No," a voice demanded from the shadows of the room.

Ernest "Rock" Evans stood up from his seat to walk over to his newborn daughter that wasn't even a few minutes old. He untied his purple label tie as the jewelry on his body shined, playing hide-and-seek with the lights in the room. The heel of his pure alligator shoes pattered as his fingers ran across his freshly shaved beard. His six-foot-three stature flashed shadows on the wall as the smell of his signature cologne followed his every step.

He looked around the castle-like room as his loyal goons respectfully watched him approach the bedside of his beautiful wife, Anoki. He kissed her forehead as a thank you for giving birth to his first daughter, then moved down to her lips. He grabbed the ice chips on the marble-topped nightstand next to the California king-sized bed and softly rubbed them around her chapped lips.

Anoki panted slowly as her hair, as black as the darkest skies, rested wildly underneath her on a plush pillow. The imported silk sheets gushed with bodily fluids as she squirmed around to look directly into her daughter's eyes. Her bronzed skin glistened under the light of the diamond-encrusted chandelier that hung from the high-end ceiling above as she rubbed her freshly manicured finger on her little girl's soft cheek.

"She's perfect," Anoki spoke out softly, her body exhausted from the delivery and pain she had just endured as her husband sat next to her, his slacks used as a towel, soaking up the fluids on the sheets.

"I can see that." Rock grabbed his daughter and gently held her in his arms. "So this is the little girl that's going to make me kill a lot of little boys?"

"Yes," Anoki whispered as she managed to sit up, "she's already beautiful."

"She has your eyes," Rock said, referring to his wife's soft greenish-brown eyes. "She has your skin tone, too," He stood up to get a better look at his future daddy's girl. "Welcome to the world, little girl, I'm your pops, and as long as I'm here, you won't need for anything; this I promise you."

"Please, I need to leave," the doctor pleaded as fear rushed on his face.

Pow!

Before the good doctor could fall and hit the floor, Rock snapped his fingers and a bullet pierced through the man's head, killing him instantly. His body was caught in mid-air stopping it from falling, then carried out of the room before a sprinkle of blood could hit the Italian marble floors.

"See how Pops had to end that disrespectful motherfucker's life?" Rock asked his daughter as he kissed her on the forehead without a hint of remorse in his voice. "That's what happens when niggas forget who I am."

"A name," Anoki called out as someone pulled the straw she was sipping on away from her mouth, "we need to choose a name for her baby."

"Let's let Junior choose." Rock decided as he signaled for someone to go get his firstborn.

Junior busted through the door walking with his hands in his pockets. He was only four years young, but his posture and facial expressions mimicked his father's. The perfect mixture of both of his parents, he stood there with a serious face as his eyes, the exact eyes his mother and new little sister shared, paced back and forth around the room.

"What?" Junior asked as he held his hands behind his back.

"We want you to meet your little sister," Anoki said, smiling at her erratic son.

"I don't want a sister. I want a brother," he yelped.

"Junior," Rock said as his son looked him in the eyes. "What did I tell you about expressing to us your wants?"

"You said I can have everything I need and some of what I want," Junior responded, speaking better than every kid his age that they knew.

"That's right. So you have a little sister and that's what you need right now, so get used to it." Rock leaned down. "Come here," he signaled as Junior approached him and the unnamed infant. "It's your job as a big brother to protect this little girl at all costs. After me, you're next in line and you have to make sure she's always protected."

"I know, Pops," he said, reacting to the situation like an adult.

"Also, your mom and I were thinking you should be the one to name this little girl. She is going to be your little sister, after all."

"I like the name Willow," he blurted without thinking.

"Willow," Rock looked at Anoki for approval, "what do you think, baby?"

"That's fine with me," she said, smiling at her son's intelligence.

"It's time to bounce," Tony, Rock's best friend and right-hand man, advised as the beeper on his waist chirped nonstop.

Rock nodded his head as he placed Willow into Anoki's arms. He rubbed the top of Junior's head as he smiled at the family he built despite the duties and time-consuming work associated with being a drug lord. At that very moment he was glad he didn't keep the promise to never have a family. He kissed his wife and without explaining, which he didn't have to because she knew the job, he and his goons left.

Anoki let out a sigh of exhilaration as she looked into her children's faces. She couldn't believe that a girl from the slums of Hawaii had found love and was living the good life. She handed her newborn to the live-in nanny as she swooped to the edge of the bed, her stilettos that she kept on during her labor meeting the beautiful marble floor beneath her.

Anoki watched as the nanny walked out of the room with the newborn in her arms and her toddler's hand in her hand. As soon as the doors closed, the hired help surrounded her, cleaning her from head to toe. The clothes on her body were changed and brand-new heels, fresh out of the box, were placed at her feet. By the time she stood up, she was as beautiful as ever and no one would have believed she had just spent the last sixteen hours in labor. Her long majestic curls flowed timelessly as she walked to her large his-and-hers bathroom to fix her makeup.

The bathroom alone was bigger than any house she had ever stayed in back in her little hometown of Hata. Tears rolled down her bare face as she smiled at her first memories of Rock. It baffled her how two months of fun on the shores of Hawaii had turned into years so quickly.

She was sixteen when she first met Rock. Upon her first glance, she knew that he was a drug dealer, that he was even trouble. She had seen his kind come and go all of the time for the drug connects in Hawaii, but she had a feeling that she would be with him. When he looked at her for the first time at the little restaurant where she was a waitress, his eyes pierced through her own, and it was love at first sight. His plump lips made her heart palpitate, and when he asked her what her name was in his deep Eastern accent, her heart was taken.

Rock was just as intrigued with her. He had never seen anything so beautiful in his life. The way her babydoll-like curls bounced as her petite frame took orders to tables enticed him. Her eyes drew him in and he could see the potential in her to be his queen. She was a diamond in the rough and he was willing to buff her into perfection.

They spent the next two months on the ocean getting to know each other. Their lust blossomed into love as their bodies became one over and over again. Anoki knew that giving her body to a man was dangerous. She had been warned by every woman who had ever been in her life. No matter how hard she tried, she couldn't resist Rock's thuggish charm. He was her first and she prayed that he would be her last.

Although Rock was young, his business mind-set captivated Anoki. She had never seen a man dress so debonair and it impressed her on how clean-cut he was. He showed her that she could live the lavish life, too, and although he was only twenty, he promised to provide it for her and she believed his every word. He showered her constantly with gifts to give her a taste of what life would be like with him. He even paid her boss to let her off from the restaurant just so he could spend every free minute he had with her.

As time grew closer for him to leave, Rock begged for Anoki to follow him back to his home in Philadelphia. His pleas were like cries on deaf ears. Anoki wanted to leave, but she was scared all at the same time. Reality set in when his business in Hawaii was finally over. She accompanied him to the airport to part ways. While waiting, nausea took over her and the contents of her stomach spewed all over the place.

Taking a pregnancy test a week prior, Anoki knew that she was pregnant. Out of fear of his reaction, she kept it from him. When he asked for an explanation on her sudden sickness, she broke down and told him the cause. He insisted that she follow him and, with no bonds holding her, she never looked back. She knew that her life was about to change for the better.

It took Anoki some time to get adjusted to being the queen of a drug empire. Rock had molded her, slowly watching as she transformed from a girl into a woman. A woman that every man who crossed her path wanted and every woman hated and wanted to be. He would sit back and smile at how polished Anoki had become.

Anoki understood that staying on top of her game was a must. She had the hottest nigga in the game around their way and she didn't want to give him any reason to stray. She stayed laced up in the most lavish designer pieces, and if anybody else around could get it, she didn't want it. She was royalty now and had to remain as such in order to keep the flame between her and Rock always lit.

She smiled as memories played over in her head like a broken record. She grabbed her powder-pink lipstick, the only color she would wear, and colored her lips. She stood there, in front of the wall mirror that complemented the walk-in bathroom, four years later with no reservations. She knew that she had done the right thing by following Rock. She was just as in love with him today as she was the day she had met him. And she was determined to make sure the feeling was mutual.

Two

Rock sped through the busy streets of Philly as his jaw clenched. His grip on the steering wheel tightened as the smooth breeze from the highway massaged the pores of his face. He was late for the birth of his second daughter and the thought of him missing it enraged him.

"Fuck," he yelled out in frustration.

"Calm down." Tony lit a blunt and passed it to the left. "Hit this Mary to get your mind right."

"Good looking out, fam." Rock quickly placed the purp to his lips and inhaled.

The tires of the black-on-black Mercedes screeched, halting in front of the massive hospital that overlooked the city. With the car running, the keys in the ignition, Rock hopped out leaving his door wide open, daring any onlooker to steal it.

His mind raced, almost patronizing him in a sense as he approached the elevator. He felt like scum for what he had been doing. What was done was done; he couldn't do shit about it but to man up and accept it.

The unpleasant beeps of the elevator lit up with a different number each time, making his stomach flip.

"The fuck am I so nervous about?" he spoke aloud. "I run this fucking city."

Rock checked his demeanor, letting his mind relax as he stepped off of the elevator. His almond-colored skin and perfect smile stole the hearts of every nurse he passed. The power he possessed could be felt from a mile away, and every woman he came in contact with wanted to fuck his brains out because of it.

"Yo', you good?" Tony asked as he trailed behind him.

"As good as I can be," Rock responded as he stopped in front of a room that read "504" that was guarded by two buff Italian men dressed in black. "Can y'all niggas move?" he asked, trying to push through.

"We got to check you," one of the men advised as they blocked the entrance. "You know the rules!"

"Listen, you got two options," Rock lifted up his button-up shirt, exposing his sprayer lining his waist, "y'all can get the fuck out of my face or I can blast on y'all niggas; you choose." The two men moved aware of Rock's hot-temper. They knew his reputation in the streets and they didn't want to become an example.

"That's what the fuck I thought," he said as he slowly pushed the door.

The door crept open as the smell of Davidoff cigars rushed out. The room was dark with the light from the television casting shadows along the eggshell-colored walls. Rock and Tony entered deeper inside of the VIP room and closed the heavy wooden door behind them.

"Yous late," a voice snapped from the depths of the corner.

"My daughter was born." Rock eased his hands into his pockets.

"So was *my* granddaughter!" An Italian man huffed as he continued to puff on his expensive cigar. "I don't give a fuck if Mary was giving birth to baby Jesus. When I call your black ass, get here!" he screamed as a vein pulsated out of his neck.

"My apologies, Vinny," Rock said as he nodded his head.

Vincent "Vinny" Mancini stood stretching his round frame. His dark-black hair that had hints of gray hair was cut so low that effects of him being bald were emulated. Each finger held a certain ring and his silk Versace shirt hung open and free, exposing his hairy chest. His face had the same expression, no matter the topic. His name was legendary up East and his murder record was too many to count. He ran every drug cartel in the Eastern region.

"You and yous fat-ass friend," Vinny hissed as he pointed his cigar at Tony, "would be swimming in the sea with cemented feet if it wasn't for Evelyn."

"This nigga here," Rock said under his breath. "Look, I'm here now so where the fuck is my daughter and her mother?"

"They're at the nursery with all of the other babies."

"Thank you." Rock headed for the door.

"I don't appreciate that fat comment." Tony followed backward behind Rock with his eyes looking at Vinny. "I been working hard on my fitness."

"Well, keep trying, you fat-ass porch monkey," Vinny yelled out before the door closed.

Evelyn Mancini leaned against the nursery window as she looked inside at her beautiful baby girl. Her Italian descent shunned as her strong facial features shouted her heritage. Her long straight hair rested on her backside as her toned, tanned legs crossed one another underneath the gown she wore.

Rock eyed his first love from head to toe as he approached her. The small of her back was always his favorite part about her. As he eyed it from behind, his dick grew in his slacks. The smell of her perfume held his nose prisoner with no chance of parole the closer he got. He wrapped his arms around her waist and kissed the back of her head.

It had been seven long years since he'd met Evelyn. They were each other's first everything. She was everything he ever wanted in a woman. She was smart, beautiful, and with a father as the leader of the mafia, she had street smarts that surpassed his own. She was the perfect match for a thug.

Rock had met her when he first started pushing weight. Her father Vinny trafficked ninety-five percent of all drugs throughout Philly; it was inevitable that he would be his boss. With good loyal work, his name reached Vinny and before he knew it, he had gained lieutenant status in the biggest drug operation the dirty east had ever seen.

With the constant conversing he did with Vinny at his home, Rock ran in to Evelyn all of the time. Ignoring the warnings from Vinny, he pursued the innocent beauty and wooed her. He didn't care about his dick being cut off and put in a jar like Vinny did so many other guys who tried his daughter; he just had to have her.

Rock knew she was the one for him. He never meant for a meeting with Hawaii's drug connection to make him fall in love all over again with a new woman. He blamed Vinny for making him go to Hawaii for him being in love with two women. Without that trip, his heart would have belonged to Evelyn, but when Anoki came into the picture, he had to split it into two.

Rock was indecisive. If Evelyn would have married him like he had asked when they were younger, he would have been with her wholeheartedly. Her repetitive "no" from the fear of being disowned by her father made him find a "yes" with Anoki. He didn't want to look anywhere else, but his hidden desire for a family caused him to.

Rock never wanted Evelyn to find out about Anoki. She wasn't going to as far as he was concerned, but the birth of his firstborn brought the skeleton out of its closet. He couldn't make a child and not take care of it. That was what his father had done to him, and he always told himself he would be better than that.

He told Evelyn about Anoki. He didn't want her to find out any other way. To his surprise, Evelyn understood. She blamed herself for being afraid to be with him. She knew that she would have to share him from that moment on, but a small piece of him was enough to fill her appetite.

Deep down, Evelyn didn't want to share him. No woman wanted to share their man let alone their dick. She sucked up her pride knowing that voicing optimism would put a bullet through Rock's head. Her father would have a bounty on him the moment she admitted she didn't like the situation. She played the sideline to keep Rock safe.

"Congratulations," Evelyn moaned as the scruff from Rock's beard rubbed against the side of her face.

"Thank you." Rock replied as he kissed her soft velvet skin that always tasted like honey to him. "She is beautiful just like her mother."

"Not for her." Evelyn shoved him away. "Congratulations on the birth of your daughter that was just born that meant more to you since you missed ours being born."

"Don't start that shit, Eve." Rock turned to a nurse coming out of the nursery. "Can you bring me my daughter?"

"Yes, sir," the pale nurse replied, moving quickly back inside of the nursery.

"I thought I could do this," Evelyn cried out as her mascara began to run down her face. "I can't be this sideline bitch for too much longer. Not when I had you first. I can't keep giving you all of me and I get a microscopic piece of you."

"Calm down, baby." Rock grabbed her.

"No, fuck that!" Evelyn screamed while pulling her arm away. "It was fine when it was just me, but now we have a daughter. Am I supposed to be a single parent and raise her by myself because you're at another house playing daddy? Am I supposed to tuck her in at night and be the only one to clean her boo-boos?"

"You know I'm going to take care of my daughter," Rock promised.

"That's not the point; it's not about money. I have money, Rock. I need somebody that's going to be there for her physically and emotionally. I need someone to teach her not to fall for a man like you."

Rock could see the hurt in her brown sugar-colored eyes. He had never seen Evelyn break down over the love triangle they had woven until now. She was at her breaking point and soon an ultimatum would be coming.

"Here you go, sir." The nurse returned as she handed Rock his baby girl.

Her eyes sprang open the moment she felt her father's touch. Rock loved her the minute he looked at her. It felt the exact same way it did when he held his other children. He knew that she would be a daddy's girl and anything she asked for, he would get.

Rock kissed her softly as her little fingers gripped his. He removed the cap on her head, revealing her small curly fro with the same texture and color of her mother's. He kissed her again as he walked up and down the hall, mesmerized by his little girl's presence. The feeling he felt made him smile unconditionally.

"Her name is Melee." Evelyn stood next to Rock. "She really is beautiful, isn't she?"

"Yes, she is," Rock answered, never taking his eyes off of his little bundle of joy.

"She deserves all of you. If you can't give me all of you, at least give it to your baby girl. The love that you get from your poppa is one of a kind." Evelyn reached for Melee. "You have to choose. Us or them," she said as she stood up and walked away.

Rock watched as pieces of his heart disappeared into the darkness of the hospital hallways. He knew this day would come. Choosing was something he couldn't do. He loved both of his families. He sat deep in thought in the connected hospital seats with a heavy heart. He knew that if he couldn't choose, then Vinny would choose for him.

Rock's normally calm demeanor slowly changed as his face contorted in an all-consuming anger; his nostrils flaring, his eyes flashing and closing into slits. His mouth started to quiver and drool. Slurring words that were unrecognizable came spewing into space like a volcano releasing its pent-up emotion into the darkness.

Cold silence filled the room. The exotic fish and baby shark swam freely in the aquarium that was built into the wall. Etches of the sun peeked through the floor windows of the office, and the soft trickles of rain thudded softly against the bulletproof glass.

Rock looked at Vinny with so much hatred in his eyes. He couldn't believe what he had just said to him. Killing Anoki and their two children was something he wasn't going for. He couldn't believe Vinny had just put a hit out on his family.

"I let you take over the mafia. There's millions and millions of dollars to be made in this lucrative business." Vinny opened a drawer in his desk. "I let you be the head man in charge to provide for my daughter and granddaughter. Not to take care of another bitch and her kids that doesn't have my fucking blood."

Vinny pulled out a glass egg full of pure Italian cocaine; the same product that had made him filthy rich. He poured a pile onto his large desk. Grabbing a straight blade razor, he formed lines before he enjoyed the product through the depths of his nose.

"I'm not letting my family die," Rock said as he stood up.

"I'll reason with you." Vinny snorted another line while immediately feeling the high. "I'm a family man. As a man I always wanted a firstborn son, someone to leave my business to. So with that being said, I'll let your firstborn son live. Evelyn will act as his mother effective immediately."

"There's no reasoning behind my fucking family," Rock said as he punched the desk.

"You don't have a fucking choice. This is my last request as the leader of this organization. Once Anoki and her daughter is worm food, I'll give you full control. Until then, follow what the fuck I say."

"What if I say no?"

"You don't want to do that." Vinny smiled as an AK-47 pressed the back of Rock's head. "I'm warming up to you, but I'll have your brains cooked into my next meal in a heartbeat. If you say no, then they will die anyway. The only thing that will change will be you, Tony, and whoever else you care about will join them."

"Evelyn would hate you. You wouldn't have anyone to take over." Rock spat as the pressure from the gun on his head increased. He knew Vinny desired to retire from the mafia and him fully taking over was a part of that reason.

"Rock, let me explain something to you." Vinny stood up and walked around the desk. He placed his mouth directly in Rock's ear and whispered, "You're replaceable." He kissed Rock on the cheek and waved him off to leave.

"So that's it?" Rock asked as his frustration grew.

Vinny sat back at his desk with deaf ears. When he was done talking about it, he was done. There was nothing that Rock could say that could have changed his mind. The hit was called and Vinny would die before he called it off.

"This shit isn't over." Rock stood up, the machine gun still pressed at the back of his head.

"If you're going to pull a gun out on me," Rock said as the bodyguard lowered his gun, "you better use it."

A loud crack boomed throughout the room as a bullet ejected from Rock's gun into the bodyguard's head. Blood splattered all over Rock's Armani shirt and slacks as he watched the lifeless body fall and lie in the pool of its own blood. He stepped over the corpse and left without a thought; with no remnants of him but his cologne.

Vinny sat with his back turned to the door of his upscale office as a smile emerged on his lips. No matter how much he hated Rock, he had never met anyone so ruthless and he liked it. He knew that Rock was a killer and was the perfect person to take over his business.

One day, no matter if it was a day or a month or even years, the killer that he had trained would kill him for Anoki's and Willow's murders. And when that day came, he would accept it like a man.

Rock ran into the doors of his two-story home with his lungs working in overdrive. The only thing on his mind was seeing his family even if it would be for the last time. As he ran up the spiral staircase, he prayed he wasn't too late.

Vinny had him busy that whole day and he was hoping that it wasn't to execute his plan and slay his family. He couldn't walk into the room and see them in a pool of blood. He had to see them breathing, once more.

"Anoki?" he called out as he made it to the second level of the home. "Anoki?"

"Rock, why are you screaming?" Anoki appeared out of the master bedroom with their baby girl in her arms.

Anoki walked closer to Rock as her heels clicked with each step that she took. Her form-fitting Chanel dress complemented her hair, which was a rich shade of black. It flowed effortlessly to accent her glowing bronze skin. Her soft eyes, shining like a million stars in the sky, seemed to lighten the hallway.

Rock snapped photographs in his mind of his island beauty wife and daughter. He knew in the core of his soul that it was the last time he would see them alive and breathing. It pained him that he couldn't do anything but accept it.

As he looked at them more, Rock thought about killing the whole mafia, but he was only one man. The thought of fleeing crossed his mind, but Vinny ran Philly for the time being and he wouldn't make it outside of the city limits. He knew that saving one of them was his only option, and it ate at his psyche. It was going to be him and Junior versus the world.

Rock grabbed Willow into his arms as guilt struck his body. He didn't want to fathom the thought of life without his baby girl. The last two months with her didn't seem long enough. She hadn't even begun to live and Rock wished he could trade places with her.

"Are you okay?" Anoki saw something in Rock's eyes that she'd never seen before.

"I'm good," he lied as he softly kissed her lips as if it would be the last time.

Anoki didn't know how to handle Rock's answer. She knew he was lying. She had never seen her husband so shaken by anything in the years they had been together. There was a reason behind the light slowly leaving his eyes. She didn't question it. Whenever he was ready to talk about it, then she would know. Until then, she would take his word for it.

"Let's go to the bedroom," Rock whispered as they made their way to their suite.

Rock looked into his daughter's eyes as he walked over to the crib on the other side of the room and placed her in it. He knew as he watched Willow's little chest go up and down through her onesie that her lungs would soon stop working. Vinny would leave no remnants of his loved ones so he cherished the moment.

"Come to bed," Anoki called out as she hung seductively off of the bed with only her heels on.

Rock looked back at his wife as she slowly patted her freshly shaved womanhood inviting him in. Rock bit his bottom lip as all nine inches tucked away in his pants showed as if it would burst through the zipper. He walked over to Anoki while he removed his clothes.

Anoki licked his six-pack as the Armani button-down covering Rock's upper half fell onto the floor. She softly kissed through his slacks as her hands removed his belt. She looked at Rock with lustful eyes as she unbuttoned his pants and watched them fall to his feet.

Rock's dick pulsated, thumping wildly as Anoki lowered his boxers and took every inch of him into her mouth. Rock loved how her mouth felt like wet pussy. He slowly fucked her throat as Anoki got more into it. He looked down at her and her eyes looked back up with him begging for pleasure.

Rock raised her up as his hands passionately opened and closed her slit while he kissed on her soft brown nipples like a newborn baby. He softly bit them, making Anoki moan as her pussy gushed with wetness. Anoki was in heaven as her pussy creamed all over Rock's fingers.

Rock eased down her body until he reached her cherry box. He danced around her pearl with his tongue like a professional. In and out, he fucked her as her pussy gripped his tongue as cream escaped her slit, falling into his mouth. Rock slurped it all up as Anoki's orgasms continued nonstop.

"Daddy!" Anoki's legs shook uncontrollably.

Rock grinned as he continued eating away. Pre-cum oozed out of his manhood as the moans rushing from Anoki's lips enticed him the louder they became. Rock couldn't wait any longer; he raised Anoki's body as if it was paper and laid her onto the bed.

Rock entered every inch of himself inside of Anoki, making her toes curl. He could feel the head of his dick hit the bottom of her opening as her walls tightened more with each stroke. Their bodies moved in unison as their strokes matched and changed every other minute.

Rock's mind was blown at how good Anoki's pussy was. They had made love so much and each time it had gotten better. Of all of the women he had ever fucked in his lifetime, he was sure Anoki was the best he'd ever had. Evelyn's pussy was nowhere near as good as Anoki's, even after bearing two children.

Rock turned Anoki over as he held her hips steady with his hands while he continued to dig into her. Cream aligned his dick as he watched it go in and out of her pussy. He sped up his stroke as he felt his nut coming.

"I'm about to nut, baby," Rock roared out as his seeds released into Anoki. Their bodies collapsed and fell into one another, landing on the silk sheets covering the bed beneath them.

"That was so good, Rock," Anoki moaned as she struggled to catch her breath. "Come take a shower with me, daddy," she said playfully as she stood up as naked as the day she was born and ran to the bathroom.

"I'll be right there," Rock called behind her as he stood up. He peeked out of the window as headlights flashed on and off in the round driveway in front of their home.

Rock watched as an army of men rushed out of two black vans with guns in their hands. They were there to kill his wife and daughter. Vinny had taken precautions and sent more men than what he normally would have in fear of Rock retaliating.

"Fuck." He punched the air.

Rock rushed to put his clothes on. He had to get Junior out of there fast. He had to get away before his anger caused everyone he loved their lives. He had to get away before a hint of Anoki's scent hit his nose to remind him of what he would never smell again.

He walked over to the crib and looked into Willow's eyes. He wanted to pick her up and take her with him. She had a piece of his heart that she would never know existed. He glared at her as his emotions got the best of him.

"Baby, hurry up. Don't let the water get cold," Anoki called out, stopping him in his tracks as he headed to the door.

"Hold on," Rock called. His eyes began to water. "Wait for me."

Rock stood there as his conscience fucked with him. A man was supposed to protect his family. A man was supposed to make sure everything was okay. He had never felt less than a man than at that moment. He didn't think he could feel so low. He had every mind to go blast every man he saw in his driveway, but he couldn't end both of his kids' lives.

Rock dashed for the door and walked to Junior's room. With one motion, he picked Junior up in his arms as slobber ran down his little mouth. He walked down the rural staircase and headed toward the door.

"Hide," Rock told Nicole, his favorite overnight maid, as he opened the front door.

"Mr. Evans, what's going on?" Nicole asked as she watched sorrow release itself as tears down Rock's face.

"Nicole," Rock said before the front door closed, "run and hide now!"

Rock eased out of the door knowing if Nicole didn't hide, she would die. He already had the blood of his family on his hands, and any more would have broken him even more. Nicole had a little girl to go home to.

"What's up, Boss?" one of Vinny's workers said as he smiled at Rock as he approached the men dressed in black.

Rock released the gun from his waist while still holding Junior in the other as he pressed it against the forehead of the worker. "This is what's up," he said as he released two rounds into his skull.

"None of y'all bitch-ass niggas say shit to me," Rock spat with anger. "Whoever kills my wife and my little girl, I'm killing them, so remember that."

Rock pushed past the group of men with a football player's force. He dared any of them to say something to him; anything at all and he would have put something hot in whomever. He was itching to kill all of them, and if the consequences weren't too high, he would have.

Rock opened the door to his Mercedes. He laid Junior in the passenger seat while his little body continued to snore. He couldn't help but to feel like he had failed him. He knew he wouldn't be able to replace his mother, and the pain killed him on the inside.

Rock started his whip as he watched the men enter his home. In a matter of minutes, the love of his life and the mother of his kids would be dead. His little girl would die also.

"I'm sorry." He zoomed off into the night with a broken heart. He couldn't bear to stay and hear the screams and cries to come.

Four

"Rock, what is taking you so long?" Anoki asked as she called through the open bathroom door. "Rock?" she called again as she cut the water off.

Anoki grabbed the towel hanging over the walk-in shower as she stepped out onto the marble floor. She wrapped the towel around her as she walked into the mirror while removing her shower cap. *His ass done fell asleep again from the way I put it down*, she thought to herself as she ran her fingers through her mane.

Anoki removed the towel as she walked into the bedroom hoping for a round two. The half-moon lit the room dimly as she looked around and realized Rock was nowhere to be found. A chill took over her body as Willow started to cry from her crib.

"Rock, where you at?" she called as she picked up her whimpering baby girl, who was restless. "Your daddy is hiding from us," she told Willow as she kissed her cheek.

Anoki kept having a feeling that something wasn't right. Rock never left without letting her know even if it was to go downstairs. Her stomach turned knots as she slipped on her robe and heels without ever putting Willow down.

She eased into the hallway with alert ears. Although it was late, it was still too quiet for her liking. She crept into Junior's room across the hall from her own as the sound of the door opening screeched throughout the hallway. She quickly picked up her pace as she rushed to his bed.

Anoki closed her eyes when nothing but pillows and race car sheets filled the bed. Her intuition was never wrong, and everything in her being was telling her to get out of the house. She didn't know exactly what, but she knew something was up.

Her feet raced back into her room as she placed Willow into her crib. She only needed a few seconds to find the gun that Rock hid for emergencies. Anoki kicked off her heels as she went to the drawer that held the gun. She maneuvered quietly around the room not wanting to make any sounds.

She opened the drawer and raised the boxers and socks inside revealing a small door. She reached in as three guns stared her in the face. She picked the one Rock always made her practice with before closing the drawer. Her heart beat through her fingertips as she held the gun in her hands.

She held her breath trying to be as quiet as possible as she walked over to the window and took a peek through the large blinds. Anoki's heart dropped as she saw Rock holding a sleeping Junior get inside of his car and drive off while men dressed in all black entered the home. Tears ran down her face as different thoughts ran through her mind.

"Baby girl," she approached the crib wiping her tears, "Mommy doesn't know what is going on, but it looks like your daddy is trying to kill us." She spoke freely as a tear escaped her eye. "I love you and I'll be right back," she whispered.

Anoki's body language changed as she walked back to the gun stash. She picked another pistol out of the drawer before closing it with her hip. She held the guns out in front of her and made her mind up that she would shoot anything standing.

Sounds of footsteps and voices outside of the bedroom door stopped her in her tracks as she rushed over to the crib and picked Willow up. She ran to the deepest closet in her bedroom and hid a now sleeping Willow in there with a blanket over her.

Anoki knew she had the advantage. Whoever came to her thought that she was in the dark; that she didn't have a clue that they were there. She had the element of surprise and was going to use it fully.

She slipped behind the door as it opened. The smell of death entered along with the same group of men she saw outside of her window pane. She watched them search the bathroom and under the bed. As their attention focused on the closet that held her daughter, she had to act fast.

Anoki kicked the door closed as she aimed and shot, giving the three men no time to react. Body after body fell until she was the last one standing. She rushed to the closet as she reloaded her guns praying that no one else was in the home other than Willow.

"Anoki," a familiar voice called out as the door swung open.

Relief filled Anoki's soul as Tony walked through the door. She knew deep down that Rock wasn't trying to kill her and that he would send someone to save their lives. Her emotions ran wild as she released the guns from her hands.

Anoki ran to Tony as her heartbeat slowed down to its normal pace. She wrapped her arms around him as tears fell from her eyes onto his tie. He stroked her hair in a way to let her know she was safe.

Tony pulled Anoki's face out of his chest. He glanced down at her and even with her crying face, she was the most beautiful woman he had ever seen in his life. He softly stroked her face, which was something that he could never do under any other circumstance. He took in her presence as the job he was there to do escaped him.

"Are you okay?" Tony questioned as reality set in and he focused on his mission.

"No." Anoki rushed toward the closet. "I have to get Willow and we have to leave."

Pow! Pow!

The gunshots were not as loud as Anoki had anticipated. The metal fragments, spiraling through the air, pierced her chest and arm without consideration, without real meaning of relevance, and with more speed than the fastest of living things. The small wounds in her flesh leaked blood much like the way crying eyes leaked tears.

It wasn't so much the pain, but the shock, the betrayal, the surprise, of almost anticipating, feeling the hot wet pain in her chest, the hole the bullets made. It wasn't what Anoki expected. She had thought it would be more pain. She stumbled, taken aback; still looking dully into the air, not knowing what may come next, and realizing that it was the end.

Anoki was stunned to know she was dying. She was shocked that she wasn't overwhelmed by the emotion she had assumed would accompany such a violent end. She knew her life would end like this with Rock, but knowing it and experiencing it were two different things.

Anoki was amazed by all that surrounded her. She looked down at her hand and flexed it. She was astonished at how the muscles flexed back and forth perfectly and would soon move no more. Her ability to move was drawing near.

"I'm sorry." Tony leaned down to check her pulse. "It's just business."

"Why?" Anoki asked as blood ran out of her mouth onto her pink-colored lips. "I thought we were family."

"It's business," Tony repeated nonchalantly as he stepped over her. "I'll make it quick with the kid. I'll end it with one shot. She won't feel anything," he assured her as he headed to the closet.

"Wait!" Anoki screamed, using every ounce of her energy. "Don't hurt her! She's a baby; she's your goddaughter, T!"

"It's business," Tony reiterated as he opened the door and pointed the gun at Willow. "I have to finish the job, Anoki. You know how things work," he assured as he stood at the door of the closet.

"Please," she coughed uncontrollably, "leave her. Don't hurt her. Let her starve, T. I beg you. Please!"

Tony looked into Anoki's eyes as he lowered his gun. He had never killed a baby, but he would have. He let what Anoki said contemplate in his mind. He knew if he left them that they would both die; Anoki from her wounds and Willow from starvation and dehydration. He put his gun in his waistband before heading for the door.

"Thank you," Anoki panted.

Suddenly, everything went completely silent. All movement around Anoki slowed down to an excruciating pace. She could feel her pulse pounding through her body and escaping torrents through the open wounds. At that moment she didn't feel any pain, only sorrow.

There was something altogether serene as she bled out, losing consciousness with a smile on her face. The images swirled before her right until the end, leaving memories of Junior, Willow, and even Rock imprinted upon her mind without the oxygen to sustain it.

"Rock didn't want this," Tony said as he stopped halfway through the door. "Don't leave this world thinking that nigga didn't love you because he does. This was out of his control," he said as he walked out the door.

Tony exhaled as he walked down the stairs of the mansion. He didn't think he could have pulled it off since he was so close to Anoki and Willow, but for what he was being paid, he would have killed his own mother if he had to. The half a million was all his now.

Tony thought about Willow as he walked over to the phone in the kitchen. He had bonded with her and given her gifts almost daily. He had love in his heart for his goddaughter, but it was his life or hers and he chose to live.

"Hello," a voice answered on the other end of the receiver.

"It's done," Tony said into the phone as he looked behind him. The gloves covering his hands seemed to get tighter with each minute that passed.

"Are you sure? Are they dead?" the voice grilled.

"That's what 'it's done' means," Tony snapped while his ears stayed alert for the sound of sirens.

"Good job. I'll let Poppa know of your good work," Evelyn said as she hung up the phone.

Evelyn smiled as she set the phone down, missing the receiver. She leaned over and kissed Junior on the cheek; he was still sleeping peacefully. "I'm your mommy now," she whispered as she squeezed his little hand with her own.

Evelyn stood up tying her hair into a ponytail. She walked over to the mini bar and poured herself a glass of champagne that was chilling on ice for this very occasion. She took a sip as a celebration for the deaths of Anoki and Willow. With them out of the way, she and Rock could finally be a family. She could finally have his last name and be his one and only woman.

Five

Eight Years Later

The sky was ablaze with color as hints of fiery orange and searing reds beamed down on God's creation. The sounds of birds and waves were alive while the smell of the fresh water lingered all around. The caress of the midday breeze felt just right as the fish played flopping in and out of the water; some even landing in the small boat filled with people that trailed the outskirts of the ocean.

"We're almost at the big island of Punalu'u," the captain of the boat screamed.

"I thought we were going to Hata, Mommy," Willow said as people rambled to get their stuff together, waiting to get off of the boat once it hit shore.

"We are," Anoki said as she inhaled the air of her home, which left a familiar tingle on her nose. "Your aunt is meeting us here and then we are going to Hata."

"My aunt?" Willow asked as she twirled her fingers in her dazzling hair. "Like Aunt Nicole back in Philly?"

"No." Anoki smiled at Willow. "This is my sister. She is your aunt by blood."

"By blood?"

"Yes, baby," Anoki responded as she saw the enormous island approaching from afar.

"She's your sister like Kail is my sister?" Willow asked as she tugged on the strap of her pink overalls.

Anoki smiled as she looked at the little girl sitting next to Willow. She stuck her tongue out at her youngest daughter as the horns on top of the small steamboat started going off, alerting them that they had reached their destination.

"Yes, baby, just like you and Kail." Anoki removed the straw hat from her head and let it hang by a string around her neck.

Anoki opened her eyes. The sunlight bathed her skin as the boat approached the dock. She tried closing her eyes. What had happened in Philly was something she didn't want to deal with today. Thoughts bit at her brain, forbidding her to gather her thoughts.

She was worried for Willow and Kail; they were innocent. They shouldn't have had to go through any of this. She rubbed the scar the bullet left on her arm, her stomach growling. She reached in her backpack, and then counted the wad of money she had brought with them. She dug in once more and found her pocket-sized mirror. She looked so different with short hair. She had to cut it if she didn't want anyone to recognize her back in Philly or there in Hawaii, for that matter.

Anoki touched her chest. She winced. She could still feel the pain from it all. Flashbacks danced in her head like a two-step. She saw Nicole, the housekeeper, running to her side as her vision went in and out. Memories of hospital staff surrounding her with panicked faces played in her mind. She remembered waking up after an extensive surgery. As if living through what she had experienced wasn't enough, she was told that she was pregnant and that her baby would live.

That year she spent in the hospital seemed like a decade. All of it seemed worth it once her baby girl Kail was born. When she looked into her little girl's face, she knew that fighting for her life was her only option. She had to be a trooper for her kids. Although she considered Kail a blessing, she couldn't believe that her and Rock's last time making love had produced a child.

Anoki stood there grateful for everything Nicole had done for them. Making sure her and Willow's existence was unknown, and going with the façade that they were dead was no easy task. Hiding them out for years and treating them like family was something Anoki never could forget. She couldn't repay her if she wanted to; she would forever be appreciative.

Anoki quickly gathered their belongings, then placed the straw hat back in place on her head. She had to wear it in case somebody noticed her, even with her hair cut short. She reached on the collar of her shirt to grab her shades to put on her face. She could never be too careful.

"Aloha," beautiful Hawaiian women greeted them as Anoki guided her girls off of the boat.

"Aloha," she replied as she held the back of her girls' necks. "Stay close," she whispered as she released her grip to focus on the luggage dangling on the inner part of her arms.

Anoki looked down at the warm crushed, black glass sand that got darker at the water's edges that slid off and on her feet while she walked. She looked back at the volcanic rocks spiking from the water. She could see sea turtles basking on the hot sand and more grazing on the algae growing on the rocks.

Anoki was home as she watched fishermen cast their nets hoping to bring home a delicious catch for dinner. The smell of coffee being roasted in the coffee plantations hit her; assuring her she had really made it back. The palm trees casting their soothing shade on sunbathers, who watched the red sun drop into the ocean, hoping for the famous green flash, finally convinced her that it wasn't a dream and after twelve long years, she was really home.

"What does 'aloha' mean?" Willow asked as she sunk in and out of the black sand.

"It's how Hawaiians greet each other. It's the way we say 'hello.'"

"Why can't we just say hello then?" Kail asked as they made it off the sand, and onto the street.

"You can greet people any way that you like," Anoki said as she saw her sister pulling up.

Anoki smiled as she saw Mahina slow down in front of them. She screamed as she ran to the driver's door and opened it. She hugged her big sister as tight as she could, and for as long as she could stand. Mahina embraced Anoki and their reunion grew emotional.

"I missed you," Mahina repeated, kissing all over Anoki's face, leaving traces of the powder-pink lipstick that covered her lips.

"I missed you, too," Anoki wiped the lipstick from her skin.

Anoki stepped back to take a look at her big sister, who was only eleven months older. Most people who saw them said they could pass for twins, but Anoki never thought so. She always thought Mahina had more natural beauty.

Anoki looked past her sister at the expensive Lexus that she had pulled up in. From the designer clothing Mahina was wearing, Anoki knew she was still living the fast life. Mahina was still a part of what she had left Hata for in the first place, The Pink Lip Bandits.

"They look just like we did when we were kids," Mahina said as she approached Willow and Kail, "I'm your auntie."

"You're pretty," Willow said as she grinned, "almost as pretty as Mommy."

"Is that so?" Mahina half laughed.

"You two have on the same lipstick." Kail's eyes went from Anoki's lips to Mahina's.

"I know," Mahina hugged them, "if you're lucky, one day you two will wear the same color."

"Mahina," Anoki warned, signaling her to shut her mouth with only her eyes.

"I'm just saying." Mahina hissed as she walked back to the car and got in. "You coming or what?"

Anoki bit her tongue and reminded herself to give Mahina a piece of her mind when they were alone. She signaled for her girls to walk to the car as she picked up the luggage to follow. She loaded the car, got in, and before she could close the door well, Mahina sped off.

"Gino is going to be so happy to see you," Mahina rolled down the window to let in the cool, island breeze.

"We can talk about this later." Anoki ended the conversation before it started. She looked in the backseat at her nosey little girls.

"Okay," Mahina rolled her eyes.

Mahina was shocked at how censored Anoki had become. She couldn't believe how much she had changed. If it wasn't for her looks being the exact same, she would have sworn a stranger was sitting next to her. She knew her sister was a different person, but it baffled her how much she had become someone new.

Mahina looked through the rearview mirror at her nieces. She wondered if they were the reason for Anoki's cautiousness. She wondered if it was all worth it. She rubbed her stomach in deep thought as if she should have kept the baby by Gino that she recently had carried.

Mahina always wanted a family. She always wanted to be the

mother she wished her mother was to her and Anoki. She would have kept the baby if it was by anyone else. She knew the minute she told Gino, he would have made her take care of it. She looked at Anoki with envious eyes, and realized she finally had something to be jealous of her sister for.

"Okay, they're sleep," Anoki said, referring to her snoring cubs in the backseat. "Now, what's up?" she asked, waking Mahina out of her daydream.

"You still down to make some money?"

"Doing what, Mahina?"

"What do you think?" Mahina stopped at a light. "You gon' have to join The Pink Lip Bandits again. You got two kids," she said as she watched Anoki's facial expression change. "You know what I mean." She knew that Anoki still counted Junior as one of her own.

"I know I have kids." Anoki ignored her last comment. "I'm not gon' ask you or nobody else for shit. I've always made my own money and I can provide for mines."

"You better because I sure ain't." Mahina sped off. "It's bad enough y'all about to be in my spot taking up space and shit."

"Mahina, you working my fucking nerves."

"The truth hurts." Mahina smirked.

"Let's talk about truths." Anoki kicked her heels off and turned to Mahina. "I remember sending you ten stacks a month just on the strength that you were my sister. The whole time I was with Rock, you lived how I lived. You were miles away and I made sure when I ate, you ate. So don't be petty because the roles have reversed. Until you throw me ten stacks a month for four years," Anoki said with her finger pointing directly at Mahina, "don't say shit to me about being up in your space that I paid for in the first fucking place."

Mahina knew she had hit a nerve. She was thankful for Anoki looking out for her. She had never seen her sister so vulnerable, and she couldn't pass up the chance to throw some shit up in her face even if it was petty. She was happy to see her, but her envious ways made it nearly impossible to show it.

"I didn't mean it like that." Mahina pulled into the driveway of her two-story, multicolored brick home.

"Yes, you did," Anoki opened the door, "but it's cool. I'm going to meet with Gino tonight and start stacking paper. I'm gon' get in this shit one more time. Me and my girls won't be in your hair too long."

Anoki knew as she got Willow and Kail out of the car exactly what she had to do. She would have to join The Pink Lip Bandits even if it was for a few months, despite how much she didn't want to. She promised herself that she would get in and get out. Once she had enough money, she would disappear and never look back like she did before.

Six

noki sped down a dirt road as the sun had completed its tour for the day, and had now been replaced by myriad stars, which dotted the inky canopy. A low, waning gibbous moon hovered tenuously in the twilight firmament, bestowing a very dim light upon the small town. It was a cool, windy night; the swaying of trees and rustling of leaves could be heard but not seen, as the encompassing darkness had blotted out all but the faintest light.

Anoki stopped abruptly in front of the small restaurant that instantly brought memories to her. Dust from the road's gravel colliding in between the tires floated upward, forming a large brown cloud in her mist as she got out of the car. Her neat short hair clung to her scalp as she made her way toward the building that appeared to be deserted, but she knew better.

"Gino," she called out as she knocked at the front door. Her eyes cut at the "sorry, we're closed" sign. "Gino, I know your ass in there!"

"Like fine wine that gets better with time." Gino peeked through the blinds. "And girl," he opened the door, "time has been on your side."

Gino Mancini leaned back in the wheelchair he used as he wheeled himself closer to the entrance. His face was handsome for a man his age. His hair was as dark as tar, and hung over the back of his wheelchair. His skin was pale, and from being in his chair constantly, the weight had piled on over the years. He pulled a cigar out of his front Versace shirt pocket as he looked at Anoki the way a lion looked at its prey.

To anyone around town who didn't know him, they would tell you he was the owner and manager of the small restaurant that sat directly in the middle of town. To anyone who knew him personally, they would tell you something different. They would tell you that Gino was the man behind The Pink Lip Bandits and every drug cartel in and off the shores of Hawaii.

Not wanting to put his hand in the pot, he put together an organization of overly beautiful women and trained them to be whatever the job required them to be. Any and everything illegal that could be done, Gino could get done. Branding them by powder-pink lipstick, he knew that they could get away with a lot of things men couldn't. Murder, larceny, escort services, whatever request he received, he would fulfill if the money was right.

Gino had met Anoki and Mahina on the beach on a cold summer's night. He could tell from the way that their clothing had holes in it that they were dirt poor, but he could also see their beauty through the dirt. He made them an offer they couldn't refuse; shelter and money. He took them in at fourteen and thirteen and had kept his promise to always put money in their pockets if they worked for it.

"Yous know you still owe me," he moved out of the way inviting her in, "a lot of fucking money."

"Whatever I owe you," Anoki said as she started to slide the straps of the little white dress she wore off of her shoulder, "I'm sure we could work it out."

Anoki was far from stupid. She wasn't the least bit attracted to Gino, but she knew what kind of man he was. Pussy was his weakness and for some good pussy, he would do anything. She laughed on the inside at how Gino's ignorance would eventually be the death of him.

"I don't know, Anoki." Gino closed the door to the restaurant and locked the doors. "I'm flattered but you caused problems for me; big fucking problems, Anoki!"

"Daddy," she purred as she walked toward him seductively, "can we just work this out like we used to?" She sat on top of his wheelchair, her legs wrapped through the openings as she moved her hips up and down on him.

"The one assassination job that I gave you," Gino barked as Anoki rubbed her breast in his face, "yous fall in love with the dude and disappear on me. This was a special job; it came from my brother."

While being in The Pink Lip Bandits, Anoki had never gotten a murder gig. She always got robberies or jobs that were designed for no bloodshed unless it was necessary. As much as she tried to fight what she started feeling for Rock, she couldn't. She knew from the moment she'd met him at the restaurant that she couldn't kill him. Getting away from Gino's reign and finding true love were the only good things that came from that job.

"I'm sorry, baby," Anoki cooed in Gino's ear.

"I hope the dick was worth it," Gino continued, "I hope it was worth every fucking cent."

"Let me make it up to you."

"My brother cut my fucking legs off because of you," Gino hissed.

"I know," Anoki reached down and unfastened his slacks.

She rubbed his tiny dick as the trail of straight black pubic hairs surrounded it. She was disgusted, but played it off. Anoki could make him cum just from the excitement of getting in her pussy.

She had been giving him hand jobs since she was thirteen; she knew exactly how to touch his dick to make it explode.

"Fuck," Gino called out as Anoki's warm, soft hands stroked him up and down.

"Cum for me, baby," Anoki moaned.

Gino's body tightened up, and his hips started to thrust. Anoki's stomach flipped as thick white globs of cum rushed out of his tiny penis. She quickly stroked it again, and watched cum run off the side of her hands as it fell to the floor. She knew Gino would have asked her to lick it up if she didn't do that.

"I'm sure we can work something out," Gino zipped his slacks back up. "Matter of fact, I have a special assignment for you right now."

"How much does it pay?" Anoki asked as she found a towel to wash her hands.

"Thirty large," Gino lied with a menacing grin.

"I'm in."

Anoki paid attention as Gino told her about a job that didn't exist. Anoki didn't have a clue, but that night she would die. Gino was going to make sure there was no coming back from the dead this time.

"It's in place," Gino said on the phone as he watched Anoki drive off.

"Make sure she dies. You failed to get my pain-in-the-ass son-in-law killed when I asked you to, little brother," Vinny demanded. "She stops breathing, or this time, it will be your fucking arms, *capisce?*"

"*Capisce*," Gino said as he hung up the phone.

Gino sat in his wheelchair as his mind raced. He hoped that Mahina could fulfill the biggest job he had ever given her; killing her one and only sister. He pulled out a cigar, and lit it before disappearing into the door that led to the restaurant's real contents.

Money, drugs, and naked women appeared as he wheeled down the ramp leading to the bottom level of the restaurant. Music blasted through the soundproof walls as he wheeled himself to his favorite spot in the room. A woman with pink lips, that glowed through the room's darkness, handed him a glass with scotch. He sipped, using his arms to hold the glass, hoping that he would get to keep them.

Anoki stalked down the hallway of the house Gino had given her the address to for the job. She was told to get inside, steal a briefcase, and get out. She heard light-paced treading from above. She dared not look, but the curiosity was killing her; as with the cat. She looked above and saw the door to the attic slightly open. She eased the ladder down as shadows from above danced on the walls.

The curiosity in her got the better of her. She slowly climbed the old wooden ladder, and peered into the dark, dimly lit attic room as she scrunched her small dress down with one hand, using her other to aim her gun. Her eyes were wide open, heart beating fast as if some unforeseen circumstance was about to arise.

A cool shudder trickled down her spine. Glancing around nervously, she saw somber portraits staring at her from behind layers of dust, seemingly penetrating her very being. Cold, hesitant light streamed in through a cracked window from an old streetlight, casting eerie shadows on the walls. As she walked forward, she couldn't help but feel that someone was following her. Whirling around, she saw nothing but the faces in the portraits staring at her, their eyes telling her to leave.

The wail of a thousand screams could be heard as the wind beat down on the old latched window weaving its way through the cracks that had formed over time. The moon's light shone down on the dusty panes of glass illuminating the room ever so slightly.

Even though fear was rooted deep within Anoki, the quick money she was about to make made her inspect the attic a little more. There was something familiar about the room that drew her in; all that antique wood that painted a picture of former glory intrigued her.

"Brings back memories, doesn't it?" Mahina asked, appearing from the shadows.

Anoki didn't remember; at the time she was too young to. In the very attic where they stood, they had played all of the time as kids. The house they were in once belonged to their grandparents. Mahina remembered it all, and deemed the attic as the one place she could go to with no worries. It was the only time in her life when she was truly happy.

"Shit," Anoki exclaimed while pointing her gun at Mahina. "You scared the fuck out of me, Mahina. What are you doing here?" She lowered her gun. "Gino thinks I went soft and can't finish the job?"

"No," Mahina cocked the butt of her gun, "I'm here to do my job so throw your gun down."

"I'm the job?" Anoki tossed her gun at the floor.

"Why did you come back, Noki?" Mahina's palms grew sweaty.

"Please," Anoki pleaded. "Don't do this."

"I have to. Besides," Mahina shrugged her shoulders, "it's you or me."

"What about your nieces? Your blood? Are you going to kill them, too?"

"No."

"Can you promise that to me?" Anoki looked into her sister's eyes waiting for her truth.

"Promise me!"

"I promise."

"Do it," Anoki screamed as she started praying for the well-being of Junior, Willow, and Kail. "Lord, look over my children for me. Take them under your wing and protect them, Lord. Please forgive me as well, God, for I have sinned." She continued with her eyes closed, "Do it."

"Forgive me as well, God." Mahina pulled the trigger releasing a bullet into Anoki's head and killing her instantly.

"I'm sorry it had to be this way." Mahina cried hysterically as blood flowed underneath the corpse of her one and only sister. She lay next to her, held her close to her body, and she stroked her face with her hands. She kissed the side of her face as her hands shook uncontrollably at what she had just done.

Mahina walked into her home as the sun began to rise and set. The smell of the murder she had committed lingered on her clothes. She shook her head as visions of Anoki's lifeless body entered her mind. She eased into the guest room to check on her nieces whom she had just left motherless in this world.

"Mommy?" The creaking of the door awakened Willow.

"No, it's your aunt," Mahina answered, sorrow present in her voice.

"Where's my mommy?" Willow sat up, wiping her eyes.

"She went away," Mahina responded quickly.

"To where?"

Anoki would never return, Mahina thought. Her sister was dead, but she could never tell Willow and Kail the truth. She would take the truth to her grave.

"She will be back," Mahina lied. "Now go back to sleep."

"Aunt Mahina," Willow said, stopping her in her tracks, "can I try on your lipstick? Mommy never lets us."

Mahina was aware of her nieces' future. One day they would wear the shade of lipstick that cursed her and Anoki's lips. It was inevitable. One day that blood would be on their hands as well.

"Sure." She pulled out a small mirror and her lipstick that was hidden in a golden-colored tube.

Willow smiled as she felt the creamy substance rub all around her lips. The tingling sensation made her face feel funny, but her eagerness was undeniable through her smile. Mahina coated her lips perfectly as she put the golden tube back in her compact.

"I look pretty." Willow blushed as she looked at herself in the small black mirror that Mahina held in front of her face.

"Yes, you do," Mahina agreed sincerely, "just like your mother."

"Really?" Willow questioned as her eyes grew big with excitement.

"Yes." Mahina started to wipe the lipstick off with her thumbs. "I need you to promise me something, Willow."

"Okay." Willow looked into her aunt's eyes.

"Promise me you will never trust anyone," she said as she grabbed her chin.

"What about Mommy?"

Mahina shook her head no.

"Kail?" Willow asked.

"Sisters do backstabbing shit, too." Mahina grabbed Willow's hand, releasing her chin while leading her to bed.

"What about you?"

"Never trust me." Mahina tucked her under the sheets.

"I guess it's a good thing that I don't." Willow scooted her body down into the sheets.

"It's a damn good thing," Mahina agreed as she walked toward the door. "Oh, and Willow," Mahina stuck her head back through the door, "remember that you would rather have four quarters than one hundred pennies." She smiled and walked away. "Less is more sometimes."

Willow sat in the bed wondering, letting what her aunt had told her play into her mind. She didn't understand what she meant. Her eight-year-old mind couldn't process the message and wisdom behind those words. One day it would all make sense to her. But Willow would be the type that would have rather had a whole dollar bill, and she would soon realize that you only have yourself in this world.

The Present

Happiness is not something you postpone for the future;
it is something you design for the present

Seven

The luminous full moon glowed in the midnight sky as the two women began their sparring boxing on the rooftop of their exquisite condo that overlooked the beautiful city of Honolulu. They stood there in boy shorts, a tank top, and a pair of Giuseppe heels with their hands out in front of them forming fists. Both as beautiful as sin, each waited to catch the other one off-guard.

Willow, twenty-two, decked a twenty-one-year-old Kail in the eye, resulting in a grotesque squelching noise making her eye immediately water.

"Pay attention," Willow yelled.

Kail shrieked in pain, grasping the gaping wound where her eye was, and in a frenzy, she grabbed Willow's arm. Willow moaned in agony as Kail twisted it 360 degrees with sickening cracking noises.

"You have to do better than that, baby sis." Willow panted as she released herself from Kail's grip by punching her rib cage.

With her left arm, Kail pulled a revolver out of her cleavage. She pointed it at Willow in frustration. She had never won one of the sparring matches with her big sister, and it made her mad. Kail raised her tank top exposing the medium-sized red circle from where Willow's fist had landed.

As Kail paid attention to her wound, Willow seized the opportunity, diving forward and pinning her to the ground, making the gun fly in the opposite direction. Kail wasn't going down so easily, and in a fit of hulk-like rage, she punched Willow's face until they both sat there going blow for blow.

Kail nearly passed out from the pain, but instead grabbed Willow and head-butted her off of her. Willow was sweating fire and salt that soaked her shirt at the crevice of her breasts, and told her sister, "You better make your hands a weapon, Kail." Kail stared in the eyes of Willow, watching for the moment she'd second-guess herself, watching for her moment of godliness.

There, in that moment, Kail's eyes faltered. It was maybe less than one second, but she was an animal now. Things were slowed down like she was a cheetah and Willow was a gazelle that'd lost its footing.

Kail swung her fist. Flesh met flesh; Willow stumbled, and fell like a drunken transient before God himself, confused and unaware. Willow struggled to her feet, as she started to smile. She took the rubber band around her wrist and tied up her auburn-colored hair in a messy ponytail.

"That's what the fuck I'm talking about," Willow said as she tossed a rubber band to Kail to tie her hair up for round two.

Willow closed her eyes as the night air became therapeutic to her. She smiled at how easy their life had become. Filling the shoes of their mother and their aunt, she and Kail were now members of The Pink Lip Bandits. With unlimited money at their disposal, they never knew the meaning of the word *struggle* and could buy whatever their hearts desired.

Raised by their Aunt Mahina, and her soon-to-be husband, Gino, they had learned the ways of the streets before they were ten. Instead of getting an allowance like normal kids their age growing up, they had to earn it. No matter if it was stealing, drugs, or whatever crooked things Gino asked them to do, they did it without asking questions.

Willow became the brains of The Pink Lip Bandits and Kail became the force. As their deadly combination grew more and more, the money and control they had in the streets grew. Letting their beauty be mistaken for weakness was a price a lot of hustlers paid.

Willow's and Kail's names became feared on the islands of Hawaii. They were everything their reputation said they were plus more. People knew if they saw them coming, to go the other way. Wherever you saw the two together, their lips as pink as taffy, you knew they were there on business, and any business done by them ended badly.

Although Mahina filled in for their mother—they'd always wondered what happened to her—she never instilled feelings or emotions in them. She trained them to be cold. She raised them to be the perfect soldiers for the organization and it paid off. Although there were more than twenty girls in The Pink Lip Bandits, Willow and Kail were the only two who mattered to Mahina and Gino. They were making more money than the other girls put together.

"I'm about to beat your ass now," Willow called as she held her fist out in front of her.

"Wait." Kail's cell phone started ringing. She walked over to the railings of the rooftop and grabbed her phone. "It's Mahina," she called.

"Answer it," Willow walked closer, "she's probably making sure we are there on time tomorrow for their damn wedding." She shook her head as she sat on the railing.

"That better be all." Kail hit the answer button. "'Cause I ain't down with working tonight. Hello."

"What is she saying?" Willow put her ear close to the phone.

"I think she called me by mistake." Kail looked at Anoki as a familiar voice caught their interest.

"Do yous think they gon' try to overpower us?" Gino's voice came booming through the receiver of the phone.

Willow put her finger up to Kail's mouth, telling her sister to be quiet as she hit the speaker phone button.

"I don't know," Mahina said. "But, if they do, we can just take care of them like we did Anoki."

"Could you kill them like you killed your sister?" Gino asked in a malicious tone.

"In a minute," Mahina replied as static started to take over the call. "It's bad enough that their father took over the mafia and we have to listen to him regarding the drug cartel here." She spat. "If those little bitches ever got from under my control, I'd kill them."

"But they make us so much money."

"They are just common bitches from the streets of Philadelphia. We could always find two more bitches like them."

"You're right," Gino agreed as they laughed.

Kail threw the phone over the rooftop in anger. She sat silently, hunched over and with a sense of loss so powerful that her muscles wouldn't respond to commands. Her gaze was into the far distance, unseeing but fixed on some imaginary future of a life with her mother. Although it was naïve, she had figured her mother had left at will and would return someday.

Willow wasn't as naïve; she had grieved for the loss of her mother when she was a little girl. She knew deep down that she was dead. The story that Mahina had always told them about their mother leaving to go find herself didn't make sense to her. Her mother had been taken from the world a long time ago, but she'd never suspected Mahina.

Kail's throat tightened and a short intake of breath forecast the explosion of emotion, which to date, she had managed to keep buried deep inside. Not any more though, that image of things shared with a love which were not to come, was too powerful and gut-wrenching to be kept in check; the tearing at her soul was too compelling and energetic to be contained. The vision she had began to swim in front of her as tears welled from deep inside and coursed down her cheeks.

All the pent-up hysteria and dread of loss was let loose in a paroxysm of choking and sobbing, so powerful in its intensity that it shook her body until she could barely breathe.

"I want that bitch dead," Kail said, her voice shaking.

"I know, but calm down." Willow grabbed her sister's shoulder. "I feel the same way. How about we give that bitch a wedding she will never forget?"

"I'm down," Kail agreed as she bit her bottom lip.

They both sat there under the moon thinking of a master plan for revenge. Their lips shined with pink essence as they put together a plan that would end The Pink Lip Bandits for good. They would leave traces of no one affiliated with the organization. The wedding of Mahina and Gino would be a bloodbath like Hawaii had never seen.

"Ms. Melee Evans?" the stout limo driver screamed, holding up a big sign with her name neatly written on it.

"That's me," a woman called out as she handed him her designer luggage.

Melee waited for the limo driver to put the luggage in the back, and open the door for her as her light-caramel skin tone glistened under the Hawaiian sun. Her hazel-brown eyes hid behind her Fendi sunglasses. The lengthy beige Alexander McQueen dress that fitted her body perfectly split up the side showing off her beautiful toned legs. A small breeze made her long, straight hair blow softly as the scent from the peppermint shampoo she used mixed with the natural smells of the island.

She was the kind of woman that gay men went straight for; the kind who could make a man run into walls staring at her as she walked by. The type who you have to take an extra breath between sentences while talking to her. A gaze at her face and you could get lost in a daydream. There was a beauty as pure and captivating as this and she was it.

"Have you been to the islands before?" the limo driver asked as he held the door open.

"Please don't speak to me," Melee said as she gracefully entered the limo like she had done it a thousand times. "An acquaintance is with me so we will wait for him. He went to the bathroom."

"Yes, ma'am," the limo driver said as he softly closed the door. "What a bitch," he mumbled under his breath.

The limo door opened and Melee slid over to let her travel partner inside of the limo. Craig Price entered the limo as his tapered faded head scuffed the top cloth of the seat. With skin that was nearly blue, he was the darkest man most people had ever seen in their life. His Evasion sunglasses hid his dark-colored eyes. The opened white Gucci shirt and shorts to match complemented the white loafers that made a home to his feet. He was handsome and his swag attracted every woman he passed.

"Didn't I tell yo' ass to wait by the restroom?" he barked, the pearly white teeth in his mouth appearing and disappearing.

Melee ignored his rant as she gazed out of the window at the gorgeous sites.

"You think this shit is a game, but if something happens to you, then yo' pops would kill me," he said.

"That sounds like a personal problem." Melee checked her cell phone. "All I'm here for is to attend my uncle's wedding, stand in for my family, and that's it. Just chill the fuck out and we'll be back in Philly before you know it."

"You try telling that to Rock." Craig grabbed her cell phone. "He doesn't have any understanding behind his baby girl. So look, I don't give a fuck what you here for. I was asked to watch you so, that's what the fuck I'm gon' do. So where you go, I go. You got that?"

"Yes, goddammit," Melee huffed as she snatched her cell phone back.

"Where to?" the limo driver asked as the window in the middle console let down.

"The Halekulani Hotel on Kalia Road," Craig yelled.

"I'll get us there fast." The limo driver nodded as he rolled the window up.

Melee leaned against the door of the limo with her chin resting on the palm of her hand. She felt like a kid with a babysitter. She was in this beautiful place and couldn't even enjoy it due to having a constant shadow. She loved her father, but she longed for the day to do things on her own. She felt like she couldn't even go to the restroom by herself. She was tired of being chaperoned.

Willow and Kail prepped in the presidential suite with the rest of the bridesmaids as they got ready for the two o'clock English

Garden wedding. They stayed calm as they looked at each other, and then out of the window of the Halekulani knowing that it would be their last day in Hawaii. Willow had bought the two first-class tickets, and their plane would leave at the stroke of midnight. There was no turning back now.

"I'm so nervous." Mahina looked at herself in the mirror; the makeup artist she hired painting her face.

"You'll do fine." Willow rubbed her back and looked at Kail for backup, but she simply stood on the balcony of the oversized suite.

"You'll be okay. It will all be over before you know it." Kail smiled as she held a half-empty glass of chilled champagne in the air.

"I hope you're right." Mahina smiled as she stood up. "It's time to get dressed."

Mahina wore a simple gown with crystal and pearl accents by Camille La Vie and the bridesmaids were outfitted in kiwi cocktail-length Alfred Angelo dresses as they entered the carriage waiting for them in front the of lavish hotel.

Mahina carried kiwi-centered pale-pink gerbera daisies with crystal accents in a Victorian silver bouquet holder, and the bridesmaids carried hand-wrapped bouquets of the same flower. Kail was the exception. She was the flower girl in a sense and she carried six long-stemmed flowers. She would give one to each mother and grandmother who stood in for Mahina since she had no living relatives besides her and Willow.

The carriage pulled up to the front of the biggest church in Hawaii. The church was once the mansion of the town's founder. It had a beautiful garden at the back, so it went perfectly with Mahina and Gino's theme for their wedding. The driver let the door open for them as they all exited the carriage.

The garden was naturally beautiful, so there wasn't much in the way of decoration. White wooden folding chairs filled with guests split by a petal-marked aisle awaited. Mahina made her way down the aisle as the bridesmaids who had walked seconds earlier waited on the side of the arch. The elderly woman standing in for Mahina held their flowers tightly that Kail had given them as tears formed in their eyes. Onlookers admired Mahina's dress and countless gasps could be heard aloud.

They all looked in the handmade programs, which included a beautiful Cherokee prayer that was translated for one of the many ancestral touches as the sounds of a harp echoed throughout the garden. Mahina walked into the opening of the beautiful white arch as Gino, who was dressed in an all-white tux with the same flower his bride was holding hanging out of his top pocket, smiled as he leaned up in his wheelchair.

The ceremony began as they exchanged beautiful vows followed by a reading they both loved from a book. The piece was an old Apache wedding vow that Willow knew. Following the ceremony's end, they were announced husband and wife, and everyone headed to the reception.

"You got everything packed?" Willow asked Kail as they dipped through the busy streets of the island.

"Yes, we good," she replied.

"Let's change." Willow pulled in front of their condo. "Then we will head there."

Kail complied as they went upstairs to get out of the bridesmaids dresses. They scurried everything they would need after they got dressed and loaded it in the trunk of the car. Jewelry, clothes, Kail's car, and other things were all left behind at the condo that would soon become abandoned. The person who cleaned it out would make a grip off of the stuff that they left behind.

They swung in and out of lanes in a rush to make it to the reception. They wanted to make it there on time; every minute counted. Today was the day they would get their revenge and nothing was going to stop them.

Eight

Willow and Kail parked a couple of blocks from the building where the reception was held. Willow rolled down the driver window of her midnight-blue Range Rover as they watched countless people go in and out of the establishment. They staked it out and eyed their surroundings like they did every job they worked.

"I say we go shoot every fucking body." Kail pulled an AK-47 from in between her legs while rubbing on the barrel with her neon-orange nails.

"Think, Kail," Willow responded as she leaned in the backseat to grab a box, "we don't want to make a scene; just get in, kill, and get out." She opened the box revealing two AAC Evolution 40 suppressors. "Just do what we discussed."

"Silencers." Kail reached over and grabbed one. "This is legit," she said as the cool from the steel shot goose bumps through her skin making her anxious to use it.

"I know, let's go," Willow ordered as she opened the door with Kail following.

Their feet paced calmly as they crossed the busy streets. They both held their clutches in their hands, the guns on their person hidden perfectly under their black babydoll Chanel dresses. Their hair flowed well past their shoulders as they approached the greeter at the door.

"Names, please?" the security asked, stopping them.

"They're VIP," Mahina said as she appeared through the double glass doors inviting her nieces inside.

Bright lights filled the room like a million fireflies on a cold summer's night. A band played as waitresses and waiters walked around in black server clothes with top-shelf wine and hors d'oeuvres on their trays. It was a high-society event, and since Gino was over most of the businesses in Hawaii, everyone who was anyone was in attendance.

"You girls look beautiful," Mahina said as they reached a table filled with small diamonds surrounding the plate settings, "please take a seat."

"Look at my nieces." Gino wheeled behind Kail and Willow and hugged their necks from behind. "We have an announcement," he said as the smell of liquor escaped from his mouth.

"What is it?" Willow asked.

"We're about to announce it now." Mahina signaled for Gino to follow her to the stage.

Kail scoped the surroundings to check out the security. It was a habit of hers anytime she was on a job. In three minutes flat, she had counted everyone in the room.

"Thank you all for coming." Mahina held her wedding ring in the air for all to see. "We are finally married, and since everyone we care about is in the room," she said as she pointed toward Melee, "including my beautiful niece-in-law that came all the way from Philly."

"She's pregnant," Gino interrupted as he grabbed at Mahina's stomach.

"This changes nothing," Kail whispered to Willow as she gulped the wine in her mouth softly.

Everyone in attendance gave their congratulations as a barrage of claps overpowered the soft jazz music that was being played by the band.

"Do it now," Kail mumbled to Willow as she continued clapping, letting a fake smile take over her face, exposing her beautiful innocent smile.

Willow stood up as the lights from the chandeliers sparkled the diamond tennis bracelet around her wrist. She clapped as she approached the microphone standing next to Mahina and Gino.

"We been with Mahina, and Gino, since we were younger." Willow turned to them and smiled. "They are the only family me and my sister, Kail, know and we really want to give them something special to show our appreciation. Especially for all that they've done for us. So Mahina, Gino, if you two and the rest of our extended family," she said, referring to all of The Pink Lip Bandits, "could follow me and Kail to the back room, we have a surprise for you."

"This is going to be good," Mahina said as she approached the microphone. "Don't worry; we will share with you guys when we return of what it was."

Kail stood up as they all headed to the back room of the venue. Kail smiled as Gino's normal security that followed him everywhere stood still. She had paid them double not to hear or see anything, and it was money well spent. She knew Gino wouldn't notice because of his intoxication.

Willow closed the double doors of the back room as Kail stood next to her. This was it, this was the moment they had been waiting for, and this was justice for their mother.

"Okay, you guys," Kail sashayed over to the light switch, "close your eyes and don't open them until we tell you to."

They all obliged as the lights went off. Kail tossed Willow the night vision goggles that she had stashed there the night before as darkness filled the room. They pulled out their guns as they saw their targets in a optic green color.

"Surprise, motherfuckas," Kail screamed as she aimed and shot, starting with Mahina and Gino. Willow joined as a stampede of bullets filled the air.

An eerie silence took over the room as the bullets stopped. Willow and Kail checked pulses with their guns never leaving the aiming position. They had hit heads and hearts, so they knew no one should have been left breathing.

"You ungrateful bitches." Mahina panted as she crawled toward the door, her nails breaking in the beautiful marble floor as she pulled her weight. "After I took you in, this is how you repay me. Fuck you."

"No, fuck you, bitch," Kail said as she stood over Mahina, "and your unborn bastard child. See you in hell." She released two rounds to the back of Mahina's head.

"Hello," a voice called out from the entrance of the room, "Uncle Gino?"

"Who the fuck is that?" Willow asked with a whisper.

"I don't fucking know." Kail hissed as the lights flashed on.

Melee stood there as her eyes adjusted to the lights. Tears filled her eyes as she looked around the room at the massacre that had taken place only minutes earlier. She dashed for the door when two guns filled her view, pointing directly at her.

The bullet came at the speed of light. Everything started moving slowly around Melee as a pressure forced through her back, exiting her chest. She fell forward, her eyes rolling around in their sockets as a strange feeling of unusual pain took over her. Her lungs produced two more breaths for her until her vision went completely dark. She was dead.

"Let's go." Kail tossed the goggles and headed toward the emergency exit.

Willow's eyes looked at the beautiful woman as blood flowed out of her mouth onto the buffed floor. Willow saw herself in the woman as her lifeless body lay frozen with a bullet inside of her that wasn't meant for her.

"Willow," Kail shook her out of the trance, "in and out."

"I know," she said as she walked toward the entrance of the room. "I'll meet you outside in five minutes. I forgot my clutch."

"Leave it and come on," Kail suggested.

"I'll be right out." Willow disappeared through the doors.

Willow eased through the crowd as she saw her clutch from afar. She leaned over the table and picked it up as an urge to drink took over her. All she wanted was a chilled glass of Grand Marnier.

Willow made her way to the open bar as the images of the woman's life they had just taken haunted her brain. The woman didn't even know what she had died for. She was at the wrong place at the wrong time.

"Hennessy straight up," a voice bellowed next to Willow as she sat down on a stool at the bar, her heel tapping the floor to the beat of the music.

Damn, Willow thought to herself as she eyed the chocolate thug next to her. Their eyes met as he smiled at her, exposing his perfect smile. Willow was impressed by his appearance; a dark-skinned man dressed in all white made her pussy wet, especially since it was designer.

She eyed him once more as he took sips from the cold cocktail glass that the bartender set in front of him. She watched his lips as she wondered what all he could do with them. His hands looked strong as they held the glass and it drove Willow crazy.

"And what can I get for you, pretty lady?" the bartender asked Willow as he gave her all of his attention.

"She'll have Grand Marnier, straight up," the chocolate gentleman said as his thuggish charm intrigued Willow.

"Is that so?" the bartender questioned.

"What the fuck did I just say?" the man snapped, feeling disrespected.

"Coming right up." The bartender's face turned bloodshot red.

"If that motherfucka spit in my drink, that's your ass," Willow said, never looking in his direction.

"No, if dude spit in yo' drink, that's his ass. Ya mean? All men are accountable for their own actions." He took another sip from the light-brown liquid in his glass.

"Agreed." The bartender set a glass in front of her. "So what made you think that this would be what I wanted?" she asked as she sipped through the straw.

"I know the difference between a woman who would enjoy a forty, and one who would enjoy the taste of Grand Marnier. Seeing that the bracelet around yo' wrist cost you about one hundred fat boys, I'm sure you never had a forty in yo' life." He took a sip of the Hennessy as he undressed her with his eyes.

"You would be right." Willow rubbed her fingers through her hair.

"So what does the tattoo of that locket on your ring finger mean?" He looked down at her soft, moisturized hands.

"It's not worth talking about," she lied. "So what is a man like you doing in Hawaii?" she asked to change the subject.

"I'm working," he said with a sly grin, "I'm on a job."

"What kind of job is that?"

"The kind that pretty women like you wouldn't understand because it involves getting my hands dirty."

"You'd be surprised." She stood up, drinking the last of the liqueur through the straw, leaving small traces of her pink lipstick on the tip. "Don't judge a book by the cover. I'm sure whatever you do is a walk in the park next to my profession." She smiled and walked away.

"Wait," he walked after her, "I didn't get yo' name."

"That's because I didn't give it to you."

Willow exited the building as she eyed the blocks for Kail. She needed to get out of there as soon as possible. The last thing she wanted was to be questioned about the surprise that she and Kail had given Mahina and Gino. She didn't need anyone to remember her face. She looked backward out of the corner of her eye as the man from the bar walked up on her slowly. She smiled as she continued piercing down the dark searing streets.

"I'm Craig," he said as he stood directly next to her.

"Willow."

"So do you have a nigga?"

"No, I do not." A Range Rover with Kail driving pulled up and put her mind at ease.

"I'm only in Hawaii for tonight," he walked toward the curb, "and, I would love to spend it with you."

"I don't even know you." She opened the door to the car.

"You can get to know me." He smiled at her.

"If it were any other time, then maybe." She closed the door as she climbed into the car.

"No number?" he asked as she rolled the window down.

"I'll make a deal with you; if I ever see you again in life, it's a date," she said through the window as the car sped off down the street.

Craig stood there captivated by Willow's beauty. He had never seen a woman so beautiful in his whole twenty-three years of life.

He had a main shorty back home, but for a woman as breathtaking as Willow, he would have replaced her. He wondered if he would ever see her again.

A ripple of screams escaping the doors of the building grabbed Craig's attention. People running from a mass hysteria, falling and being crushed by others stampeded out of the door. Craig pushed through the crowd as expressions of panic filled the room.

Craig stepped into the room that he saw waitresses point toward as he felt its icy gesture as the air adjusted around him. Sprawled on the ground, covered in blood, was Melee. He looked around the room and eyed the other dead bodies covering the floor.

Ring-Ring-Ring!

The realization struck him like a bullet as his phone started to ring and Rock's name appeared on the screen. He couldn't tell him that his attention was focused elsewhere and as a result, his baby girl was murdered. There was no way he could mouth those words to Rock without digging his grave.

He ignored the call as he reached down and picked up Melee's lifeless body. He needed to get her out of sight before the police showed up and discovered the massacre. The last thing he needed was to be caught on the scene of a bloodbath.

He looked down at Melee's face as he walked through the emergency exit doors that led to an alleyway. The blood from her wounds stained his white shirt as he walked and thought of a plan. He had to figure out what to do by morning. If he stepped one foot on Philly soil without Melee, he would be killed immediately.

Nine

"You know the plan for Philly, right?" Willow asked Kail as they walked through the double doors of Honolulu International Airport.

"We lay low for some months," Kail opened her Louis Vuitton luggage to grab their tickets, "then we resurrect The Pink Lip Bandits, and start making some crazy dough again."

"I mean lay the fuck low, Kail," Willow warned as they approached the terminal. "We don't need to make our presence known until shit here cools down."

"I know." Kail nodded in agreement. "So are we going to meet up with Nicole, Choice, and everybody else we use to fuck with when we were kids?"

"In due time," Willow assured.

Kail nodded her head as they stood in the long, bustling terminal. Willow could sense the excitement of tourists and vacationers waiting to be flown to their far-flung dream destinations. But, she couldn't share that excitement because she was saying goodbye to a place that she had called home for the past fourteen years of her life.

They queued at check-in desks. Willow could see groups of people all with their suitcases talking about the once-in-a-lifetime opportunity to travel and what they would do while they were staying in Hawaii. Their faces brimmed with happiness, grinning like Cheshire cats.

As they approached the check-in agent to retrieve their boarding passes and check in their luggage, Willow could feel her stomach pulsating as a piece of her didn't want to go. She was thinking of all ways possible to tell Kail that they should stay. She wanted to make a scene and scream that she had a bomb just so they wouldn't board the plane. But, she knew there was nothing left for them in Hawaii, and Philly would be their fresh start. Philly would be the beginning of their new lives.

After passing through the security checkpoint, they settled in the waiting area.

"G-15 is departing in fifteen minutes. G-15 is departing in fifteen minutes." The speaker called out to let them know it was time to board after they had waited an hour in the uncomfortable blue connected chairs.

After boarding, the flight attendant pointed toward first-class as Kail and Willow located their plush seats.

"Would you ladies care for something to drink?" she asked with a smile.

"Something strong." Kail yawned as she leaned back into her neck pillow that she had brought on the plane.

"And, for you?" the same flight attendant asked.

"She'll have Grand Marnier," a voice interrupted from behind.

Willow turned her head as Craig walked into first-class, his eyes locked on her. She smiled on the inside, never changing her facial expression. She eyed him as the sound of the Timberlands stomping on his feet got closer and closer. She basked in his scent as he took the seat across from her. His smooth, dark Egyptian-like skin shined as he made himself comfortable for the eight-hour flight.

"Now if I recall, you said if we ever met again in life, it was a date." Craig smiled at Willow. "So what's up, shorty?"

"I said that had it been a coincidence, but it seems like you're stalking me."

"Stalking? Girl, I am Philadelphia. What you know about my city?" Craig asked as he looked at the flight attendant. "I'll have—"

"Hennessy," Willow finished his sentence.

"You remembered?"

"I have the mind of an elephant, Craig." She looked at Kail, who was now snoring. "I remember everything."

"I see." He looked past Willow. "Damn, shorty cuttin' up." He laughed.

"Hey, now leave my baby sister alone." Willow chuckled. "She's tired; we had a very long day."

The sound of the captain advising everyone to fasten their seat-belts over the intercom interrupted their conversation. Willow could hear the engines start to roar as she got pushed gently back in her seat as the plane accelerated to over 140 miles per hour.

When the plane lifted in the air, she could feel a slightly different push against her seat since the plane was accelerating forward but also upward. After a minute, the engines started to quiet down and slowly level off.

Willow watched out the window as the plane started to reach its altitude. She wanted to lie back and relax, but knew she couldn't with Craig sitting across from her and Kail snoring next to her.

Craig was not paying attention to her at the moment. He was playing with his sunglasses that hung from his shirt's front pocket. He was waiting for the plane to get up in the clouds. He loved the view of the beautiful sky. When Willow took a deep breath and looked out the window again, they were high in the sky, and she could see what had silenced Craig. Her breath was taken away.

"This view is relaxing," Craig said. "It gives you a reason to take yo' mind off that other bullshit."

"I know what you mean, and right now I need something to clear my mind," Willow said as she continued to gaze out of the window.

"What could be pressing a woman like you who seems to have it all?" he asked.

"I told you earlier that you'd be surprised about the life that I live."

"You'd feel the same way about me," Craig assured. "Damn, I wish I had some Mary Jane right now."

"You got a rillo?" Willow raised her eyebrow at him.

"Straight up." He looked at her. "If you about to ask me what I think you're about to ask me, you truly are a completely different shorty than what I thought."

"I told you." Willow pulled a small sack of dark green leaves out of her clothing and tossed it his way. "Don't judge the inside of a book without having read it."

"How we gon' fire this up?" he asked with a smile.

"Here," she said as she tossed him the pack of matches that she'd pulled the staple out of to get it past the detectors, "roll that shit up."

"You crazy as hell." Craig threw the weed and box of matches back at her. "You gon' have a nigga in some handcuffs for real, fucking with you."

"Scared?" Willow questioned.

"I'm just smart, shawty." Craig pulled out two pills from his pocket and handed one to Willow. "This will do the same thing that weed will do."

"What is it?"

"Something that won't have the air marshal harassing us." Craig put the pill in his mouth, using the chilled Hennessy as a chaser. Willow followed his lead.

Willow and Craig talked almost the whole flight as they enjoyed each other's company. Secrets that they'd promised never to tell anyone were discussed with no judgment with how they made their money being the exception. In a matter of hours, they went from feeling like strangers to potnas that had known each other since the sandbox. Their chemistry was magnetic.

"That pill made me horny as hell," Willow blurted out as she reached over and touched Craig's leg while sipping the liquid that danced around the glass she was holding through a straw. She had paid the two first-class flight attendants to keep the drinks coming, and they were doing just that.

"I feel you." Craig put the rim of the glass to his lips and sipped. "You should let me handle that fo' ya."

"You wouldn't know what to do with it." Willow seductively stood up. "I have to use the little girl's room. I'll be right back."

Willow swayed down the aisle as Craig's eyes watched her booty go up and down in the small dress around her frame. He stood up, letting lust take over his mind as he walked down the aisle following her every move. She could feel him behind her; it's exactly what she wanted him to do.

"It's one at a time." Willow looked back at Craig with her glossy eyes; his body on hers as they stood outside of the small airplane bathroom.

"Go inside." He moved her body with his from behind. "I wanna show you something."

Willow willingly accepted his offer as they went into the small, compact room. They were standing close together facing each other; the room was warm. He gazed into her eyes, gently kissed her forehead, then she raised her head to the kissing position, put her arms around him and was breathing heavily with her head resting on his shoulders. His hands wandered toward her breasts, and she moved a bit tighter with her lower limbs, and heaved a huge sigh.

He brushed his fingers across her shoulders, letting the straps of her dress fall. Pulling her into a gentle embrace, his lips caressed hers as they tumbled into the toilet, her long hair framing her perfect face. Running his hands down her curvaceous body, Craig looked deep into her greenish-brown eyes and knew that in a matter of hours, he had fallen in love. Slowly, they took turns removing each other's clothing; until all that separated them was Willow's excited breathing blowing gently on his chest.

Craig leaned down and licked on her breast as his fingers explored the diamond between Willow's legs. He slowly went in and out with his fingers as he felt her body tense up. He took his fingers out of her pussy as he picked her body up, her pussy now directly in his face. He licked on it, and slowly nibbled on her pearl making her lose her senses until he felt her release her juices onto his tongue.

Craig massaged all eight inches of his massive manhood as he slowly guided Willow onto it. Sucking and biting on her breast, he went in and out of her, her moans soft and gentle as she fucked him back and rode him with intensity. She could feel him in the bottom of her stomach as the feeling was electrifying.

Willow turned around on Craig's pole with it still inside of her. She started throwing her ass back into his dick as she controlled her muscles to get tighter. As Craig sped up, so did she, knowing that he would nut soon. Grabbing her hair, Craig went as far in her as he could go as he released his spawn deep inside of her.

"I don't usually do this." Willow looked back at him, his member still inside of her. "I don't want you to think I'm a hoe."

"I know what kind of woman you are." Craig pulled out of her and wiped himself off with an undershirt he had planned to dispose of.

The captain buzzed over the speaker. "We will be making our landing into Philadelphia International Airport in approximately twenty minutes. Please fasten your seat belts and make sure your trays are in an upright and locked position. Do not leave your seats until we are safely at the gate. Thank you for flying Honolulu Airlines."

Craig studied Willow's face for a moment as she put the strap of her dress over her shoulder. Her eyes seemed to roam around the tiny restroom as if she was expecting something to happen. She stood there as he saw regret on her face. It wasn't that she didn't enjoy it; it was good. It was the fact that she was feeling him just as much, and felt like she'd given it up too soon.

"Ma'am, sir, you have to return to your seats immediately," a flight attendant ordered as she knocked on the door.

"Fuck." Craig opened the door. "We are about to return now."

"Also," the attendant looked past Craig and at Willow, "this is a restroom, not a motel!"

Willow rushed by Craig as embarrassment took over her. She didn't make eye contact with anyone as she strolled down the aisle. Her high coming down, she sat down, looking straight ahead until she connected the navy seat belt around her waist.

She could see Craig sitting in his seat out the corner of her eye. Embarrassment wasn't present on his face, but Willow could sense that he shared the same feeling as her as eyes stared at them. She signaled for him to put on his seat belt.

The 727 tilted slightly to the left and began a slow and steady turn. Down below, the ground looked like square plots on a huge map of some kind. Gradually, everything began to come into view. As they neared the ground, small cars heading down the black ribbon of long highways came into view, as well as various colored homes of different sizes and shapes. A sudden bump alerted the landing gear was released. Willow jumped slightly at the sound.

Feeling his ears pop, Craig opened his mouth in an attempt to release the pressure. Trees and rooftops whizzed by as the aircraft made its final turn onto the waiting runway and ended with a mild rumbling as the tires kissed the tarmac. A loud rush of air giving pressure to the brakes slowly brought the plane to an Indy 500 speed, culminating into the final act of landing and then taxiing to the arrival gate.

"I guess I'll see you around." Willow smiled his way.

"What about a number?" he asked as he smiled back at her.

"This is Philadelphia; we'll see each other again," Willow said as she shook Kail to wake her up.

"You may now exit the plane," the flight attendant's voice said on the loud speaker as the seatbelt light went from on to off.

Willow and Kail stood up, reached up to grab their carry-on bags, and exited the plane. Willow could feel Craig looking at her. His eyes piercing through her made her short of breath. She could feel his energy vibrating through her body.

Craig leaned back in his seat as other passengers passed him. He looked at Willow thinking maybe his lust had run her off. She looked back at him as they stared at each other for several moments. There was passion in their eyes that was more intense than just sex. She said goodbye without mouthing a word.

Willow and Kail exited the plane as lights shined above their heads. They headed to baggage claim, using the white arrows as their guide, to collect their belongings. They collected their luggage, picked the keys up to the car they had rented in advance, and before they knew it, they were on the streets of Philly headed to their five-star hotel room to lay low.

Craig was on Willow's mind as the flashing traffic lights hit in and out of her eyes as she drove through the empty streets. It had been a long time since she had felt this way about a man. As she pulled into the entrance of the hotel, she wondered if she would ever see Craig again.

Ten

Craig's heart pounded like a jackhammer as he saw Rock approach him with a sinister smile. He tried again to free his hands from their bonds; this time in hysterical desperation as he saw him slowly pull something from his pockets.

Rock inched forward, taking his time to enjoy the moment, and Craig's helplessness. His wrists burned from the constant scraping. Fresh beads of sweat started to form over his already drenched body as he saw a silver glint from the corner of his eye.

His body started shuddering and heaving when he saw what his sick instrument of torture was: pliers. Sadistic as Rock was, he laughed out loud when he saw Craig's realization. Rock came in close, and whispered in his ear, "I haven't spoken to or seen my daughter in three fucking months, and I think you know more than what you've admitted to me, boy."

His words were strongly laced with malice, which sent a cold shiver down Craig's spine. Rock gently took hold of his hand after failed attempts of jerking away due to the bonds being too tight. Slowly, but firmly, he opened his fingers one at a time.

"Do you have something you want to admit?" Rock asked.

Craig shook his head no, never screaming from the pain as he felt the blood drain from his face as black spots danced in front of his eyes. He could feel the cold steel pincers around his middle finger.

"Tell me!" Rock screamed.

All Craig could do was squeeze his eyes shut, and bite down hard on his gag, waiting for the inevitable pain to end, as he started to feel the pressure build. His vision went in and out from the blood he'd lost. He never screamed but met his fate with silence.

"I don't think he knows anything, Pops." Junior walked up to them. "Maybe Melee has gone away somewhere."

Junior's height trumped his father as he stood next to him. The business suit specially tailored for him fitted his body perfectly. His hair was cut into a fade, and from first glance by his demeanor, he could easily be mistaken for a lawyer.

"Fuck that," Rock spat. "She would never leave without telling me."

Rock leaned on his desk as the watch on his arm slid down onto the top of his hand. His jaw clenched as he saw the picture of Melee looking at him, taunting him in a sense. He couldn't believe that his baby girl was gone without a trace, and the thought of her lying dead somewhere in a ditch or ocean infuriated him.

"Get this motherfucker outta my face," Rock ordered the security as he took a seat behind his desk.

"She will show up." Junior sat across from his father, his hands intertwined. "Melee is probably across the country shopping in a mall somewhere," he said with a fake smile.

"You're probably right," Rock agreed with hope. "Did anything turn up from the private investigators in Hawaii?" he asked as he gazed out of the window.

"Nothing at all."

"Something just doesn't feel right." Rock looked at his son. "Do you think she's dead?"

"Honestly?" He leaned back in the chair. "I don't know but to leave without a trace isn't like her."

A knock on the door interrupted their conversation as Tony

entered the room. He pulled out a cigar and lit it before taking a seat next to Junior. He took off his hat and set it on the desk as he puffed on the brown stick.

"Did I see Craig getting carried away?" Tony asked as he blew smoke out of his mouth.

"Yeah," Junior stood up to leave, "Pops tortured him trying to get some information."

"You still think young blood know something he not telling you?" Tony slammed the door closed behind Junior.

"I know he knows something and whatever he may know is the only reason he is alive." Rock stood up to head to the meeting. He was late.

"I saw Vinny earlier," Tony said as they entered the hallway to make it to the conference room.

"Are you sure?" Rock asked, never looking at him.

"I'm sure," Tony assured as they approached the room. "And, by the time I looked for a second time, he had disappeared."

Rock and Tony entered the conference room as a large square wood table sat directly in the middle with a group of his most loyal workers surrounding it. Rock took the head seat as the women surrounding the room poured drinks and passed out cigars. He eyed his workers as they all lit up their cigars.

The room was spacious with black-and-white photos covering the walls. There was everything a man in their line of work could need in the room. Smoke filled the air as gulps from men drinking their liquor could be heard.

"We have a problem." Rock looked around the room. "Vinny has been spotted and as all of you know, I want his head," his teeth started to show, "on my fucking wall. So with that being said, the first man to bring me the body of Vincent Mancini, will receive one million dollars in cash."

The group of men all looked at each other with cold stares. Never in the Mafia history had a bounty been worth so much money. They all sat and observed the words coming out of Rock's mouth knowing that he was letting his personal feelings cloud his business mind.

"Also," Rock closed his eyes, "the apple of my eye, Melee, is still missing. Anyone who can find her, give me a lead to find her, or give me any kind of information regarding her whereabouts, I'd pay two million dollars cash."

"Make it five," Evelyn said as she entered the room.

The men gawked at her appearance as she walked over next to Rock and leaned down. "Can I speak to you outside?" she asked with her lips, as red as a rose, almost touching his ear.

"Tony," Rock stood up, "can you handle this?"

Tony nodded as they exited the room.

Evelyn walked a little bit quicker than Rock on purpose as her hair bounced to the rhythm of her heels. The lengthy white Prada dress hugged her body as it flowed gorgeously with each step that she took. The breathtaking diamond earrings that hung from her ears matched the wedding ring that hugged her ring finger.

"What's up?" Rock asked her, stopping in the middle of their wide, long hallway.

"Did I just hear you call a hit out on my father?" Evelyn asked as she folded her arms.

"I did," Rock said calmly. "Your family is notorious for them, so I'd just thought I would take a page out of your book."

"Why would you do that?"

"Evelyn, I don't have to answer shit you ask me. I'm the godfather around this motherfucker and if I want to call a hit on your ass, I can," he said as he started to walk away.

"Don't forget who helped you get here, Rock." Evelyn screamed after him. "I love you, but don't think for a minute that you can't be overthrown!"

Evelyn pulled out her cell phone as she went out the front door of their mansion. She hit the alarm to her BMW and got inside. She dialed a number as she drove around the fountain parking area, cutting on the air conditioner and making her hair blow wildly.

"You've been spotted, Poppa," Evelyn said as she headed to the strip club that she owned.

"I know, Evelyn; I still have eyes everywhere in this city," Vinny said.

"Just be careful; there's a large amount for your life, and if you're seen, it's over. Bye, Poppa," she warned as she hung up.

Evelyn cruised down the streets as the thought of her one and only daughter, Melee, stayed on her mind. She always thought about if she was okay or not. As a mother, she had to keep hope in order to make it. As a businesswoman, she had to think of her as dead in order to conduct business. Already mourning for Melee, she hoped to see the day when it would have been for naught.

Willow looked over the city from her and Kail's spacious condo where they had recently moved. She looked down from the balcony, thinking of how they were going to make some major figures like they had done in Hawaii. With no connections in Philly, she had to figure out a way to get clientele.

"I'm tired of sitting in this house," Kail said as she joined Willow on the balcony. "Look at this city," she shoved her sister with her shoulder, "you know how much bread we can be raking in right now?"

"Kail, I know this." Willow leaned over the rail, enjoying the tangent breeze from the snowstorm.

"We have been hiding out for three months. Three long months, Will; ain't nobody looking for us so let's get back to this money." Kail handed her a golden container.

"Making money for me has never been an issue." Willow grabbed the container and opened it, revealing the never-used powder-pink lipstick inside. "But, we don't have clients like we did in Hawaii. We need to build a rapport with these big names here."

"So let's do it."

Willow slid the smooth lipstick up as she put her lips together. She put the cold mush on her lips perfectly without a flinch. She had been putting on this lipstick for thirteen years; she didn't need a mirror. She put her lips together as the color that she loved, and hated at the same time, once again marked her identity.

"It's a strip club I heard about before we even made it back here." Willow walked into the condo with Kail trailing. "Can you get a rifle scope?" she asked as she thought of a plan.

Willow's eyes slowly adjusted to the dim lights in the room. She looked at the small fire burning on one side of the wall, surrounded by a huge, brown couch and a rocking chair with red pillows. She looked to her left and saw a large dining table, with several chairs around it, a small closet with lots of dishes and glasses behind it, and several mirrors on the sides of the partially separated room.

Near the middle of the living room were three large red sofas forming a "U" with a low table in front of them. Only a large vase sat with three beautiful red roses in front of the sofas with a big TV stand with two units on each side.

"I can find anything." Kail took the scarf off her head, letting her long, delicate hair that she'd wrapped earlier fall into place.

"I know." Willow went into the kitchen and took down two wine glasses from a rack. "Listen closely, because this should get us some quick cash, a new Pink Lip Bandit, and some clientele."

"A new Pink Lip Bandit?" Kail watched Willow pour their glasses half full with Moët. "You know I don't work well with others."

"Don't worry." Willow handed her the glass. "It's somebody you would like."

"So what's the plan?" Kail took a sip from the wine with her ears completely open.

"Are you down to make a move tonight?" Willow asked.

"Like shoes." Kail leaned back on the countertop and listened to the plan that took Willow five minutes to devise.

W illow walked into Sweet Lips, an upscale strip club off the beaten path of northeast Philly as the Fendi dress hugged her petite frame. Her hair was a rich shade of mahogany, which flowed in waves to adorn her glowing, porcelain-like skin. Her eyes, framed by long lashes, were a bright hazel with hints of emerald-green that seemed to brighten the world. A straight nose, full lips; she appeared to be perfection and she knew it.

From around the corner, she could hear the somnolent buzz of the eponymous neon-red lips out front, providing a backdrop for the clinking of glasses and drone-like chatter of hundreds of niggas who were ready to spend their money and bitches who would do anything for it. She bit her lips from the excitement of the dough she was about to rack up.

The brisk cold wind from the snowstorm entered the joint with her as the intermingled smells of smoke and sweat and too many people instantly assaulted her nostrils as she inhaled deeply. *Ahhh, it's good to be home and out the house*, she thought aloud while pushing her body through the pulsating crowd as her heels clicked with anticipation.

Finding her way to an empty barstool in the corner, she caught several men's eyes. She shook her head and smiled downward laughing to herself at the nonstop glances she received. She wasn't new to the attention. She was used to men gawking at her.

"Grand Marnier straight up," she mouthed to the bartender; he nodded and melted away into the cries of a hundred other thirsty customers.

By now, Willow's eyes were adjusting to the intimate darkness, tomblike and womblike at the same time. Bright spots of neon beer signs on the wall stood out, illuminating the faces and bodies of the crowd, while others disappeared into the contrasting blackness. She pierced through the crowd to see if she recognized anyone, but her efforts were in vein.

A moment later, before her thought was even finished, her Grand Marnier slid in front of her, and the bartender was gone before she could look up to mouth the word *thanks*. She clearly understood that one spoke to a bartender with cash, not words, so she didn't take it personally. She just simply put her money down on the wood bar.

Willow took her first sip of the elegant mixture, cold and icy, slightly sweet and tangy against her full lips, which were accented by a small beauty mark. She held the drink in her mouth for only a moment and let the ice, Grand Marnier, and lime pulp wallow against her tongue. The sensation alone made her inside's tingle and she knew she would have several more before the night was up.

She felt a pair of hands on her waist, making her jump at the sensation. Turning quickly, her eyes locked with Duke's, a dope boy from around the way. There were no words that could sum up the intense wave of attraction as she looked at this man. His hands fell from Willow's hips, and her skin bristled at the touch. The small hairs on her arms rose, despite the cold air circulating the establishment.

Willow eyed Duke up and down to check if the gear matched the face. She studied his whole ensemble in less than ten seconds.

Armani, she thought as she eyed the stitching of the button-down adorning Duke's body. She knew designers simply from the stitching. *A Girard-Perregaux watch*, Willow kept thinking as her eyes wondered, *that watch cost ten stacks.*

"Let me get ten bottles of Dom," Duke said as the bartender gave him his full attention. "Just have them sent to VIP."

"I'll get right on that," the bartender replied.

Duke looked at Willow with the same intentions. He looked her up and down to see where her level was. He let off a small grin as he turned around and walked away, disappearing through the crowd. Although he liked what he saw, he was on a date and she was eyeing his every move from the glass VIP room that overlooked the bar.

Willow looked up at the chocolate beauty that was looking at her with disgust. She winked at her and held her half-empty glass up in her direction. The woman rolled her eyes at her and flipped her off before moving out of view. Willow smiled as she finished the concoction, leaving nothing but ice and a straw in the oval glass.

"Bartender," she waved him over, "let me get another one of these, and send something fruity to the dark chick upstairs in VIP that's wearing the canary yellow."

Willow grabbed her drink as she watched a waitress go up the stairs into the VIP area. She smiled when she saw the same waitress return with the drink still on her circle carrier.

"She said she doesn't drink cheap shit." The waitress set the drink in front of Willow.

"Well, she sure as hell wears cheap shit," Willow thought aloud as she chugged the remainder of her drink and made her way through the crowd, leaving the fruity mixture on the bar untouched.

"Next up to the stage is Choice," the DJ spat through the microphone as the crowd went wild. "All y'all niggas and bitches get yo' wallets out for this sexy-ass woman. Get your dough out and tip this woman."

Willow made her way to the enormous square stage directly in the center of the first level. She eyed all around her as the lights dimmed and a crowd rushed to the stage. She put a piece of her mane behind her ear as she eagerly waited to see what all the commotion was about.

The lights flashed on as the music boomed throughout the club making the floor vibrate. Willow focused on the silk curtain that was in between two stage mirrors. She knew that Choice, her childhood friend, would enter through the curtain. She wasn't new to the strip world; she had been to several strip clubs.

The curtain swung open as a girl with longish, brown hair that cascaded over her shoulders appeared. It contrasted with her gray-blue eyes well. Her skin was pale; not in an anemic way, but enough so that it suggested she didn't go out much. Her smile was small and shy, but it spread across all of her features, making her eyes twinkle.

The girl started dancing as her legs, bowlegged as could be, shined without a mark on them. Her small waist was complemented by the colossal-sized ass that was unbelievable for the petite frame she owned. Her breasts were firm and her soft light-brown nipples stood erect as she cavorted around the stage.

"She bad." Willow smirked. "She would be perfect."

Willow watched as the stage went from brown to green from all of the money that filled it. There were some big-baller-type men in the building and she'd chosen the right night to come out of hiding to make some quick cash. She heard the song that was playing getting ready to end as she made her way to the DJ booth.

"Can I help you with summin,' sweetheart?" the DJ asked, removing the headphones from one side of his face.

"Can you play a song for me?" Willow asked.

"You dancing?" he asked as claps erupted throughout the building as Choice made her way off the stage.

"Yeah." Willow slowly unzipped the front of her Fendi dress. "Play 'Pop That' by French Montana," she requested as she handed him her six hundred-dollar dress.

"You didn't even tell me yo' name, ma." He threw the dress over his shoulder.

"I'm unknown." She smiled as she went through the doors that led to the curtain.

Dirty looks took over the faces of all the other dancers that were waiting their turn. They all looked at Willow with hateful eyes and it pumped her up. *That's right,* Willow thought to herself as she smiled at the dancers. *I'm at yo' job about to eat off yo' plate.* She laughed.

"Yo, who the fuck is that?" the girls whispered amongst themselves.

Don't stop, pop that don't stop, pop that pop that pop that don't stop, came booming through the speakers and Willow knew it was her cue. "Don't worry, bitches," she said as she opened the curtains, "I'll leave a few dollars in their wallets for you."

Willow looked into the crowd and as the music grew louder, the closer she got to the pole. She wasn't nervous; she knew she looked better than every woman there. She had never stripped before, but for the money they were throwing, she was about to learn. She started with skilled precision moves using her body and the pole. She slid down it, climbed up it, hung upside down from it as she controlled the muscles in her ass cheeks.

She removed her top, revealing her breasts as money started hitting the stage nonstop. She kept up her routine as the money flowed. Playing off the fantasy, she licked her lips at countless men as she massaged her nipples. She lay on her back and folded a hundred-dollar bill in half the long way. She put the bill down on the front of her g-strip and moved her legs in a circular motion. The crowd went wild as the hundred-dollar bill flew into the air off of Willow's pussy.

"Yo, did you see that shit?" Tristan, a neighborhood hardhead, said to Duke as they watched from the VIP window. "I ain't never seen no bitch do no shit like that."

"Me either." Duke removed his fitted cap and rubbed down his fade. "Tristan, make sure Cocoa gets home," he said as he headed for the door.

"Why do I have to go home?" Cocoa asked Duke, stopping him in his tracks. "I'm good right here." She fixed the sleeve of her deep-yellow dress.

Duke ignored her as he walked through the double doors. His Armani black button-up made shadows on the wall with each step he took. His jewelry played off the strobe lights as he made his way down the metal staircase. He approached the stage to get a close-up view on the bombshell that had caught his attention for the second time that night.

"Yo," Duke yelled at Willow, her eyes reading his lips. "Let me get at you for a moment."

"That was Unknown," the DJ spat with excitement through the microphone. "Yo, whoever shorty is, she need to be a regular. Now, next to the stage is Kisses."

Willow collected all of the money on the stage before she walked over to the DJ booth to get her dress, with Duke close behind.

She eased the dress down over her body as she tossed the two large wads of cash—that had nothing but hundreds, fifties, and twenties inside—on the booth.

"Yo, Unknown, that shit was fire." The DJ gave her a couple rubber bands for her money.

"Thank you." She started to roll her cash. "Thanks for the song," she said as she tossed some money to the DJ.

"So, your name is Unknown?" Duke asked from behind.

"Isn't that what the DJ just said?" Willow responded as she hid the money on her body.

"I wanted to let you know that you're too beautiful to be stripping. I think only one nigga should have the right to see yo' body." Duke handed her a wad of money. "But, since that's your profession, I guess I'll tip."

"You good." Willow handed him his wad of money back. "Plus, I don't strip. I came here to find a friend and I couldn't resist making some quick cash."

"Is that right?" he asked as he looked her up and down.

"So do you know this woman, Duke?" Evelyn asked as she walked up on them with two bouncers surrounding her.

Evelyn had to pause and look at Willow a second time as she got closer. She looked so much like Melee to her. They had the same kind of skin, the same expression, even the same chin that mimicked the bottom of a heart. She was floored at the resemblance.

"I don't know her at all, Evelyn," Duke said.

"Well, somebody better know who the fuck she is because she just danced on my stage without permission." Evelyn looked at Willow. "How much money did you make?"

"That's my business." Willow started to walk off. "I didn't see your old ass up there dancing."

"Grab her," Evelyn told the bouncers as they dashed for Willow.

"Get the fuck back." Willow turned around, her gun pointing at the bouncers.

"So you're a thug?" Evelyn asked with her hands on her hips as she wondered where the gun could have been hidden on the girl's body. "I don't think this is a game you want to play. Lower the gun, give me the money you made, and we will call it even. I'll even let you live."

"No, no deal," Willow said with a smile. "Why the fuck would I give you the money that I just made?"

"Because," Evelyn said, smiling back, "if you don't, you're going to die where you stand; I promise you this."

Evelyn pointed at the small red dot that was aimed at Willow's chest as a small laugh overwhelmed her. Willow lowered her gun as the bouncers grabbed her quickly, taking her gun from her. They held her arms and pressed them, getting revenge for her pointing a gun at them.

"Yo, y'all being too rough with her," Duke said.

"See, this is why you don't play with grown-ups." Evelyn smiled. "Take her ass to my office."

"If this is what you call being grown, then I would consider you to be an infant." Willow yelled out, "Where's the red dot?"

Evelyn looked at Willow's chest and the dot disappeared before her eyes. She looked up at the bodyguard from the near top of the building that she'd hired to scope out the place, and she could see his lifeless body lying face-down. Willow nodded toward her chest as a red dot was now aimed at Evelyn.

"Let her go," Evelyn said as sweat poured from her forehead. "I said, let her fucking go," she yelled.

"Willow?" Choice squinted her eyes. "Is that you?"

"Outside," Willow told Choice as she grabbed her gun from the bouncer's hand.

"Choice, you have two more dances tonight." Evelyn pointed her finger at her. "If you leave, you're done."

"It's more money for you with me so I suggest you come on," Willow said, walking through the crowd to exit the building.

Choice followed her through the crowd. She was tired of stripping and after lying to her man telling him that she had stopped, she figured now was the time to. She wanted to hear Willow out to see if it was legit or not. If it wasn't, she could always get her job back with Evelyn; she made her the most money.

"Yo, when did you get back to Philly?" Choice asked as the door to the club closed behind them. "Where is Kail and yo' moms? Why y'all ain't tell us y'all was coming back? We ain't heard from y'all in years."

"Follow me." Willow stalked down the street, her heels going in and out of the snow sticking to the ground.

Willow and Choice walked in silence as the winds from the storm cut them like a sharp knife slicing into a tomato. Although it was cold, and they had on small dresses, they kept walking, showing no signs of discomfort. They reached a black Range Rover and Willow got inside signaling for Choice to get in the back. Although Choice hadn't seen her in fourteen years, she trusted her, so she got inside.

"Look who I found," Willow told Kail as she put her hands in front of the heat blasting from the vents.

"Choice," Kail looked at her from the rearview mirror, "It's good to see you, girl."

"Y'all look the fucking same from when we was kids." Choice observed her surroundings. "So what y'all doing back in Philly?"

"About to make a whole lot of fuckin' money." Kail turned around and looked at Choice.

"Doing what?" Choice asked.

"Doing whatever's required. Listen, we not trying to put you on to nothing that you don't want to do, but it's money to be made and we can make it together." Willow looked back at Choice.

"How much money?" Choice asked.

"More than this." Willow took the two wads of money out of her clothes and tossed it on the dashboard. "No offense, but I know I made more than you, and this shit," she said as her manicured nail pointed at the money, "couldn't buy me a decent pair of shoes."

"This y'all whip?" Choice asked.

"This is my whip." Kail pointed at Willow. "This bitch got a Mercedes."

"I drive a Cobalt." Choice admired the interior of the car.

"A Cobalt." Kail shook her head. "Listen, me and Willow a part of something. It's kind of like an organization, but we think of it as a sisterhood. Me and her are the only two members left and we need at least another person."

"An organization." Choice leaned back against the cushion.

"Yes, you can say that. We call ourselves The Pink Lip Bandits. We take request from clients for a high price and fulfill those requests with no questions, no feelings, and no complications," Willow said.

"What kind of requests?"

"Murder, sex, robbery," Kail replied, facing forward, checking the mirrors and their surroundings. "If the money is right, we will do anything with a few twists."

"And, I can get paid like this?" Choice asked.

"Paid?" Kail turned back around. "I guarantee you that the Cobalt that you driving will be parked while your ass flosses around the city driving in a luxury car that you bought in cash."

"I'm in." Choice leaned her head in the front seat. "So what do I have to do?"

"First," Kail dug in her purse and pulled a golden container out, "let us see how you look with this powder-pink lipstick on."

Willow sat in the front seat as her mind raced. She was finally three deep and her plan to resurrect The Pink Lip Bandits was now in effect. All she had to do was sit back and wait for the clients to reach out to her. And, after the little show she'd put on at the strip club, she knew word would get out about her.

Twelve

E velyn sat at her cherry desk that seemed almost superfluous, since there was little to no paperwork to be seen. A deep-burgundy leather desk chair, which reclined to an almost obscene angle, held her up as she got her thoughts together. There were two small table lamps—one near the door atop a wicker table that clashed with the rest of the room's executive motif, and another on the cherrywood desk with a long brass pull-cord. The absence of overhead light cast shadows into the corners, spilling under the desk and over top of the framed black-and-white pictures on the wall.

Evelyn blinked a few times as her long lashes went up and down. *Is that Rock's daughter?* she thought to herself. She could have sworn that she was dead. *Tony said she was dead,* she thought as she looked at the baby-blue walls that had pictures of unfamiliar people scattered throughout the façade.

"You wanted to see me?" Duke walked into the office.

"Yes, have a seat." Evelyn opened her hand toward a chair.

Duke sat down with an uneasy feeling. He knew that Evelyn didn't like him. He'd known ever since he and Melee got together a few years back. If it wasn't for his loyal work for Rock, Evelyn would have disposed of him. And, since Melee was missing, he hoped Evelyn didn't suspect him.

"So you didn't know that woman?" Evelyn asked.

"No, tonight was my first time seeing her."

"Interesting." She tapped on the desk. "Do you think she resembled Melee?"

"A little bit."

Evelyn put her hand over her mouth to stifle a scream; she could hear her heart hammering in her ear, echoing through her head. As she realized that she was holding her breath, she eased the air out of her lungs slowly, and then the reality hit her. She tried to prevent the bile rising in her throat as the putrid truth invaded her thoughts.

The thought of Anoki and Willow being alive made her sick to her stomach. It was like a bad dream that she couldn't wake up from. She had Rock exactly where she wanted him, and although their marriage wasn't perfect by any means, it worked for her and she didn't need anything or anyone to mess it up.

"I have a job for you." She looked at Duke. "That girl that was just here; Willow is what Choice said her name was. I need you to get close to her."

"Close to her fo' what?" Duke asked.

"It's none of your fucking business; just do it." She waved him off. "Don't tell anyone about this. Keep your mouth closed and report to me on everything that she tells you. You hear me?"

"Yes, I hear you."

"Evelyn, it's clear," one of the bouncers said as he walked through the office door. "All the top levels of every building within a mile radius in every direction have been checked. There's no one waiting for you to leave."

"Thank you." Evelyn stood. "And, Duke, one more other thing," she said as she wrapped her body-length trench coat around her, "don't think I didn't notice that bitch you had in VIP with you. I don't give a fuck what you do when you're not around me, but the next time you disrespect the memory of my daughter in my place of business, you will be killed."

Evelyn walked by the security, her long knee-high boots marking the floor as she made her way toward the back exit. She hit the alarm to her car as she got inside, immediately blasting the heater. She drove off and got on a main street to go see Vinny. She needed some advice on how to take care of the situation she was in and her Poppa always had the answers.

"Hello," answered Tony through the phone.

"Can you explain to me why Willow just showed up at my club alive twenty-two years later?" she barked, holding the phone away from her ear and close to her mouth.

"That's not possible. Are you sure? How do you know it was her?" he asked.

"Because, it was like looking at Melee, and oh, did I forget to mention that her name was Willow?"

"I'll handle it."

"No, you won't." Evelyn pulled into a retirement home on the outskirts of town. "You would die trying, because I don't know how, but this little bitch is like her father when it comes to the streets. I had a mark on her, the next thing I know the shooter ended up dead, and I had a mark on me," she screamed. "You hear me? A mark was on me."

"I hear you."

"I'll take care of her. You just focus on Rock never finding out," Evelyn said as she parked her car.

"I'm on it," Tony said. "Is Anoki alive, too?"

"I don't know yet." Evelyn hung up the phone.

Evelyn got out of the car as she made her way to the entrance of Angel Arms, a retirement home for rich and famous people's loved ones. Evelyn knew that Rock had connections with every realtor in the state. There was no way that she could put anything in her name for Vinny without him knowing. Putting him in a place that had no interest to her husband was her only solution.

It was past visiting hours, but with the agreement she'd made with the director, the extra million a year that she was paying, Evelyn could visit Vinny whenever her heart desired. She walked up to the door as she gently buzzed it for entrance. She looked up at the security camera as the door made a swoosh sound and opened in front of her.

Evelyn's arms swayed, simultaneously, back and forth, as her thick legs seemed to be carrying her from point A to point B; mechanically in motion one leg thrust forward as the other tried, rhythmically, to catch up. She was in a rush to make it to his room. She had so much on her mind that she had to get out.

She made it to the door to her father's room. She knocked twice but no answer. Without waiting for a response, she opened the door and then closed it fast at what she saw. A frown covered her face as the door opened and a member of the staff rushed out while fixing her clothes.

"Nasty," Evelyn said to the worker as she scurried down the hall.

"You should have knocked, baby," Vinny said as Evelyn entered the room.

Vinny's face was serious with lines of worry, tears, happiness and joy outlining his cloudy dark eyes. Stubble crossed his chin and lip as if he hadn't shaved for lack of time or incentive, yet there seemed to be lightness about him as the corners of his mouth lifted into a small smile. His short, light-gray hair played along his forehead as he stood up to greet his daughter.

"How you doing, Evelyn?" He kissed her on the cheek.

"I'm good, Poppa," she said as she took a seat. "And, seeing as you're getting special treatment from the staff, I would say you're doing well, too."

"I have to live, baby." He sat on his bed. "I have needs and I shouldn't even be in this fucking place," he said angrily.

"I know, Poppa, but if not here, then a funeral home."

"To think that Vincent Mancini would be hiding from a coon." He hung his head. "The shame my ancestors must be feeling."

"Poppa, you can sulk later." Evelyn set her purse down. "Rock's daughter is alive."

"Melee's back?" he asked.

"Not Melee, she's still missing. I'm talking about Willow. You remember his wife and child, that you ordered the death of? Well, Willow just showed up at my club."

"Why did you let her leave alive?" He reached on his night-stand and grabbed his Scotch and a cup.

"It was my life or hers," Evelyn spat. "She brought someone with her to hide in the shadows that had a mark on me, so I didn't have a choice."

"Sounds like someone who has Rock's genes," he said as he poured a cup. "I don't like the bastard, but he thinks every move out before he goes into something. If this is his daughter, then she got it from her Poppa."

"That's the problem. What if she knows about Rock?"

"You're the daughter of Vincent 'Vinny' Mancini, the most notorious godfather to ever live. Don't ever show fear, especially to a monkey. And besides, what makes you so sure it's her?"

"She looked just like Melee." She grabbed the bottle of Scotch from him, taking a shot to the head straight from the bottle.

"It probably is her," Vinny admitted as he stood up. "I knew she was alive when she and Anoki showed up in Hawaii. I didn't tell you because I handled it. I told your Uncle Gino to get rid of her and he did."

"So Willow lived?"

He nodded his head yes.

"That's not all," he looked at Evelyn, "there's another daughter that Rock doesn't know about. When Anoki was shot, she was pregnant, and when she was saved, so was the baby she was carrying. Anoki's sister, Mahina, who is the woman your Uncle Gino married, raised them and they have been a part of The Pink Lip Bandits ever since."

"So not only do I have to deal with one of Rock's offspring, but two?" Evelyn held her hands up above her head. "What the fuck am I going to do? These girls were a part of an organization that killed for a living. They know the game."

"Evelyn," Vinny raised his voice, "no matter what your last name is now, you have Mancini blood through your veins. Take care of those two fast, because if you don't, it will be trouble for you down the line. Trust me."

"Can Uncle Gino give you some information on them?" she asked, walking toward the door.

"He could if he wasn't dead." He took a sip of his liquor.

"Dead?"

"Gino, Mahina, and twenty others were killed at their wedding reception. They were shot in the middle of the event and no one knew until it was almost over."

"Silencers," Evelyn whispered to herself. "Wait; was Melee one of the bodies they found?"

"No, I've already checked. All of the girls that died were wearing pink lipstick and none of them were her."

"So they killed everyone associated with the organization and moved here to Philly? But, for what?"

"Whatever it is, they want it bad." Vinny poured another round of Scotch.

"I'll talk to you later," Evelyn said, rushing out of the room and pulling out her cell phone, her heels clicking loudly from her walking so fast and hard.

"Talvin," she huffed into the phone as she paced down the long hallway to the exit. "I have a job for you, so be at the spot in thirty minutes."

Evelyn got into her car and sped off leaving snow melted behind her from the exhaust. She had to end the reign of Willow and her sister before it started. She had to put them six feet under before she was the one in a casket. She only used Talvin's skills for extreme jobs, and now knowing their reputation, he was the perfect person to put a bullet in their heads.

Willow glanced over at Kail and Choice; all three of their lips branded with pink lipstick. She gave them a sly smile as she carried her bags onto the escalator that led to the second level of the mall. They had been shopping all day to get Choice's style in line with their own and the task was more difficult than they'd expected.

"See, it's easy." Kail smirked as they stepped off the escalator.

"Y'all spend crazy money on clothes," Choice said, referring to the thousands she'd just witnessed them spend.

"You have to spend in order to look how you should look," Willow said as they made their way into a shoe boutique. "Why should we have to shop at the dollar store when we can shop where the hoes who got real cash can shop?" She held up a six thousand-dollar shoe in Choice's face. "If you had a choice between a steak and a cheeseburger, what would you choose?"

"The steak," Choice responded.

"Exactly, and with clothes that concept is even more enforced. No one wants clothes from a thrift store; they get that shit because they have to. Let us show you that you don't have to." Kail grabbed the shoe and handed it to the sales associate. "Can I get these in a size...what size are you?" She looked at Choice.

"I'm a seven, but I didn't bring that kind of dough."

"Seven," Kail said to the sales associate. "I got you, Choice."

"These are six thousand-dollar shoes." The sales associate looked at Kail in shock.

"Did I ask you the fucking price?" Kail asked, raising her voice. "I can see, bitch, I know what they cost. I didn't ask your seven-dollar-an-hour-making-ass shit, so just go get the shoe, come back, and don't say shit else."

"I'm sorry," she said as she ran off to get the shoes.

"I hate when these motherfuckas act like you don't belong here." Kail looked at other shoes.

"You see that shit?" Willow said to Choice, referring to the sales associate. "See how they treat us when we come to these stores to spend money? Now, how do you think it feels to walk out of here in a shoe that none of these hoes that work here can afford?"

"It would make me feel good," Choice said as they all started to laugh.

"Is your name Willow?" a girl who looked no older than sixteen asked as she approached them.

"Who wants to know?" Kail looked at the girl.

The white girl wore heavy black lipstick. Her hair was cut in a short boy cut and her pants were big at the bottoms. Chains hung from the loops on her belt line and fell onto the skulls that were stitched into her pants.

"I have something to give you." She handed Kail the envelope.

"Yo, who the fuck was that?" Choice asked as they watched the girl walk out of the store.

"I don't know." Willow grabbed the envelope from Kail's hands.

"Ma'am," the sales associate said as she returned with the shoes, "I can ring you up over here."

"Didn't I tell yo' ass not to speak?" Kail said, walking to the counter.

"Open it," Choice told her as she stood next to her.

Willow ripped at the edges of the small cream envelope as curiosity possessed her. She didn't know who the envelope could have been from, but she was certain to find out. She took out a white piece of paper that was stuffed neatly inside and unfolded it. She held it up, looked at the front and back of it, and read the small paragraph.

"I have a job for you. I know who you are and what you do. Call this number from an unmarked phone and I will give you all of the details, V." Her eyes skimmed over the number as she memorized it before tearing up the letter.

"Who is V?" Choice asked.

"A potential client." Willow walked up to Kail as she finished her transaction. "That envelope was a job."

"From who?" Kail handed the expensive shoes to Choice.

"Someone named V. He or she knows who we are, and what we do. They want us to call the number on the envelope from an unmarked phone," Willow said as they left the store.

"Do you think it's a job or is someone playing with us?" Kail asked, her adrenaline pumping at the thought of doing a job.

"Let's find out." Willow cut through the food court to escalators, throwing the torn pieces of paper in her hand in a random trashcan.

"What if it's a setup?" Choice asked with a nervous tone.

"Don't worry," Kail told her as they stepped outside of the mall, "Willow will know."

Willow led them outside to the payphone that was inside a small opening surrounded by plastic. She held her hands out for someone to give her quarters as shoppers passed them left and right. The sounds of the cars' tires in the parking lot fighting with the snow could be heard as Choice placed three quarters into the palm of Willow's hand.

Willow stood there with the door to the payphone nearly shut to drown out the sounds from the busy mall parking lot. She put the quarters inside of the payphone and dialed the number as she mouthed each number with her lips. She let the phone ring as the breeze from the cold joined her inside of the booth.

"What took you so long to call?" V asked after picking up the phone.

"The job," Willow said, cutting the small talk from the conversation.

"Strictly business," V said from the other end of the phone. "I like that."

"The job," Willow repeated with a good mind to hang up.

"It's an assassination job. I need someone dead by the end of the night."

"Payment?"

"You will find one hundred thousand dollars under the driver's seat of your car."

"It will get completed." Willow took the phone away from her ear to hang up.

"Wait," V said, causing Willow to put the phone back to her ear. "Don't you want to know how I know about you?"

"If it will change how much money we get for this job, then maybe. But, seeing as I already got payment, how you know me doesn't matter. It won't change the fact that you do know me and what I do." She hung up the phone.

Willow walked past Choice and Kail to get to her car. It didn't sit well with her to know that someone that she didn't know had been inside of her whip. She had to see if the money was there. She looked around her as she felt herself being watched.

"So is it legit?" Kail asked, catching up to her.

"Let me see something and I will let you know." She hit the alarm to her car.

Willow put her purse and bags in the seat as she reached down to feel underneath it. She pulled a medium-sized envelope out as she turned around to show it to Kail and Choice. She opened up the envelope as she revealed its contents. One hundred thousand dollars, and a small piece of paper with a name, a photo, an address, and other information peeked through the opening.

"Assassination, one hundred thousand." She looked at Kail and Choice.

"By when?" Kail looked inside at the money.

"Tonight," Willow answered as she closed the envelope and tossed it in the seat.

"Let's get it," Kail said with a smile.

"Choice, we will get you up to speed on the way to the crib to switch out cars," Willow said as Choice nodded.

"Switch cars?" Kail put her bags in the backseat. "We can just go work this now and be done with it."

"Kail, someone was in the car. Whoever this person is we don't know. They could have bugged the car or anything. Let's be smart. We get in this car, keep our conversations mild, and once we get to the house, we will get Choice up to speed on the plan we use for all of our assassinations." Willow got inside of the car.

"You right," Kail agreed as she went around the car to get in. "I wonder what this Tony cat did to deserve this."

Willow sped off after Kail and Choice got into the car. She didn't trust this V character, but she knew that she needed him just as much as he needed her. If she did enough jobs for him, then the name of The Pink Lip Bandits would spread, and word of mouth was the only way to promote their kind of business.

Willow, Kail, and Choice staked out the address that V had given them on the paper. They had been outside of the building observing for two hours and their target had been in and out of the building multiple times. They waited for their chance to make their move. When they saw him not coming out after another hour had passed, they knew it was time.

"We have the element of surprise." Willow got out of the car, Choice and Kail following her lead. "He doesn't know he has a hit on him, and by the time he realizes it, he will be dead."

"One shot from each gun," Kail said to Choice as they crossed the street to get to the building.

Willow glanced wearily at the dull gray cement walls, knowing that she would commit a murder inside. The bright flowers outlining the walkway seemed to droop a little more. The ivy fighting to find purchase on the smooth walls had lost their spirit due to the snow. Willow scuffed her heel on the perfectly trimmed green grass that had snow recently shovelled from it as they made it to the entrance of the building.

Willow pulled her jacket tighter around her, as if seeking warmth from the unforgiving leather. She buzzed a random button at the entrance and waited for someone to respond through the wholly white-colored intercom box that had all of the apartment numbers.

"May I help you?" a voice chimed through the intercom.

"We're here to see a friend, but we forgot what apartment he's in."

"Do you have a name?" the voice asked.

"Tony, but we wanted to surprise him; it's his birthday, so please, don't tell him that we're here," Willow said while the door slowly swung open.

"You got it, and please enjoy your friend's birthday."

"We sure will," Willow said as they entered the building.

Kail led the way in her thick, navy blue trench coat, with bronze-colored buttons that ended just above her waistline. Underneath the long coat was a large black skirt that billowed around her in the cold, winter air. A red scarf was wrapped tightly around her neck, the tails of the scarf dripping down to her thighs. Her wide brownish-green eyes reflected the gentle harmony of the season as small flakes of snow had fallen onto strands of her long, lovely hair.

Choice was next in line—her new six thousand-dollar heels felt good to her feet as she walked behind Kail. Her stomach was flipping like flapjacks on the grill at a diner, but the money she'd seen earlier motivated her to shake it off. She had never made thirty thousand dollars in one night and the thought of it made her eyes twinkle. She was used to making three thousand dollars a night and now that she could keep her clothes on, there was no way she was going to mess up the opportunity to get paid real money.

Willow was last in line; she was the back man. In her mind, she was the smartest and if something went wrong, with her in the back she could easily think of a plan to get them all out of there safely. All of the assassination jobs they had ever done were two-people jobs, but now with Choice, it gave them that extra security.

Kail slowed down as planned. Choice passed her, leaving her and Willow around a corner from their target, Tony's apartment. They watched as Choice knocked on the door. They grabbed two baseball bats from in front of the door where they were standing. They checked her face for any signs of nervousness, but to their surprise, she seemed to have it together.

"Do you think she can pull it off?" Kail asked, never taking her eyes off Choice.

"She better," Willow watched Choice bang on the door again, "this is her one and only test."

Tony wrinkled his nose at the sound of the door. As a precaution, he pulled out his pistol, and made his way toward the wooden door. He peeped out of the peephole and when he saw a beautiful woman on the other end, he opened it with a hurry, hiding his gun with a part of the door as it opened.

"Can I help you?" he asked.

"My friend needs help moving some furniture next door and she told me a strong-looking man stayed next door." Choice bit her bottom lip. "I was hoping you could give us a hand."

Choice was no stranger to getting men to do what she wanted. Although she had a man, before him she had dudes from the hood wrapped around her fingers. Seducing a man was in her genes and it was something that she did well.

"I would love to," Tony said, looking her body up and down. "Let me put something up and I'll be right out."

Choice waited as Kail and Willow made their move and stood on each side of the door. Things were going exactly how Willow had planned. If things continued to go smoothly, they would be out of the building in less than ten minutes. The door opened, and Willow and Kail swung the baseball bats at Tony at the same time with all of their might, sending him flying backward.

Tony saw it coming, but it had caught him off-guard. He felt the steel substance make contact with his muscle, watching it smash his entrails together like a rogue freight train. He felt blood vessels burst and his diaphragm collapse under the force the fist packed behind it. His breath instantly left his body for dead as he doubled over. His knees buckled from the force of the blow, and as he went down, he could have sworn he heard a cracking noise ricochet between his ribs. Fire ran through every fiber of his abdomen, and he tasted bile, adrenaline and a hint of blood.

As his crumpled body hit the ground, he gasped for air, but

oxygen eluded his grasp. His head was swimming as his organs regained their original volume: going from a pancake-like mass to their original life-saving state. He somehow managed to roll over and vomit.

"Handle that." Willow looked at Choice.

Choice advanced slowly, the gun in her hand trembling slightly. Tony crawled slowly until he reached a corner, trying to create distance between himself and his soon-to-be killer. He smiled, knowing that there was nothing he could do to change what would happen.

She lunged forward, hitting his face with the butt of the gun, hitting his shoulder. He screamed in pain and darted to the left of her, tripping and falling to the floor as he tried to stand up. She lunged at him again, this time slicing his head open. Blood poured, spattering his face and chest. He moaned in agony, knowing the worst was yet to come.

Choice stood over him, watching as his tears met blood, creating small red designs on his face and neck. His eyes weren't on her. They danced furtively around the room, looking for something that could save his life. There was nothing.

Tony looked at the other two girls that entered the room whom he hadn't really noticed yet. His eyes glued to Willow's and instantly he recognized her. He knew what he had done back then would come to haunt him one day. It was karma and it was time to pay the piper.

"Willow," he huffed. "You sure have grown up."

Kail looked at Willow as she looked at the man. She didn't recognize him, even from her childhood in the projects of Philly. She didn't know him, but he said her name with so much conviction that a stranger would have thought they had history.

"How do you know my name?" Willow asked.

"I've known you since you were a baby." He wiped the blood that was gushing down from the open wound off his face.

"He's just talking shit." Kail looked at Choice. "Handle that."

Choice exhaled as her index finger rested down on the trigger. She closed her eyes, hoping to take the idea of her taking a man's life out of her mind. The area between her finger and the trigger grew sweaty making her finger slide up and down. In a moment of panic, she pulled the trigger as the bullet spiraled out of the barrel and into Tony's head.

He laughed and then the echo of the bullet striking through his skull hit him. A blank expression took over his face. A small smile of surprise curved on his lips, and a blanket of red splattered over his shirt. The rest was hazy, as he hysterically screamed. His body dropped to the floor like a rock sinking to the pitless dark-blue ocean, entombed in a world of silence and darkness, forever to wait in its place, slowly decaying.

The world gradually sped up as his body convulsed and the scarlet liquid gushed out like a waterfall staining the rest of his shirt. His eyes fluttered open and closed, trying to block out the gory image that was playing in front of him. His dark lashes desperately trying to shield him from the horror that lay within.

"Let's go." Willow turned around after Tony took his last breath.

Choice ran over to the sink and threw up. The trauma elicited her gag reflex, making her spill everything in her stomach through her mouth. She had never killed anyone and the fact that she had just taken someone's life was overwhelming. Tears rolled down her eyes as she cut on the faucet, letting the warm water run her vomit down the drain.

"You good?" Kail approached her and rubbed her back.

"Yes." She wiped her mouth.

"Let's go," Willow yelled and they all headed for the door.

They exited the building as the guard lights illuminating the streets came on in their direction. They never looked back, only kept pushing forward, trying to make it to the car to make a clean getaway so their mission could be completed. They didn't want to be seen, and the quicker they got away, the better.

"Willow is your name, right?" Duke asked as he pulled up next to the Range Rover when they were getting inside the getaway car.

"I'm sorry, do I know you?" Willow rolled down the window.

"You know you remember me." Duke smiled. "So don't play that dumb shit with me, shorty."

"Let's go." Kail reached over and started the car.

"Come take a ride with me." Duke rolled the window up to his car as if he knew Willow would come.

"You can't be serious," Kail said as Willow got out the car. "You don't even know that nigga."

"Kail, I got this." Willow walked around and opened up the door to Duke's car. "Yo, and make sure she aight," she screamed, referring to Choice.

Willow watched as the Range Rover sped down the street. She rubbed her lips together as she got into the imported seats of Duke's Ferrari. Heat immediately warmed her up as the door closed behind her. She leaned back in the seat, letting the job she'd just done escape her mind.

"You okay?" Duke accelerated the car.

"I'm fine." Willow put her right hand in front of the vent.

"It seems like something is on your mind."

"I'm good." She looked at him. "You didn't even tell me your name."

"You didn't ask." He cut the music down in the car. "But, since you want to know, I'm Demarcus, but everybody calls me Duke."

"I'm Willow."

"I knew that already." He smiled.

"You thought you knew, but I just confirmed it. You shouldn't take everything people say to heart. Just because you heard some-one address me by that name, doesn't mean it's my name."

"You right," he said impressed. "So what was up at the club that one night? I ain't never in my life seen Evelyn so shook."

"The club owner?"

"Yeah." He pulled in front of a waffle house. "You hungry?"

"I can eat." She smirked as they got out of the car. "And, I was just looking for an old friend, that's all. She made it something, so I had to cook that beef real quick."

"A thugette." Duke laughed while holding the door open for her.

"You can say that."

By the end of their meal, as their eyes locked on each other sev-eral times, something reacted in a way neither one of them had known. There was a strange need that made them want to be close to each other and just make physical contact. It was instant attraction in the most extreme of cases, love at first sight, the need to know this person so much better than anyone ever could dream of.

Duke was falling for Willow. He couldn't figure out if it was her resemblance to his girlfriend Melee or not. But, deep down, he knew that they were two different people. Willow was like one of the boys, but with beauty to go on top of it, and he was feeling every part of her that the two hours at the diner allowed him to.

"Can you take me home?" Willow asked, then laid the money on the table to cover the tab and stood up.

"I could have paid for it." Duke stood with her. "You didn't have to do that."

"I can take care of myself." They walked out the door.

"I can see that." He grabbed her and spun her body around facing his own.

They stood there, their bodies becoming one. The smell of Willow's alluring fragrance rode the waves of the night wind and entered Duke's nostrils at full blast. He could feel his manhood growing as the soft silk Willow called hair rested on his face.

He shifted her body so that their faces could meet. He wrapped his arm around her waist with their lips locked. All of their kisses that Duke had stolen earlier in the diner were sweet and gentle, heartfelt and meaningful, but this one was different. It was still meaningful, but the way he pressed his lips to Willow's so passionately sent a wave of heat running through her.

This kiss was hot and filled with longing satisfaction. He broke away and left Willow breathless, feeling as if her knees might just give in. His gaze set on hers and she knew immediately what was going to happen next. Closing the distance between them, she returned his kiss and gripped his jacket as it intensified. They held the kiss for as long as they could, neither one of them wanting to break away until it got to the point where they were both out of breath and clinging to each other.

"I want you now," Willow whispered in his ear, and with that they were back in Duke's car, driving fast down a dark street, the world outside a blur as they zoomed past unknown houses. Four streets later they arrived at his apartment, all the windows dark and the curtains drawn.

Duke pulled Willow's hand and led her toward the pitch-black bedroom. They kissed again, wasting no time to cut on a light as they hurried to the bed, leaving little time to think. Stumbling into the darkness of his room, not bothering to turn the lights on, turned Willow on even more. Undressing, kissing, moving the mattresses on the bed, she clung to the sheets, sweating, from what seemed every pore on her body as they moved in time as raw passion spurred upon them.

Willow stroked Duke's cheek and kissed his lips. Their lips moved in time with each other. He tangled his hands in her hair. He raised his shirt up moving her lips to his neck, pulling her closer to him. He placed his hands on her lower back, slipping them into her panties after he lowered her skirt from its desired place. She was dazed. He kissed her jawline, moving down to her collar. He pulled down her panties as he slowly licked on the hood of her clitoris with his tongue. He reached up and licked her neck, then slowly kissed her stomach while pulling his dick out. He brushed his fingers across her shoulders, making the bra he had unfastened earlier fall to the floor, revealing her perfect breasts.

Willow could barely breathe; he made it hard for her to move or breathe. Her heart started pounding and she started breathing heavily. He leaned up from eating her fruit and kissed her roughly. He pinned her down and took off the rest of her clothes for a moment of passion that neither of them would forget.

Three hours later, Willow was awakened by the sound of tenants entering the apartment next to the one they were in. She looked over at Duke. Although it was dark, the glow from the moon shone on his face; no other spots in the room, only his face. She softly kissed his forehead as she got up to get dressed.

She eagerly eased out of the bed as gently as she could. She didn't want to wake him. She didn't want to do the whole goodbye thing. She wanted to remember the night for what it was and saying goodbye would ruin it. It was perfect the way it had ended; her experiencing orgasm after orgasm.

Willow exited the apartment building as she adjusted her clothes. The sun was waking up as its eyes slowly opened, alarming everyone who had slept through the night that it was time to start their day. She felt groggy, dirty even. She didn't think as she walked; all she wanted was a shower and to lie in bed.

"Where have you been all night?" Kail asked Willow as she walked through the door of their condo.

"Out." Willow set her purse on the countertop.

"With that one cat?" She followed Willow to the bathroom.

"Yes, Kail, goddamn," she exclaimed out of irritation. "I'm really not in the mood. Especially since I had to take a fucking cab here because you didn't answer your phone."

"I hope you ain't let that nigga fuck 'cause you don't even know dude." She folded her arms while leaning on the entrance of the bathroom.

"Yes, we fucked for hours."

"Just nasty." Kail tossed an envelope at Willow. "That was here waiting for us under the door when I got here. It's another job from V."

"The job," Willow looked at Kail, "did you give Choice her cut?"

"Yes, and I'll give you yours whenever you ready for it."

"I'll get it when I wake up."

"What about the job?" Kail held her arms up.

"I'll handle everything when I wake up."

"That's cool and all, Will, but I hope you ain't gone let a nigga with a rented Ferrari sell your ass a dream, and knock you off your hustle. Remember that we feed ourselves and we all we got. Don't fall in love." Kail walked off into the hallway.

"Too late," Willow whispered as she looked at herself in the mirror.

She didn't know what she was feeling for Duke, but every time she thought of him, the feeling of a thousand stars shooting wildly took over her body. She felt like a little kid after writing the name of their crush all over their journal. She couldn't deny the feelings that she had developed that night; she just hoped they were mutual as she lay down in her bed with her head under her pillow.

Fourteen

W illow walked into the bank, her clutch tightly snuggled underneath her arm as she made her way to the clerk that handled the deposit boxes. Her hair was in a tight bun and her body was dressed in business casual clothing. Her mind was focused. She needed to get in, get whatever was in the box that V wanted, and get out within fifteen minutes.

This was a job that V had given more instructions on than usual so she wanted to make sure she got it right. She listened inventively and she knew she would have to change her whole persona in order to play a widow. She was this dead man's wife for the next fifteen minutes and not a second more.

Willow tapped on the large square desk as she removed the sunglasses from her eyes. A tear brushed down her cheek as the clerk looked up from the paperwork that had her attention and was scattered all over the place. She motioned for Willow to sit down as she handed her a box of Kleenex.

"I'm sorry for my tardiness." Willow sobbed, taking her seat. "It's just so hard living without my James," she said as tears rushed from her eyes.

"I do apologize for your loss," the clerk said with a saddened face. "Now Mrs. Reyes," she said, referring to the last name of the deceased man, "because your husband did not have you on his account, we would have to verify everything with documents. Did you bring a marriage license?"

"Of course," Willow said, opening her clutch and revealing the counterfeit documents V had sent along with the job. "Here you are." She handed her a driver's license, a marriage license, and a social security card. "I hope that will be enough."

"It should be." The clerk stood up. "Let me go make copies and I'll be right back."

Willow sat with her legs crossed. Her fingers clenched to her palms making fists as she watched two cops walk in and approach the clerk. She stopped breathing for a few moments, leaving her chest really tight and her eyes became as wide as could be. She leaned back into the chair, looking around for the nearest exit.

Willow stood up as she pulled down the pencil skirt that hugged her stomach. She eased over to the stairs to go to the bottom level of the bank. She looked back and the cops were looking at her along with the clerk. She eased down the stairs as the clerk chased behind her.

"Wait, Mrs. Reyes," the clerk screamed from the top of the stairs, "I'm sorry about that, my husband had to drop me off something and his partner came up with him. We can go to the box now if you want to; everything checked out fine."

"I was looking for a restroom." Willow turned around and headed back up the stairs with her heart in her throat, "but, that can wait."

Willow sighed eternally as she watched the clerk kiss her husband in uniform before he and his partner walked down the stairs. She signaled for Willow to follow her as she walked to the door of a small room after handing her the documents that she'd copied.

"Do you have the key?" the clerk asked while opening the door.

"Yes." Willow removed the short wide key out of her clutch.

"Perfect." The clerk closed the door behind them. "Box 352, here we are." She grabbed the box and placed it on the table in the center of the room.

Willow stood over the box with the key in her hand. She didn't know what was so important about the contents of the box, but she was about to find out. She put the key in the box turning it slightly. She heard a clinging noise and used her free hand to open the box. A small black tape recorder was the only thing inside. She removed it, tucking it away in her clutch as she walked to the door.

"Thank you." Willow opened the door.

"You're so welcomed and again, I'm sorry for your loss." The clerk rubbed the top of Willow's back.

Willow smiled as she left out of the bank, the wind whipping her bun out of place. She opened up the clutch as she walked down the pale street. She wondered what was on the tape and why it was so important to V. Whatever it was, he didn't want anyone to hear it. She closed her clutch as she crossed the busy street to get to her car.

She got in the car as she wondered how Kail and Choice's job was going. She sped off to go to the spot where V had told her to leave the tape when her phone started vibrating in her hand. It was Duke and seeing his name appear on her screen made her smile. She was reluctant to answer; she was in a middle of a job but she couldn't resist.

"Where are you at?" Duke's deep baritone voice asked through the phone.

"About to finish up some work," she said as she pulled up to a park.

"You coming through?"

"Yes, I'll be over when I finish this."

"Bet." He hung up the phone.

Walking through the green-painted, wrought-iron gates, Willow saw a concrete pathway stretching out in front of her like a gray ribbon meandering through the verdant shrubbery. Over to the right, she saw a children's playground, with a sandpit, swings and roundabouts all being used to their full extent by a myriad of squealing and laughing youngsters, obviously enjoying the cold and wind of the winter day. Parents, seated nearby, were watching their offspring with the intensity of a mother hen nurturing her chicks.

Conversely on the opposite side of the path was the lush vegetation of the many trees, with their welcoming shade, and the colorful plants, their heady scent filling the air mixing with the smell of the snow.

As she walked further into the park, she saw benches, painted green to match the foliage, with people sitting on them, some resting, others enjoying a sandwich or hot drink. Once she passed the play area, she noticed the peacefulness and quiet environment she now found herself in, and she felt an inner calm that God's beautiful creations had given her.

She breathed in deeply, savoring the freshness and perfume of the oxygenated air and it gave her both peace and exhilaration at the same time. She made it to the end of the park, spotting the small birdhouse where V had told her to put the deposit box's contents. She took the tape out of her clutch and placed it into the empty birdhouse; never stopping her feet from moving as she headed to her car to go see Duke.

The night was not only dark but calm; the air was crisp, cold and awakening; the trees stiff and frozen-like. The stars could be seen for miles in the pure, perfectly landscaped sky. Snow was a sight from a picture, so perfectly layered by nature, no imperfections except for their own footsteps. The moon so bright it lit up the whole street as though they were carrying a lamp with them.

Kail's and Choice's breath looked as though they had just puffed on a cigar as they walked up the four stone steps into the church's entrance. They opened up the beautiful maroon-colored door as two fonts full of holy water greeted them. To the right was a door leading to the bathroom. To the left was the door leading to the choir loft, which they were standing directly beneath.

They entered another set of doors; the snow boots on their feet leaving little trails of melted snow. Beyond those doors were four columns of pews. There were about twenty rows. It was then two steps up to the altar. Inside the altar table were some valuable relics, unavailable to be seen without special permission from the priest.

Over to the right was the baptismal font, and next to it was the Paschal candle; the candle that is lit during Easter, funerals, and baptisms. Further to the right, there was a statue of St. Agnes, the church's patroness, and the candle that indicated the presence of the Holy Spirit.

"Is he here?" Choice whispered to Kail as they looked around the church.

"He's the priest, of course he's here." Kail looked over at the confessional area.

They never wondered why V wanted the priest dead and they didn't care. When he offered them two hundred thousand upfront, they didn't care if they had to kill the leader of the free world, they would have done it with no questions asked.

"He's in there," Kail pointed to the confessional, "stay here, make sure nobody comes in, and I got this."

"I got you." Choice headed to the doors to guard them.

Kail entered the white-walled booth and she kneeled before a tiny screen. It was no odor to speak of as her knees touched the soft cloth so the priest could not see her. She couldn't see the priest, and he couldn't see her, but she knew he was there. She began praying for what she was about to do.

"In the name of the Father, and of the Son, and of the Holy Ghost," the priest said as they both made the sign of the cross.

"Bless me, father, for I have sinned," Kail made the sign of the cross over her head and chest. "It has been a long time since I have last confessed and these are my sins." Kail continued as her eyes watered. "I am guilty of murder. I am a liar. I steal and do other bad things that I am not proud of, but it is all that I know. No matter how bad I may want to stop committing these sins, I can't. I've tried."

"Are you truly sorry for these sins?" the priest asked in a non-judgmental tone.

"Yes," she whispered.

"You would need to make an act of contrition."

"Contrition?" she asked as the priest began to pray out loud.

"Your sins are forgiven; you may leave in peace." A door at the bottom of the confessional opened and an open Bible slid through. "Read that aloud, the highlighted verse."

Kail sat and looked at the verse: Corinthians 6:9-10. She knew the scripture by memory; she knew all the scriptures by memory. The church was silent for it was only her, the priest, and Choice. She took a deep breath and closed her eyes before she started to read.

"Do you not know that the wicked will not inherit the kingdom of God? Do not be deceived: Neither the sexually immoral nor idolaters nor adulterers nor male prostitutes nor homosexual offenders nor thieves nor the greedy nor drunkards nor slanderers nor swindlers will inherit the kingdom of God." She opened her eyes and slid the Bible back into the opening.

"And, what does that mean?" he asked.

"I don't need an intervention."

"I'm just trying to help."

"By judging me?" Kail raised her tone.

"By praying for you," the priest responded.

"Do you remember this scripture from the Bible, priest?" Kail asked him as her grip on her gun tightened. "Judge not, that you be not judged. For with the judgment you pronounce you will be judged, and with the measure you use it will be measured to you. Why do you see the speck that is in your brother's eye, but do not notice the log that is in your own eye? Or how can you say to your brother, 'Let me take the speck out of your eye,' when there is the log in your own eye? You hypocrite, first take the log out of your own eye, and then you will see clearly to take the speck out of your brother's eye," she whispered.

"I assure you there is no speck in my eye," the priest said.

"There has to be something in it." Kail pulled her gun out of her clothes. "Why else would someone hire me to kill you?" She rose and released her clip into the other half of the confessional. She ran out, opened the door leading to the priest, checked his pulse, and ran over to where Choice was.

"Kail, let's get the fuck outta here," Choice screamed with panic.

Sirens blared in the distance getting closer with each ragged breath. The cold night air coursed through Choice's lungs and dried her already parched throat. Her heart was beating so fast, she was scared it would lead the cops right to them; that or it would burst out of her chest.

Kail let her hands rest upon her knees as she took two deep breaths. In through her nose, out through her mouth, she repeated this until her breathing returned to normal. After wiping away the beads of sweat on her forehead, she took in her surroundings.

The blood pounding in her ear clogging her brain, she ran through the empty pews and launched for the side door with Choice following behind her. They ran down the alley at full speed. Their arms were stretched out in front of them as they ran. They could feel them chasing them; the sound of their heartbeats filled their ears, their adrenaline pumping like ice in their veins.

They were vulnerable; they had never felt so mortal. Kail's survival instincts, buried deep down beneath the morals and etiquette associated with humanity, were pulsing through her like a second heartbeat. She could not fight or hide. She didn't know how much longer they could keep running. She could sense them behind her, rapidly catching up to them.

Their pace picked up and they thanked God when they saw the dim shine of a dying street light on the other side of the alley illuminating the car they'd parked. Without ever looking back, they jumped inside and zoomed off before the car could fully accelerate. They drove into the night as Kail realized her gun had fallen along the way.

"Fuck, fuck, fuck," she said, hitting the wheel each time she cursed.

"What's up?" Choice's heart continued to race.

"The gun." Kail pulled behind a business and parked. "I dropped the gun."

Kail sat behind the wheel for a couple of hours as she let the trail run dry. She had never been so clumsy since she started working jobs. She blamed Willow for not being there. She figured that she had snuck off to go see Duke. If Willow would have been there, she wouldn't have dropped her weapon; Willow would have caught it when it fell.

Kail ran up the stairs of the condo; her vision as red as the devil's skin. She flung the door widely, letting the doorknob bang into the wall, leaving a hole in the plaster. She wanted to punch Willow for letting a man mess up their hustle, and she intended to do just that as soon as she saw her.

Kail was furious; Willow could see it in her eyes as she walked into her bedroom without knocking. But Kail didn't want to talk; she wouldn't. Willow didn't know what to ask her. If she knew it was going to start a fight, she probably would have closed her door.

"You okay?" Willow asked.

"You would know if your ass wasn't so far up in that nigga's ass." She stopped. Willow could see her eyes get darker. "Are you choosing that nigga over family?"

"No," Willow swallowed hard, "y'all didn't need me and besides—"

"I don't give a fuck if Choice needs you, but I damn sure did," Kail said as she banged her fist against the door.

"Kail, it's cool; we'll go back and find it." Willow was aware about the gun being left from a phone conversation she'd just had with Choice.

Kail didn't listen, and she pushed Willow to the floor. Willow swung back around and gave Kail a full blow to the ribs. She howled in torment but still tried to fight her. Willow grabbed her as she tried to talk some sense into her. Sparring was one thing, but they had never had a fistfight in their life; especially over money.

"Step back, Kail; I really don't wanna hurt you." Willow licked her lips, her voice was dry and her brown eyes were blazing.

Willow stood up as she pointed her gun that she'd grabbed off her nightstand forward; the tip of the gun directly aimed at Kail. She knew she probably wouldn't be able to talk sense into Kail with only her fist. She was past the point of talking.

Willow backed away a couple of steps, the cold wind blowing through her hair as if it was trying to calm her down through the cracked window.

"That's enough, Kail; come on, let's think this through," Willow whispered.

Kail felt like Willow was treating her like a little girl. Her tone was implying she expected Kail to do whatever she said, with no hesitation whatsoever. Willow had lowered her gun. A mocking grin had formed on her face, the sort of grin you'd give a child when you wanted them to do something.

That thought sickened Kail; how could she think of her like that, like a child willing to do all her work? She looked out the window and saw a bird fly through the gaps between the branches, being free as what she wanted to be from Willow's pity. Kail took a breath and tried to think of a way to get past Willow. She glanced over at her momentarily; she'd started to walk over to her, the sickly grin still plastered on her face, her arms parted slightly as if she were asking for an embrace.

Willow was off-guard and Kail took the opportunity.

Kail put her hand on the top of the gun and quickly snatched it away, quicker than she ever had done before. She bit her lip and charged at Willow like a ravenous wolf chases a lamb. Before she knew it, she heard the sound of Willow's flesh being pierced, and the bullet from the gun was locked loose in her shoulder, her crimson blood splattered up, staining the pure white carpet.

Kail bit her lip harder as it started to shake. The harsh reality had just sunk in. *Did I just shoot Willow?* she thought. She looked down at her; her eyes were cold and dark and her face was an eerie pale. Kail's eyes then flashed to the gun and Willow's shoulder, then back up, then down again.

"Kail," Willow murmured, placing her hand on her shoulder blade, "why?" She grunted as she tore the bullet out of her flesh, blood oozing down her chest.

Kail opened her mouth, but no words would come out; she felt numb all over. Willow forced her gun out of Kail's hand and dropped it to the ground with a metallic thud. Kail's body started to shake as Willow drew another gun. Her eyes were blazing again like sparks, and she could see the lust in her eyes. She'd never felt so hated in her life.

"I'm sorry," Kail whispered, stepping back slightly. She took a jerked breath and picked up the other gun off the slightly blood-spattered carpet.

"Sorry?" Willow snapped, her grip tightening on the handle of the gun, so tight her knuckles had turned red.

They both stood there with the gun deep in their palms. They didn't say anything; only the sounds of Willow's pain could be heard and the soft whistle from the ceiling fan above. Kail dropped her gun as a tear fell from her eye. She dashed out of the room, and before Willow could process a thought, the sound of the front door closing echoed throughout the condo.

Fifteen

Evelyn's heart raced as she closed her eyes while Talvin led her to the secret place he always told her about with promises of taking her one day. He took his hands away from her eyes and she gasped at the beauty. The moon was shining over the enchanting waterfall he took her to six hours away from the place they called home.

Evelyn and Talvin had been creeping for years; it was their little secret. Rock would have them both killed if it ever got out, so she kept it as discreet as possible. She was meek about all of their meetings, even if they were business related. She was his boss, his lover, and as long as he didn't mix the two, she didn't mind.

"This is beautiful." Evelyn ran into his arms.

"It's all for you." He cuffed her ass in his hands.

His dark hair shined in the moon's light and she couldn't help but take her hands and rub his head. That's when she saw it. Those azure eyes, just like the sky at midnight so beautiful and dark. She looked deep into them as he bent down and whispered to her three very important words: *"I love you."* She didn't have time to react, for he quickly captured her lips. It was warm, and his lips were soft. Passion burned within the kiss, desire in it, too. Their eyes were closed, both of them savoring the moment. His arms wrapped around her waist and her fingers intertwined with his.

"I have another surprise," Talvin said, pulling away from her.

"What is it?"

"Let's keep walking and see."

Evelyn had never been that deep in the forest. She didn't know how to respond to the atmosphere. Rock had never taken her on trips like this; she was a virgin to the wild. Every bird call and bush rumble caused her to jump as her senses grew fond of the area.

They weaved through the trees along the forest with Talvin's memory being their guide. He had roamed these woodlands since a very young age. His family owned the land and he had spent a lot of his childhood there.

Cresting the hill, they broke free of a dense patch of needle leafs that rolled freely down the embankment, a natural landslide that served their purposes more effectively now that it was covered in snow, and sped their escape from the observant gaze of wild animals.

Evelyn followed the constellation with her eyes, allowing it to guide her past the lightly scattered beech and conifer trees that peppered the land along the forest line as she held Talvin's hand; casting a soft shadow along the gray carpet of snow—beckoning them forward.

The night had always exhilarated her; allowed her a freedom seldom experienced in her station. Behind the cloak of darkness, she could run like the tall-horned stag, waving his white tail in a gesture of peace instead of alarm. Her laughter, breathless and sporadic, was an even cadence that mingled fluently with the nightly chorus sung by the woodland beasts.

As the canopy overhead thickened, their steps grew muffled by the pine needles that blanketed the forest floor; the ground no longer cold beneath her soles. They paused. The trees were much thicker in the lowland territories, and as they looked up ahead, there was a beautiful log cabin.

As they walked into the clearing, they saw the small and slightly abandoned-looking cabin standing right in the middle of it. It looked directly out of a fairy tale as it was covered in snow and there were small icicles hanging from the crooked roof. There was a huge chimney on top of it and as a cold breeze brushed through the woods around them and over the clearing, the smell of pine and wood smoke pinched their noses. It smelled sharp in comparison to the clear winter air around them, but also kind and agreeable. It made them want to go straight into the cabin and warm their hands by the fire inside.

Talvin grinned as the door opened at his will. He grabbed Evelyn's arm and led her inside as the heat throughout the home hit their bodies. He was happy he had come earlier in the day to set up everything for this very moment. As the door closed behind them, he knew he had made the right decision.

"This is nice." Evelyn removed her long mink and set it on the old wooden furniture.

"I want this night to be special."

Talvin lit the candles in the cabin. She could feel his hand running down her back and to her ass. It felt good. As he did this, she moaned and squeezed his head tight in her tiny fists. Her heart was beating furiously; as this was the most passionate foreplay she'd ever had. He rubbed her and then went back up, as she unbuttoned his shirt and he took off his pants.

Talvin could hear Evelyn moaning as he rubbed her soft ass with his fingers. She shuddered as he reached her; it was obvious he was too cold. He could also hear her heart. He reached up to her breasts, cuffing them softly into his palms. He started squeezing them gently as her nipples hardened with enthusiasm.

He took hold of her hand and led her to the sofa. Talvin sat down, longing to feel Evelyn against his body once more. She sat on his lap, holding his face in her hands and kissing him lightly across his cheeks and forehead.

He pulled her toward him, instantly feeling the warmth of their bodies against each other. Evelyn felt his hands grazing, oh so gently, along her thigh, his warm hand against her bare skin underneath her skirt. His hands explored her back and he eventually picked her up and gently laid her down on the old, wooden handmade sofa.

They continued kissing when Talvin stretched his fingers under Evelyn's soft cotton vest. He pulled it over her head, and then slowly removed his own T-shirt. She arched her back slightly as his lips delicately caressed her stomach. His chest was soft, and slightly rough from the sun. Talvin wasn't the type to have bulging biceps, but he was perfectly toned, with a strong hold of her. Things became more intense and hot. They clumsily made their way to an empty room. Their sweaty bodies pressed against each other, and they became one person.

"That was good," Evelyn moaned as she lay on top of Talvin.

"That shit was real good." Talvin kissed her lips.

Although Evelyn was twenty years older than him, Talvin still wanted her. In his eyes she was as beautiful and graceful than all the other women his age, but the way she ran the streets alongside her husband made Talvin that much more attracted to her. He had fallen in love with her and he couldn't stop even if it killed him.

"You think you can still handle that thing for me?" Evelyn asked, referring to Duke.

"Of course," he said as he looked into her eyes.

"When?"

"When do you need me to do it?"

"Tonight," she said as she bit his bottom lip.

"Then I will handle it tonight."

Evelyn stretched her body on the comfortable bear skin rug that she and Talvin somehow ended their sex session on as he went to fetch something to wipe up with. She could still feel his fluids on the small patch of hair between her legs as she lay there on her stomach with a smile on her face. She knew that by the following day Duke would be dead and if she were lucky, so would Willow.

Everyone and everything Duke saw was in his way, a barrier between him and his destination, the emergency room. He was resolutely focused on getting to the hospital as quickly as possible. Every possible outcome was running through his mind: one moment he was convinced that Willow was at death's door; the next he hopefully speculated that she had just a few scratches; or better still, it was not his Willow at all; a case of mistaken identity; his Willow was at home.

The hospital smelled like a synthetic clean death as he entered. The florescent lights glared on the tile floors as he spotted Willow waiting as she applied pressure to her wound. He witnessed many extremely sick people as he rushed over to her. Some were upset as they were bored. Those waiting were sad yet impatient and mad, all emotions across the board. The wait was great as it always was. Willow thought to herself, *This is why they call us patients because we must be patient before anything ever gets done.*

"Yo, the fuck are you doing out here?" he asked her as he stood over her.

"Waiting to be called." She clenched her teeth, the pain becoming too much for her to bear.

Duke's temper rose immediately at the sight of Willow's pain. He couldn't take seeing her hurt. For some reason, he could feel her pain, and as he watched small sweat beads roll down her forehead, he became furious. Duke turned around, his eyes looking for the nurses station. When he saw it, he headed over, and within seconds, he was in front of a nurse.

"Excuse me," Duke said, the nurses at the station ignoring him. "Excuse me!" he yelled as he banged on the top of the counter for dramatics. The nurses, the waiters, and the people leaving all turned around and looked at him as the room stood still, nobody moving or saying a word as silence took over.

"My girl has been shot. I need y'all motherfuckers to get her to the back now. She's bleeding, and she looks like she's about to faint," he said with a raised voice.

"Sir, we have an order to follow here and—"

"I don't give a fuck about an order."

"Calm down, sir, we will have her in the back as quick as we can." The nurse pointed to the waiting chairs. "Now have a seat and be patient."

Duke wanted to reach over and pull the woman up by her collar, but he saw the police in the waiting area, so he decided to be mild. He pulled his cell phone out as he looked over at Willow. He had to make a move quick. Her eyes were closed from the pain and if he had to call in one of his favors from the streets, that's what he was going to do.

"I need some intel," Duke said into the phone as he looked back at the nurse's badge, "she's a nurse at Thomas Jefferson University Hospital. Her name is Melissa, white chick, kind of short, thick, dark hair with dark eyes."

"I found her," the voice on the phone said. "What do you need to know?"

"Everything." Duke walked over to Willow, listening to everything the voice told him. He tapped Willow as he hung up the phone. Her eyes sprang open and he leaned down and helped her up. "Come on, we're going to the back."

He let her weight fall on him as they made their way to the nurses station. The same nurse looked their way and smirked before turning her head to engage in the conversation she was having. Duke smiled at her arrogance, knowing that in a minute, she would be hitting the button to open up the doors in the back.

"I wonder what would happen if Justin was rushed here," Duke said as the nurse looked his way quickly at the call of her son's name. When the look of worry took over her eyes, Duke knew he had her exactly where he wanted her. "Would Justin have to wait like this if he showed up with the same gunshot wound? Maybe I should go to Grover Washington Jr. Elementary School in the morning and find out."

"We have a bleeder," the nurse called out as a facade.

"That's what I thought," Duke said as the nurse rolled a wheelchair around the nurses station to allow Duke to sit Willow in the seat.

Willow's vision swam for a second before she felt a hand grip her arm.

"Please, just sit down," Duke said to her, a worried expression on his face.

She angrily pulled her arm away, a scowl on her face as she placed her hand on the nurse's thigh. "No!" she yelled, trying to shake away the dots in her vision. "I-I'm fine," she said, stumbling over her words as it got harder to see.

A still moment passed before she felt the nurse tug on her arm again. "Please, miss," she pleaded, and Willow didn't have the strength to pull away. Her knees collapsed, and the next thing she knew, the world went black.

Willow was in a heavy black cloud. There was nothing to see and nothing to hear; just this heaviness in her whole body. It was so heavy that she couldn't move. She couldn't remember how to open her eyes. Then she started to hear noises. The buzz of machines and the clicking of feet near her, quiet talking. She lay still. She strained to hear and make sense of it all. She felt some light shining on her closed eyes—a pink glow. She struggled to open them. She was in a bright white place. Someone was bending over her. He said her name twice. She tried to remember how to talk. No words came, but she blinked hard. Again, he called her. Again, she tried to answer. Suddenly, Willow cleared her throat. She thought she was about to shout. But all that came out in a tiny whisper was, "What happened?"

Willow awoke fully as she leaned up in the hospital bed. All she could remember was the gun going off at Kail's leisure. She snapped back into reality and realized she was in a hospital. She could make out Duke's face next to her.

The doctor smiled. "Good, you're awake; how are you feeling?"

With the little strength she had left, she replied, "I don't know, weak."

The doctor looked at Duke and motioned him to go outside with him. As she watched Duke walk out of the room, she got out of the bed as she walked over to the small mirror above the sink. Her wound was packed, a small needle was inside her arm secured by tape as if medicine, and fluids had been given to her. Her lips were bare, no pink on them at all, which made her feel naked. Willow couldn't believe that Kail had shot her. Her mind was still in a state of shock and almost shut down every time she tried to process the thought. Her heart was telling her it wasn't true, but her brain played it over in her head like a prosecutor wanting justice. Her heart was heavy as she leaned on the sink, tears rushing down her face at the fact that she couldn't trust her one and only living relative.

"Your girlfriend is going to be okay," the doctor said as he looked Duke in the eyes. "As long as she cleans the wound thoroughly, then it should heal nicely. I'm going to write a prescription for pain, have a nurse remove that IV from her arm, and she can leave."

"Thank you, Doc." Duke shook his hand before making his way back into the room.

"Let's go." Willow met him at the door.

"You gotta wait for the doctor."

"Duke, you can wait. I'm leaving. I don't like hospitals. Because this is a gunshot wound, it's protocol for them to call the cops, and I sure as fuck don't like them motherfuckers. So if you want to wait, that's on you." She pushed by him.

Duke obliged as they walked down the hallway. "So who shot you?"

"My sister," she responded coldly.

"Word?"

"Thank you for coming," Willow said to him, changing the subject as they made it outside.

"Come to my place; let me take care of you." Duke wrapped his arms around her gently. "I make some bomb-ass noodles." He smiled.

"I don't eat that shit." Willow grinned.

"We will find something for you to eat then." Duke kissed her forehead. "Now wait here and let me go get my whip."

Willow could see Duke's pearl-white Mercedes CLK 500 sitting on 22's pull up in front of the hospital as she adjusted the makeup on her face. The vibrations from his sound system shook the foundation of the hospital as the beat echoed throughout her eardrum.

She walked to his whip as his eyes pierced through her body, undressing her a little more with each step she took. After entering the car, the smell of his cologne danced inside of her nostrils, making her love his scent even more.

The gold in his mouth glistened from the light that came on from her opening up the door. He was wearing Polo everything and his smile was therapeutic to her in some way. His smile always put her mind at ease.

"You feeling better?" He reached over and kissed her lips.

"Somewhat," she told him as she continued to kiss his lips, "thank you for being here for me tonight; it meant a lot."

"I love you." He gazed at her. "I love the fuck outta you, shorty, and that's what you do for the people that you love."

Willow sat with chills as each word rolled off of his tongue. She was scared of love. She had never had the chance to experience it the right way, and it was true what people said: you feared what you didn't know. Her heart melted in her chest, and flowed to her stomach as her pulse slowed down. "I love you, too," she said as they drove into the night.

They pulled up to Duke's apartment building; neither of them wanted to get out. They were too caught up in their moment of love that they just sat there as Cupid's arrow shot into both of them repeatedly.

Duke was forgetting about Melee more and more. He loved her, but what he felt for Willow was way deeper, and each day that she stayed missing, made him love Willow more. He had forgotten how it felt to be connected to someone until now. He was in love, and as he looked into her big marble-like eyes, what he was feeling was real.

"Did you see that?" Willow asked Duke as she looked out the back window.

"Naw, I didn't see nothing, baby." Duke closed his eyes and leaned his head back in his plush seat.

The sound of the pistol going off ripped through their ears as if they were right next to a fireworks display, listening to it go off, with no protection. The echo of the ear-splitting bang carried on for a good minute before Willow actually realized that they were being shot at.

A burning sensation hit her like a deer caught in headlights; it felt like something slit her throat. She panicked as she ran her fingers across her neck and blood gushed onto them.

She looked over at Duke and he was shaking while holding his side. His body was in shock and from the way blood oozed out of his mouth, she could tell he had been shot.

The bullets kept coming as Willow managed to open the door and get out. With her hand on her neck, catching the nonstop flow of blood, she fell onto the hard pavement of the street. Tears filled her eyes as she started to pant for air. Her arms felt heavy and she couldn't move no matter how hard she tried.

The barrage of bullets stopped and she could see a truck speed off down the road. She recognized the brand of the truck, but the sound of Duke choking on his own blood interrupted her from thinking straight.

Willow lay there with her shirt covered in blood unable to think. Her thoughts patronized her, so close to her grasping, until they escaped her mind.

What just happened? she kept asking herself as her vision grew blurry. Her eyes started playing tricks as her vision kept going in and out. She bellowed out a loud scream, which exhausted her body, and before she could do anything else, she blacked out.

The sounds of sirens awakened her as bright lights flashed inside her pupils. Willow was on a stretcher with pressure being applied to her throat. She looked around at the EMT and the paramedic asked her questions that she didn't respond to. She looked past them and there was Kail, standing at the back of the ambulance.

"Kail, what happened?" Willow asked as agonizing heat attacked her throat with each word she managed to speak.

"Don't talk," Kail snapped while wiping her eyes.

The aides in the ambulance forced Willow to lie down as she tried to get up. The ambulance stopped and she didn't hear sirens anymore. She saw the doors open up from the outside as the aides started to pull the stretcher out of the ambulance. Her neck was still burning; it felt as though she was in a dream fighting to wake up. They rolled her inside of the back of the hospital.

Willow wanted to ask questions, but she lay there while they rolled her into an operating room. What happened to Duke crossed her mind while a group of nurses appeared around her. She tried to speak, but talking hurt, so she continued to lie there, gazing into the many lights that lined the ceiling. She felt a prick in her arm, she looked down, and there was an IV piercing her skin. A nurse told her to count to ten and by the time she got to five, her eyes closed and she drifted away in a deep sleep.

Junior walked through the front door of his parents' mansion as security nodded their heads at him in a speaking gesture. The air filled with a sweet, musky scent as he entered the room. A delightful combination of woodsy aftershave with a hint of clean perspiration could be smelled from a few feet away. It was intoxicating to the housekeepers as they found themselves inhaling deeply every chance they could when the young man walked past.

"It's done." Junior walked onto the balcony where Evelyn was sitting, enjoying her morning coffee.

"That's good news." She took a bite of the toast from the plate on a stainless silver tray. "Did he get both of them or just one of them?"

"Both of them from what he told me." Junior sat across from her.

"So, Duke and Willow are finally done for." She smiled as she stirred her coffee.

"Willow?" Rock asked as he stepped onto the balcony. He was wearing a silk pajama set.

"Just some girl that Duke was fooling around with so I had them both killed." Evelyn smiled.

"How did she look?" Rock asked, looking at Junior.

"I told you she was just some—"

"Shut the hell up," Rock said, cutting Evelyn off.

"I don't know, Pops; I didn't see her." Junior's eyes went from his mother to his father. "Why y'all making them faces?"

"Is it her?" Rock asked Evelyn as he grabbed her face, his hands squeezing her mouth together with force. "Evelyn, I swear, you better tell me the truth now or your name will be on my list right after your father's."

"Yes." She slapped his hand away. "It is her." She stood, her finger pressed into his forehead. "The little bitch isn't even supposed to be here. So, I finished what we started."

"What we started?" Rock repeated, grabbing the tray and throwing it off the balcony. "It's what you and your sick-ass father started. You knew she was alive and you didn't tell me?" He started to walk off the balcony and into the bedroom. "That's low, even for you, Eve."

"Who is this chick?" Junior asked.

"Your little sister," Rock said as he walked away. "Go downstairs and get a car ready. I'm going to get dressed and then we can go."

illow slowly lifted her heavy eyelids as the strong smell of antibacterial cleaner filled her nose. Her mouth was dry and she smacked her lips a few times to wet them. She was lying down, in a bed it seemed, and the room was bright. Light from the window reflecting off the eggshell-white walls made her want to close her eyes again.

She felt like she had slept for years, but her body was still tired. She heard the beeping of a machine and slowly turned her head toward the source of the noise. The muscles in her neck were stiff and sore. She saw Kail sitting in a chair by the window; she was sleeping, it appeared.

Goosebumps filled the skin of her arm as the cool air circulated in the room, hitting her from every direction. Squirming around from the uncomfortable feeling of the rigid bed, she tried to yelp out to get Kail's attention, but nothing would come out. The texture of the roof of her mouth felt chalk-like and speaking was futile.

"You awake? How do you feel?" Kail asked her as she woke up in the chair.

Before Willow could attempt to answer, she felt something surge from her gut and into her throat. The last thing she ate, peaches and oatmeal, unfortunately, came spewing out, covering the sheets beneath her. Her body was reacting to the anesthetic from the surgery and vomiting was one of the side effects.

"Give...me...some...water," Willow managed to say after tossing the vomit-filled sheets onto the floor beside her. Her body was weak and with every move, she discovered a new source of pain.

"Should I get a nurse?" Kail asked her as she handed her a cup with room temperature water.

"No," Willow told her as she gargled with the water, wetting every ounce of her mouth. "It's normal to do that."

"You sure you okay?" Kail asked as she examined her up and down with her eyes.

"Yes, I'm fine," she answered in a phlegmatic manner.

Willow was upset with Kail for shooting her. She didn't know how to react to her being there. She didn't know if Kail was responsible for her being in a hospital bed again for the second time within twenty-four hours. She was happy to have someone by her side, but Willow was in no mood to trust.

"So, who did this?" Kail asked in a serious tone.

"I don't know. I was going to ask you since you're trigger happy these days," she answered, trying to replay the whole scenario over in her head while her blood boiled.

"Whoever it was, I know they were after Duke." Kail sat on the edge of the bed. "I didn't do this and I didn't mean to shoot you earlier, Willow. You are my only family."

"Duke," Willow whispered softly as her priorities came back to her. "Where is he? Is he okay?"

"He's in ICU." Kail adjusted her hair from in front of her shoulders. "Dude was shot three times and it's shocking that he's breathing at all."

A single drop of grief welled up from the corner of Willow's eye and suddenly, the dam broke. Hot torrents of grief coursed down her face; her racking sobs were quiet but loud in their own right.

She sat there in the bed crying to herself with her hands covering her face.

"What the fuck," Willow moaned between cries.

"It happens in this line of work," Kail told her as she got up. "I'mma go get a nurse, but you sit in here and get yourself together, bitch." Kail left the room.

Willow sat in a sheltered room where her thoughts roamed around with only thoughts of Duke dying. She froze in fear, and shivered in disbelief. The cold air sang around her and silence ate her surroundings. The sigh of her loneliness was with each breath she exhaled. The moment she felt a tickle upon her pale, ice-cold cheeks, she knew it was just the beginning of it all. Her eyes were screaming for justice with each translucent trickle of emotions.

Knocks on the door interrupted her grieving. The knocks grew louder and louder, waking her up from the pity party she was hosting. Two men walked inside; one was slightly taller than the one following close behind him. As the door closed Willow's heart started to beat fast.

The man appeared to be really tall from afar, but as he got closer, she could see that he was an average six-feet-something; he appeared taller because he had a menacing look about him, the kind of look that made one feel insignificant with just a twitch of his eyebrow.

His narrow temples were dusted with a light gray, but the rest of his head displayed a full, bushy, jet-black mane. His face was rigid and rough with experience—life experience, crime experience, street experience. He had that kind of face that suggested he might be a dirty businessman, a criminal on the inside. His face was underscored by his steely dark eyes; they were as cold as a tombstone in the middle of a dead January night.

There were no crow's feet around his eyes; she could tell he had never laughed at a joke in his life, the really serious type. His stocky frame was hidden beneath his high-end suit. The blazer was perfect for his arms and he looked nicer than most guys wearing the exact same suit. His tie was purple and his appearance was strong.

"You've grown up," Rock admired his daughter's beauty while keeping his distance.

"Who are you?" Willow asked, her throat still dry.

"I'm your father, and this is your big brother." Rock stepped a little closer. "I can't believe you're alive."

"I don't know you," Willow said, looking past them as Kail entered the room and closed the door.

"Who the fuck are y'all?" Kail asked as she pulled her gun out.

Rock looked at her and then at Willow. In their faces, he saw Melee; all three of them looked identical to him and could pass for triplets. He looked into the girl's eyes that were clearly marked with Anoki's beauty. They were the same eyes he'd fallen in love with so many years ago.

"Sister, or no sisters, you better tell her to put that gun down unless she wants two to the dome," Junior said sternly.

"We didn't come here for any problems," Rock said as he held his hands up. "I just wanted to see my daughter all grown up."

"Father?" Kail looked at Willow with doubt. "Moms said our father died right after I was born."

"So Anoki didn't tell you about me?" Rock looked at Willow. "I don't blame her."

"How the fuck you know my mother's name?" Kail cocked the gun.

"She was my wife," he looked at Kail, "and we had two beautiful kids together. Junior," he said as he nodded his head next to him, "and Willow."

"Prove it." Willow's eyes were locked on him.

"You have a small birthmark on your right lower hip; it's the shape of a triangle. I used to see it all the time when I changed your diapers."

"Don't fall for this shit." Kail looked at Willow. "We all we got; we don't have a father."

"No, I'm all I got," Willow said, raising her voice.

Willow knew as those words escaped Rock's lips that he was telling the truth. She didn't know him, and she didn't trust him, but he seemed like a man who spoke the truth at all costs.

"I didn't want to disturb you. I wanted to meet you officially and tell you if you need something, let me know. I run this city and whatever you need is at your disposal."

"Wait," Willow said as Rock turned back around, "if you're my father, then how come you don't know about Kail?"

"Who?" he asked.

"My sister." Willow pointed toward Kail. "We're exactly eleven months apart."

"Your mother left me when you were two months old," Rock said as Junior opened the door. "I didn't know."

They left the room as the wall shook from the door's closure. Willow and Kail sat there deep in thought as they processed what had just happened. Both were speechless; figuring silence would be the only proper gesture.

As the sun left the sky and night came, Willow was alone in the room. Kail said she had some Pink Lip Bandits stuff to attend to and being alone in her solitude never bothered Willow; not even with stitches being embedded in her neck.

She wanted to go see Duke in ICU, but she was told by the staff that she couldn't. They didn't want her to walk while she was on the strong pain medicine they were pumping through her veins.

Little did they know that popping pills was one of her pastimes. The medicine that they gave her was something that she could take and function fully.

She tossed and turned on the cold mattress the hospital called a bed until she couldn't take it anymore. She searched through her things until she found her cell phone, then she powered it on. She knew she couldn't sit in the room any longer. She had shit to do and being a prisoner wasn't one of them. Willow stood up and her fingers dialed numbers.

"What's up?" Choice said as she answered the phone.

"Bitch, I need a favor," Willow told her, getting right to it.

"Where the fuck you been for the past couple of days, bitch?" Choice screamed through the phone. "Nobody has seen you or nothing. What's the deal?"

"Some niggas blasted on me and Duke." She left the fact that Kail had shot her out of the equation. The last thing she wanted to do was ruin the reputation of The Pink Lip Bandits.

Choice gasped. "Bitch, you lying."

"No, I'm dead-ass serious. My neck and shoulder fucked off and Duke is in ICU. They shot him three times."

"Bitch, you lying," she continued to say, hoping that Willow wasn't telling the truth.

"I wish I was."

"Where are you?" Choice asked.

"In the hospital and I'm supposed to get up out of here tomorrow, but I can't stay here tonight," she told her, tossing everything she had on the night of the shooting in the wastebasket. "I need some clothes, bitch, and something nice. I been having on this ugly-ass gown and I need something to slip on."

"Where is Kail?" she asked.

"Handling some business, so I'm going to need a ride home, too."

"What hospital are you at?"

"I'm at Thomas Jefferson University Hospital," Willow told her as a nurse barged in.

"Ms. Davis, you can't be out of bed," the nurse said as she sped over to where Willow was standing.

"Get here fast," she said to Choice before hanging up the phone.

"Ms. Davis, please, get back in bed."

"Look, bitch," she told the nurse, losing her cool, "get the fuck out of my face with those orders. What you can do is get your ass to that nurses station and bring me some release forms to sign."

"This is your second wound. This is your second visit here. You need to rest. The doctor didn't release you and—"

"I don't give a fuck what the doctor did," Willow interrupted, while raising her voice. "I'm leaving if I do, or if I don't, sign those papers."

The nurse left the room and returned minutes later with the release forms. Willow didn't even give her a chance to explain. She signed everywhere she was supposed to, and the nurse walked off as fast as she could out of the room. Willow followed behind her as the pain from her new wound ached as she walked to the elevators.

She hit the button to go to the second floor to see Duke. Nothing mattered more at that moment; not even her parading around in the hideous hospital gown that she was wearing. Her hair was a mess, she didn't have on any makeup, her nails were chipped, but none of that mattered as the elevators slowly lowered.

Everything started going in slow motion for Willow once the elevator beeped and the doors opened to the intensive care unit. Everything felt so surreal; the walk to the nurse's station seemed as if it took forever. At the nurse's station, her stomach started twisting. She started second-guessing if she wanted to see him as the ticking from the clock on the wall boomed in her ears.

"Can I help you?" a nurse asked as their eyes met.

"I'm here to see Demarcus Williams." Willow's cell phone vibrated in her hand.

"What is your relationship to the patient?" the nurse questioned as she looked at the gown and bandages on Willow.

"His wife," she lied.

"Right this way." The nurse got up and walked with intentions of Willow following her.

The whole floor gave off an eerie feeling. It was like death was every which way you turned. Willow didn't know what she was going to see or how she was going to react.

"Here we are," the nurse said as she stopped in a doorway with a curtain blocking it from the hallway. "He is beyond this curtain."

The nurse gave a wry smile and left Willow standing there. Fear took over her body as she stood, shaking like a leaf on a tree on a windy night. She put her hand on the curtain, but she couldn't pry it open, no matter how hard she tried. *Open it, bitch, open it*, she thought to herself as her cell phone started to vibrate again.

She clenched her teeth as she slowly opened up the curtain. She could see Duke stretched out on the same rigid bed that she was imprisoned in earlier. His body was swollen and tubes were down his throat. As she got closer, she could see how bruised his body was.

Willow swallowed hard as she grabbed one of his hands with her own. She couldn't get it together as guilt overtook her. She felt like she should have never let them sit in front of his building for that long. She thought she'd helped whoever it was trying to kill him. She'd made Duke an easy target.

"I promise you, I will find whoever did this. And, when I do,

Duke, I will make them pay," she whispered into his ear, hoping that he could hear her.

She wiped her tears away as the nurse came into the room. She had a plastic bag in her hand and a sorrowful look on her face. She approached with caution as she handed Willow the bag.

"This is all of his belongings." She looked right at her but past her at the same time.

"Shouldn't you keep all of that here for when he comes to?" Willow asked.

"It doesn't look good for your husband, ma'am. He isn't responding to any of our treatments and the doctor said it may take more than a miracle for him to recover."

"So, he's going to die?" Willow asked, keeping her composure.

"That's a possibility." She saw the tears in Willow's eyes.

Willow looked through the plastic bag and it had all of his belongings from the previous night. His wallet, jewelry, and other items filled the small bag. She gave him a kiss on the forehead and left the room.

Her cell phone started to vibrate again, but she was so emotionally drained that she couldn't answer it. It was Choice from the caller ID. She headed to the elevator and then to the main entrance of the hospital. Upon exiting the sliding double doors, she could see Choice parked in a handicapped spot with her man sitting in the passenger seat of her brand-new Lexus.

Willow was a little skeptical. Choice had always talked about her man, but neither she nor Kail had ever met him. From what Choice always said about him, he was into the streets. As Willow got closer, her heart fell to her feet. Sitting in the passenger side of the car was Craig, the man she'd met in Hawaii with whom she'd had a fling on the plane.

"Bitch, you are a mess," Choice said after Willow approached the car.

She opened the door and sat in the backseat. "I know." She looked in the bag that Choice had waiting for her. "Do you have some green?" she asked her as Choice reversed and drove off.

"Of course, my nigga, but I gotta stop by the corner store to get some cigars. But, what happened? Are you going to be okay?"

"I will be." Willow slipped into the dress Choice had brought her, with the tag still intact, while trying to stay out of the view of the mystery man. "I just hope Duke will be okay."

"He will be, girl." Choice looked into the rearview mirror. "Oh, Willow, I want to introduce you to my fiancé. Willow, this is Craig, and Craig, this is Willow."

"What's up?" Craig said, never looking back at her.

"Nice to meet you," Willow said as she looked at him sideways, the pain from changing her clothes hitting her like a dog being hit by a car.

They rode to Choice's hood and stopped at the store everyone called the green store because of its pale pea-green color. It had boosters, prostitutes, dope boys, and anything else needed for everyday hood life. Choice parked her red Lexus sitting on twenty-four's and got out to go into the store.

"Willow, you straight?" Craig asked her after moving the rear-view mirror to look.

"I guess so," she answered while freeing her hair from the pony-tail. "I never thought I'd see you again." She closed her eyes to try to endure the pain.

"I didn't think I'd see you again either." Craig turned around and looked at her. "I guess I shouldn't have judged the cover, huh?"

"I guess not." Willow saw one of his hands wrapped in bandages; her eyes now opened. "What happened to your hand?"

"Nothing," he said, changing the subject and turning back to look out the front window. "So do you know who blew heat at y'all?"

"No, I don't know, do you?" she asked, aware that he was bad news.

"If I knew," he said as he turned around to look at her, "so would you. Don't play me like I'm some bitch made-ass nigga who wouldn't tell you what I know."

"I don't know that." She ran her fingers through her hair. "I don't know you like that, so I really can't say what you would do."

"Watch out with that bullshit." He grinned, exposing the pearly whites in his mouth. "I'm real."

"A lot of niggas say they real but they not." Willow leaned back into the seat.

"I ain't a lot of niggas," he said as his mind went back to the day on the airplane. "You know that was more to me than just a fuck."

"It was?" she asked while their eyes locked through the rearview mirror.

Before he could answer, Choice came out of the store, and hopped back inside the car. She tossed the sack of weed and the cigars to Willow, because nobody rolled a blunt like she did. She drove off to a chill spot and they smoked until it was almost time for the sun to come up.

"You wanna go home?" Choice asked her as she pulled off from their smoking spot. "Or, do you wanna crash at my place with me and Craig?"

"No, I'm good; I'll just go home." Willow swung her hands softly in the air. "Besides, we've been smoking for a couple hours and after the night I just had, I need to lay in my own bed."

Choice pulled up to Willow's condo building as the sun resurfaced into the sky. Images of Duke's body convulsing in the front seat of his Mercedes flashed over and over in Willow's head as she got out of the Lexus.

"I'm gon' fuck with you and Kail when I wake up." Choice yawned. "Call me if you need anything, bitch."

"Yeah." Willow closed her door and watched them speed off.

She closed her eyes longer than normal to get a grip on the pain she was feeling as she stepped onto the sidewalk from the street. She walked groggily into the building and it seemed as if it took hours to make it to her door.

She eased the key inside of the knob and opened the door. She tiptoed to her room, not wanting to wake Kail up if she was there. Kail would have a fit that she'd left the hospital sooner than she was supposed to. Her nagging was something Willow didn't want to hear, especially since they had beef at the moment.

She flopped down onto her bed, which felt better than sex in that very second. She opened up the plastic bag that the nurse had given her and pulled Duke's wallet out. She took his driver's license out and looked at him while he was in a better state than he was in now.

She took out a necklace and fastened it around her neck. It was a thick gold chain with a Jesus charm. In some way, the necklace made her feel closer to him. It made her feel as if his arms were wrapped around her and her pillow mimicked his chest. She slowly eased out of the dress that Choice had given her and threw it on the floor. With that false comfort, she closed her eyes and fell asleep.

Seventeen

Kail walked into the small Italian restaurant, the smell of fresh pasta and mozzarella tickling her taste buds. She was finally about to meet V face to face. She felt bad for leaving Willow in the hospital by herself, but money was her first love. Business came first, and everything else, including family, came second.

She took a seat at the table where she was instructed in the last envelope she had received from V. She put her gun on top of her legs, hiding it under the table from the view of the other customers. She ordered the food V suggested as her eyes focused on the door, the wall clock, and then the door again.

Her nerves were on edge. She had no idea who this man was that she was about to meet. She didn't know anything about him, but yet she didn't care to. She only was concerned that he could pay her for her services. Nothing else mattered.

An older man entered the building as the waitress put a plate of smoking, hot lasagna in front of Kail. She opened her silverware as the man sat across from her, his eyes locked on the plate. She set her silverware down as she looked at him up and down. She was not expecting an older man; his appearance shocked her.

"Good choice." He kissed one of his hands after folding them together and waved it toward the sky. "Mrs. Vera's recipe looks and smells just as divine as always."

"Here." Kail slid him the plate, her appetite ruined.

Vinny grabbed the plate as he reached over and put the silverware into his hands. It had been a long time since he was able to enjoy the food from his childhood. With him constantly looking over his shoulder, he could never sit in a restaurant. With all of the eyes Rock had around the city, he was surprised he hadn't been spotted yet.

"I'm Vinny Mancini," he said with a mouth full of food. "It's nice to officially meet you."

"Mancini," Kail said under her breath, "Gino Mancini."

"That's my baby brother, God rest his soul." Vinny shook his head. "You and your sister really did a number on my baby brother, and his beautiful wife."

"If he is your brother, fuck you for being kin to him. Fuck his life and fuck that bitch Mahina," Kail spat as she crossed her arms. "I'm here to discuss business and that's not a part of it."

"Understood." Vinny pushed the plate and wiped his mouth. "I need a job done and you're the only one that can do it."

"Why me?" Kail asked out of curiosity.

"Because, you're ruthless, and the other ones aren't. Willow will do a job, but your feelings never get involved like hers, and Choice is too inexperienced for my taste."

"What is it?"

"I need you to kill the leader of the mafia. I am willing to pay one million dollars cash." Vinny snapped his fingers as a woman with a briefcase rushed to his side. "You have never made this kind of money on one job from anyone else. You want to keep doing that shit on the side making chump change or do you want to make some real money?" He opened the briefcase after the woman set it on the table before sliding it underneath. "The choice is yours," Vinny said. He reached into his coat, pulled out a folder and handed it to Kail.

Kail opened the folder and the picture of the man at the hospital looked at her. She closed the folder quickly as she saw features of her face on his. It was her alleged father. She put the folder into her purse as she stood up, pushing her chair under the table.

"Will you do it?" he asked as she stood there, her four-inch heels piercing the old wooden floor.

She grabbed the briefcase. "I'm takin' the money, ain't I?" Kail looked back stopping in her tracks. "You used to be the leader of the mafia, so why end something you helped build?" she asked out of curiosity.

"It's the business, kid." Vinny pulled the remainder of the lukewarm lasagna in front of him. "Money talks, bullshit walks; remember that, youngster."

Kail shook her head and exited the restaurant as she crossed the street. When she made it to her car, she put the money in the trunk, got in, and sped off through the slight midday traffic. The job didn't sit right with her and was messed up. But, money was money and she had to eat and she steady reminded herself that one key element convinced her to go along with the job.

The minute Willow woke up, she felt as if she were suffocating. A victim from her nightmares, she walked to the bathroom to splash some water on her face and get the morning residue off her lips and eyes. She sat there on the toilet, looking in the wall mirror as her nightmares haunted the core of her brain.

She needed some fresh air, so she left the condo and went outside to the front of the building, letting the midday air become her medicine to breathe a little more lightly. The neighborhood was full of life and the visual of the lively surroundings calmed her spirit.

As Willow's lungs relaxed, she saw a car that she had never seen before pull up and park. She panicked as questions ran throughout her head. It spooked her a little. She didn't know if somebody had come back to finish the job because she had survived. She thought twice about going outside, about becoming an easy target, but the fresh air was much needed.

She saw movement within the car and the beating of her heart sped up. She was frozen, unable to move, and her knees started knocking together. If she was being aimed at, she was a clear shot. She checked her body for her gun, but she had left it upstairs.

A body ejected itself from the front seat before Willow could check it out. She squinted her eyes to see if she recognized the person. It was Kail, and Willow exhaled. Kail walked up on her slowly and she could see her intimidating eyes getting more intense with each step her Manolo Blahniks took.

"When did you get that car?" Willow asked as Kail stood in front of her.

"I just bought it," she said as she looked down the street. "Why are you outta the hospital? I thought they were letting you go tomorrow?"

"I left because I wanted to."

"We need to talk." Kail wanted to tell her about the meeting she'd had with Vinny. The pink lipstick on her lips looked as if she had just applied it.

"I'd rather not, Kail," Willow said coldly.

Kail brushed past her, opened the main entrance, and walked in. Willow followed her every move up the stairs while wondering what she wanted. She entered the main door of the condo and walked over to the refrigerator and opened it.

"How are you feeling?" Kail asked.

"I don't know." Willow sat on the couch. "My man is in critical condition. My one and only sister tried to kill me."

"I didn't try to kill you, Will." Kail slammed the door to the fridge. "If I was trying to kill you, you'd be dead. You know how good my aim is."

"So you think shooting me is okay?"

"I'm not saying that." Kail's forehead grew lines. "I'm just saying, let's put this behind us, and get back to the money."

A knock at the door put a halt to their conversation. Willow opened it as Junior stood in the doorway with a dark-skinned girl. Without an invitation, he walked into the condo as the girl followed close behind him.

"The fuck do you want?" Kail walked up on him.

"Control her," Junior looked at Willow.

"Yo, Kail, chill out." Willow backed away. "So what are you doing here?"

"It's about Duke," he said, while looking down. "Pops wanted me to come tell you."

"What about him?" Willow asked as her mouth became dry.

"He died. He didn't make it." Junior looked into her eyes as a feeling of compassion washed over him.

Willow's heart stopped for a brief moment. She couldn't do anything but cry. She thought seeing him in the hospital would have prepared her mentally for this moment, but she was wrong. Kail grabbed her to hold her and she released every ounce of sadness she had onto her shirt. Kail consoled her, ran her fingers through her hair, and told her to let it out.

"Do y'all know who did it?" Willow asked Junior while she fought to keep her composure.

"No, we don't," he said. "But, we on this. Pops run this city, so trust me, if we have to make somebody talk, we will find out."

"I'll find them before they ass can." Kail's eyes pierced through Junior's.

"Get down," Junior yelled while removing his gun from his waistband as the sound of glass breaking and bullets piercing the sky filled the air. Kail removed her gun while a gunless Willow ducked down.

"What the fuck is going on?" Willow whispered aloud as the sound of their large wall mirror crashing against the floor beat inside her ears.

"Stay down," Junior said as he opened the front door and went down the stairs with Kail following.

The floor crunched under Willow as she lowered herself unceremoniously to the ground, curling into a tight ball of pain. Her eyes squeezed shut, and a strong wave of pain hit her, working its way up from her gut to spread to the ends of her fingertips and down her withered legs. She knew it would not be long. She waited, ready to welcome the oncoming darkness.

"They're gone," Junior said as he and Kail walked through the door. "Are you two okay?" He looked at Willow and then at the woman.

"Yes," Willow said, never leaving the fetal position she was in.

"I'm about to call Pops." Junior walked toward the door. "We gon' get some security over here because somebody wants you dead."

If you want something done, do it yourself, Evelyn thought as she laid the gun down in her passenger seat; her speedometer reading one hundred miles per hour. The adrenaline pumping through her veins made her feel alive. She couldn't believe that she had just shot up Willow and Kail's condo. It was something she had never done before, but she had a new-found respect for the rush that assassins felt.

She was shocked at how she had pulled the trigger, even after seeing Junior go into the building. He wasn't her son, so his well-being wasn't her concern. If she had to kill him in the crossfire, then she would. He didn't come from her, no matter how badly she wished he had.

Evelyn pulled up to her mansion as the tires screeched at her command. She got out of the car, leaving the gun she had just used in the front seat. She walked onto the porch; a rock falling from the balcony above her made her look up.

"Welcome home," Rock said, looking down at his wife.

"Hey, baby." Evelyn used her hand to block the rays of the sun.

"Where are you coming from?" He put his hand on his chin.

"Shopping."

"That's funny." Rock picked up a cigar from the box that was next to him. "Where are your bags and why is that in your car?" He pointed the cigar toward her car.

Evelyn looked back at her car as a member of Rock's entourage closed the door. He was holding the gun she had left in the seat. The gig was up. She couldn't lie any longer. Whatever she didn't say aloud, Rock already knew.

"It's a gun I used to try to kill your daughter," she said nonchalantly.

"Evelyn, you are making it very hard for me not to kill you." Rock dipped the cigar in a glass of brandy. "If it wasn't for Melee, yo' ass wouldn't be here."

"Rock, you don't have the nuts to kill me."

"No?" He pointed a gun at her, releasing a round and missing on purpose. "I'm gon' tell you this once more, Evelyn. If a hair comes out of place on them girls' heads, I will kill you personally."

Evelyn looked up at him as the ground underneath her smoked from the bullet cracking its foundation.

"You should be more worried about the whereabouts of our daughter," Rock said.

She walked into the house as she tried to make herself exhale. She had never seen Rock so angry with her. She knew that he would kill her eventually, even if it had nothing to do with his kids. It was only a matter of time.

Vinny popped a bottle of Dom Perignon as the soothing vibration of the hot tub in which he sat comfortably bubbled with warm heat. He puffed on his Cuban Davidoff cigar as he overlooked downtown Philly from the thirty-third floor of his lavish pent-house. Naked women of all races and sizes surrounded him as the rings on his fingers glistened from the light of the half-moon that filled the sky.

"Who is that?" one of the women asked Vinny as Kail approached the sidebar of the penthouse.

He snapped a finger that was layered in pure gold rings. "It's business, bitch, so that means yous hoes have to get the fuck outta' here."

The women scattered like roaches in the kitchen when the lights suddenly flashed on unexpectedly. In a matter of seconds, Vinny was left in the Jacuzzi by himself puffing on his cigar as Kail slowly approached the outside of the hot tub.

"You want something to drink, young blood?" Vinny asked as he held the half-filled bottle of Dom Perignon up in the air.

"You know I don't drink on the job," Kail said, declining the offer with her hand. "I need some more information on this organization." She took a seat diagonally in front of the bubbling Jacuzzi.

"Professional." Vinny got out of the hot tub, exposing his naked body. "That's why I keep you around, 'cause you one of them people that's about nothing but her money."

"I appreciate that and all, but can you put some clothes on, nigga?" Kail asked, looking away disgusted at the sight of Vinny's little dick flopping in front of her.

"Enjoy the view," Vinny said. "Now, how did you find this spot?"

"I have my ways. I know you didn't think I was going to think a man like you actually lived in a retirement home. Once you gave me your name, it opened the door for a lot of research."

"This penthouse isn't in my name."

"But, it's in something that's close to your name. In this business, I have learned that most people that use aliases to get houses, apartments, or penthouses," Kail looked around, "use a name that's similar to their own. So, I just search for the one thing a normal person wouldn't, and boom, you came right on up."

"Smart." Vinny puffed on his cigar using the stairs to get out of the Jacuzzi. He grabbed a towel from the edge of the hot tub and then wrapped it around his body. "So what other information do you need?"

"Is he really my father?"

"Yes," Vinny said in a low voice as if ears were listening.

"Okay, that's cool." Kail stood and checked her cell phone that was clipped to her brown leather belt.

"Can you still do it, knowing that he's your poppa?" Vinny asked in an irritated tone.

"You're kidding me, right?" Kail locked her eyes on Vinny's. "That nigga ain't did shit for me. It would be a suicide mission for anyone else. But, I'm not just anyone."

"You will be one of the only people he put his guard down for. You are the only person who can pull this shit off." Vinny snapped his fingers. Moments later, a Haitian woman draped in nothing but a pair of stilettos came walking toward them with a briefcase in her hand.

"What is that?" Kail sat back down, interested in the money she was about to be offered.

"Five hundred thousand," Vinny said as the woman handed him the briefcase. "It's insurance for his death. You can say a bonus so I'll know you get this done. So, can you do it?"

"Of course," she said, grabbing the briefcase. She walked into the night, passing the entrance of the penthouse and entered the elevator, never looking back.

Eighteen

Willow had that recurring dream again. A slumbering moon, haloed by a scattering of stars that twinkled more than a thousand diamonds, lit up the sky as dark as thick black velvet, worn and faded toward the edges. Thunder and lightning flashed throughout the ominous sky as light trickles of rain fell from the heavens. In the distance, she could see a small house, the windows of light mimicking the stars, and a church bell tolling the witching hour's melancholic start. It seemed the house was her objective; nothing else mattered.

She shuffled down a street, her eyes flickering back and forth. Every opening door and every shrill bird call caused her to jump. Her hand unconsciously tightened around something in her hand that felt like a gun. The sound of a car coming from behind forced her to turn around. Her heart froze and her stomach turned icy as she saw the vermilion red truck lumbering down the street; an unknown assailant operating it from behind tinted windows.

Turning back around, she ran down the soul-searing street, and as she turned her head, she could see the murderer speeding up. Facing forward, she began to sprint, fear clouding her mind and adrenaline pumping through her veins. However, her efforts were in vain. The pickup truck accelerated, catching up to her in an instant.

Running faster, the dirt from the streets started to accumulate around her; with every step arousing the tailing red truck. Her breathing quickened, trying to appease her need for oxygen, but it was disturbed by the dirt. Her nasal passages and eyes got a large amount of dirt in them. She felt trapped; like she was suffocating in the midst of her escape. She had to try to get away, though. Regardless of how much her body rejected, that was all she could do to survive.

Her legs became wary as her feet desperately attempted to create a form of traction—something that was lacking. She was stuck for a moment with her knees touching as she coughed from inhaling the heavy grayish-brown substance.

The sounds from the truck's horn called out from behind her as the tires' screech grew closer and closer. She looked around as goose bumps lined her pale skin as failed attempts to think of a plan escaped her brain, almost patronizing her. She looked ahead and dashed toward the alley with nowhere else to go.

Before she could make it past the alley, there he stood: Duke. She opened her mouth to say something to him. He was wearing the same clothing as the night of the shooting, and before she could open her mouth, a bullet pierced through his head and into hers. And before she could die on the street inside the alley, she woke up.

Today wasn't any different from any other days since Duke had died. The annoying shrill of her alarm clock called out, halting her faltered nightmare. Willow jolted up, her eyes squinted shut, trying to ward off the filtered sunlight drifting in; the inevitable dread of opening them to the sudden glare of a dimly lit room. She opened only one, quickly feeling the burn in her shocked retinas, before slamming it shut again. The burn—all she could think of was the burn.

She touched her face, assuring it was only a dream; it felt so real. She had broken out in a cold sweat, her silk pajamas soaked, and she was shaking in fear. She moaned from the tapping sunlight against her face, wondering how long she'd been sleeping, wondering why she kept having those nightmares. She blinked, shut her eyes, and blinked again. She yawned as her heart slowly left the middle of her throat and returned to its relatively normal pace in its proper spot, her chest.

Willow took her ponytail holder off, releasing her goddess-like curls as she walked over to make sure the front door was locked and to check around the condo. Kail was gone as usual and she was alone. She walked over to her floor entertainment system and put in Mary J. Blige's *My Life* CD, letting Mary's soulful voice be therapy to her ripping, tortured soul. She looked out the window and the same security men that had been there for the past week were still parked on her street per Rock's orders.

She walked toward her bathroom, undressing little by little, imagining how soothing the boiling-hot water of her walk-in shower would feel on her mourning skin. She desired a long, steamy session. She cut the water on to the temperature she was yearning for and stepped in with no reservations.

Great drops fell from her eyes, colliding and joining the timid water sprouting from the head of the shower; the heavy rainclouds in her mind let loose their turbulent nature and everything she fought to hold in came spewing out with no apologies. With the love of her life gone, she cried as if the entire world, and all of its beauty, had come to an end. She sobbed as if she were a mere newborn seconds after being birthed into the world.

She cut off the faucet as salty drops fell upon her velvet skin. She grabbed a towel off the rack hanging outside of the walk-in shower and wrapped it around her sorrowful body. She wiped her tears away as she passed the convex mirror hanging from the wall of the long hallway that led to her bedroom.

Willow dried off her hourglass frame and walked inside her massive closet space to find something to wear. Knowing the circumstances, she really didn't care how she would look. However, out of respect for Duke and knowing that he was all about appearances, she would have to get fly for his funeral.

She flipped through racks, going through so many brands, which all had the tags still attached. She stopped when she saw a little black dress made by her favorite label, Chanel. She slid the dress on, grabbed a pair of unworn heels from the top rack, and left the closet.

With her makeup done, her heels on, and hair gently teased with soft curls, it was time to go. Cutting off all of the lights before she left, she stepped into the hallway as her heels clicked on the beautiful granite flooring that aligned the lounges of the building.

"Are you ready?" Junior asked from the bottom of the stairs as he leaned on the railing with his hand.

"As I'll ever be. Where's Kail?"

"She left with security a long time ago to check everything out. She is going to meet us there, but I need you to ride with me."

"Okay," Willow said as they exited the building. Two black SUVs waited on them.

They pulled up to the church. Willow put her shades on and got out of the car. The sun was shining and raindrops hit her as she stared into the sky. It seemed like it always rained on days of funerals.

She saw a lot of familiar faces when she entered the double doors. Many eyes followed her and Junior as they found seats.

Men from different sets were there; it was packed. Willow knew Duke was a real dude and niggas wanted to show their respect. She found it to be admirable.

As Kail sat next to her on the pew, Willow couldn't grasp reality while sitting there; everything felt so surreal to her. She couldn't believe that she was attending Duke's funeral. It felt like it wasn't true, and no matter how sad the mood was set in, she couldn't get into it.

Time came for the services to start and the pallbearers brought the casket in and set it down. The casket was closed. Willow guessed the family had made the decision to ease some of the pain. Chances were he looked like he had the last time she had seen him, so she couldn't blame them.

Everyone stood as Duke's family entered the church and took their seats. She had never seen his family before, nor met them. They all looked alike. His family was very neat-looking and they all shared the same skin tone.

The pastor started to speak before a variety of songs were sung by the large choir. The whole box of Kleenex that Willow had was empty by the time the services were over. Her emotions really got the best of her as several members of Duke's family spoke in memory of him.

The reception started after the funeral at the church. Everyone was there eating, talking, and telling their fondest stories of Duke. Willow watched as a woman asked people who knew Duke something, and everyone pointed at her. She didn't know what it was about, but she was sure she would find out as the woman started walking toward her.

"Your name is Willow, right?" she asked, grabbing her hand as Willow stood up to greet her.

"Yes." Willow slowly pulled her hand away. "Do I know you?"

"Excuse me for being so rude. I'm Demarcus's mother, Beverly Williams." She looked Willow in the eyes.

She was a gorgeous woman and Willow knew it was taking everything in her to keep it together. She could tell she was well off from her jewelry, and that whatever Duke had been doing, he had shared it with his moms.

Guilt overcame Willow suddenly. All she wanted to do was apologize over and over again. She knew she didn't physically pull the trigger but that's how she felt at that very moment. The pain bursting through Duke's mother's eyes made her feel sick.

"Hi." Willow reached in and gave her a hug. "I'm sorry we couldn't meet under better circumstances."

"I know." She hugged her back. "I heard you were in the car with him during the time of the shooting. Thank God you came out alive."

"Yes, I was there." She looked down.

"This isn't the time or place for that." She handed her a piece of paper. "That is my number and address. Call or come by anytime you want."

"I sure will." Willow smiled as she walked off.

"How are you holding up?" Choice asked after walking up to Willow and hugging her.

"I'm good." Willow gave a fake smile.

"Who was that woman?" Kail approached them; all three of their lips coated in pink.

Rumors must have hit the streets about The Pink Lip Bandits. Seeing as all eyes were on them, Willow knew that must have been true. People kept their distance, and the fact that they were the only women in the whole church with pink lipstick, answered a lot of people's questions.

"Duke's mom," Willow said.

"Speaking of Duke," Kail looked at Choice, "you should let Nicole see what's in his bank account. Didn't you say your moms worked at a bank now?"

"Yes," Choice said as she pulled out her phone. "I'll see what I can do, but you gon' have to break her off sumthin'."

"That's cool." Kail wrapped her arm around Willow, making her jump a little from brushing her sore wounds. "When we gon' get back to this money, sis?"

"I don't know," Willow said, removing Kail's arm from around her neck. "Can I mourn first?"

"Yes, you can," Kail started to walk off, "but, don't take too long."

Willow stood with her back against the wall as she watched people come and go. She could only imagine what was being said about her since eyes cut at her so many times in seconds. She held her composure and decided to bite her tongue for Duke's family, but had it been any other setting, she would have given them a reason to talk.

"She said you can come," Choice said as she approached Willow after making a call. "She works on One Hundred Twenty-Fifth Street."

"I got it." Willow signaled for Junior as he followed her outside.

"What's up?" he asked as he approached her.

"I need to go to a bank on One Hundred Twenty-Fifth Street," Willow said.

"Just take a car." He signaled for one of the two black SUVs, and seconds later, it pulled up in front of them. "You need me to go with you?"

"No, it's cool." Willow stepped into the car.

Willow didn't know it, but her relationship with her big brother, Junior, was blossoming. He had been there for her the whole week and they'd talked about everything. She could relate to him more than Kail. She was beginning to trust Junior; she just hoped he didn't betray her trust like Kail had.

Willow looked at Choice's mama, Nicole, as she walked up to her window. She hadn't made it to see her since she had been back in Philly, and the look on Nicole's face showed her disappointment. Willow smiled at her—the same way she used to do when she was a little girl—to get her way.

"Hey, Miss DuBois," Willow said with a smile.

Although she was mad, Willow knew Nicole was one of those microwave bitches; she liked money quick, so she couldn't drain his account without breaking her off something. She could afford to spare some money, so she was going to be as fake as a three-dollar bill right now to try to lower what she would have to give her.

"Don't 'hey, Miss DuBois' me." Nicole pointed her long nail. "Yo' ass been here for months and I have yet to see you," she said with a serious face. "I've seen Kail several times, but you, I haven't seen."

"I'm sorry." Willow leaned on the teller's window. "I just have been busy."

"Busy getting shot with that nigga?" she asked.

"Yes, that was him and I was in the car." Willow lifted her head up to expose her bandages, trying to earn sympathy points.

"You got shot?" she asked, falling into her trap.

"I got grazed, but a piece of the bullet got lodged in my throat, and they had to surgically remove it." Willow rubbed her throat through the bandages.

"Girl, shut up," she exclaimed, causing a scene.

"I'm dead-ass, but that's why I'm here. I need to get them duckies out of Duke's account."

"What's in it for me?" she asked as she bit on her press-on nail.

"How much is in the account?"

"Demarcus Williams?" Willow nodded her head. "It says he has ninety-eight up in this bad boy, so that mean you want ninety back, right?" she asked, winking at her.

"I guess so," Willow said, rolling her eyes.

"That's what's up." She hopped off the stool while popping the gum in her mouth. "I'll be right back, girl. We ain't got that kind of bread up here, but I'll go get it."

Willow tapped her fingers at the window waiting for her to return. Nicole came back with a paper for Willow to sign and a smile on her face from ear to ear. Willow guessed she had just gotten ninety-eight thousand from the back, but stopped and put that eight she was getting from her in her purse.

"You want me to put this in sumthin' or just hand it to you?" she asked, flashing the money at her.

"Just hand it to me," Willow told her as she opened up her sixteen hundred-dollar Balenciaga handbag. It was the perfect size to hold the money.

"Be careful with that," she warned her as she waved her off, "niggas is crazy these days."

Willow left the bank, hugging her bag like her life depended on it, hoping she wasn't drawing too much attention to herself. She got inside the SUV and instructed the driver and guards to take her home.

A couple blocks away from her destination, she saw the red truck from her nightmares. Her mind raced as flashes of the night of the shooting came back to her. It was the same truck from that night.

As she was driving up the block, she saw a tall paper-sack-brown-skinned dude run out to the truck. He had to be at least six-five or six-six. He had on plaid shorts, a button-down shirt, and some house shoes. She saw a ring shining on every finger and a couple of necklaces around his neck. She wondered if Craig knew anything about him.

Willow made her way back to the condo to come up with a plan. She couldn't just sit by idle; she needed to know if that was the dude who killed Duke. She was deep in thought as she went to her room to hide the money she had gotten out of the bank account.

She picked up her phone and dialed. "Craig, can you come scoop me up?" she asked, stopping him from saying anything as he answered his cell phone.

"Where you at?" he asked as his voice got low. "Does Choice know about this?"

"I'm at my condo, but come to the back because security is watching me like a hawk. And, no, she doesn't know." Willow put different items on top of the purse with the money in it.

"Security?" he asked as Willow checked herself out in the mirror.

"Don't worry about all that. Are you coming?"

"I'm on my way." He hung up the phone.

He would be there in ten minutes and Willow wanted to be ready when he arrived. She grabbed a purse from a box of purses that she'd never worn. Her Christian Louboutins stomped throughout the condo as she made her way to the back exit.

She saw Craig pull up slowly to the back door. She entered the car, then ducked down when he passed the SUVs in front of her condo. She felt like a little kid sneaking off with her boyfriend in the middle of the night. She knew Rock meant well by trying to protect her, but she was a menace to society in her own right. She could only be down for so long.

"So, what's up?" he asked.

"Stop," she told him as she pointed to the house. "The dude who shot us lives here or knows somebody that does. The same truck from the night of the shooting was here."

"So, this where that bitch-ass nigga stay?" Craig parked in front of the house.

"I think so, but dude's whip ain't here no more."

"It's Saturday, baby," he said as he started to drive off, "everybody who is anybody is at the Zone."

Willow leaned back and enjoyed the ride. She cut the music up and let the wind that was seeping through the open windows cool her off. She had never been to the "Zone," but the park was infamous. She had heard stories about it. All the hard-heads gathered there to chill on a weekly basis.

Loud music mixed with the smell of liquor entered Craig's car as they pulled into the park. Women were walking around with the best knock-off pieces while men sat around showing off their new guns. Willow felt like she was in a twilight zone; she knew with or without Craig next to her, she would be okay because she had her gun, if anything were to pop off.

They got out of the car as Craig saw some of his homeboys from around the way. He mouthed to Willow that he would be right back as he walked toward their direction. Willow sat on the hood of his car as she scoped her surroundings. She calmed her scoping when she saw Choice walking toward her.

"'Sup, trick," Choice said as she sat down next to her on the hood of the car; her eyes looking back at it, wondering if it was Craig's or not.

Choice looked at Willow as she rolled down the half top she

was wearing to show off her womanly assets. The gold-colored sandals on her feet rested on the license plate bolted to the front of the car as her long hair held still in a ponytail. The small shorts hugging her body exposed her beautiful legs as every man within view gawked over them.

"What's up?" Willow responded in a nonchalant manner.

In the middle of their conversation, she saw the same red truck pull up. It was the same one from earlier. The same man from earlier got out of the car and made his way to a group of goons. Willow saw Craig on the other side of the park and when he noticed the red truck, he started to walk toward her in the parking lot.

"What's up, baby?" Craig approached Choice and gave her a kiss. "What you doing in the 'Zone'?"

"Chilling with some of my bitches," she rubbed on his dick area, making Willow feel uncomfortable.

"That's him," Willow told Craig as she looked up at him.

"It is?" He looked down at her. "That's Talvin."

They continued their conversation, but Willow's focus stayed on Talvin. She wanted to get closer to hear his voice. She finally knew who was responsible for the stitches in her neck, and vengeance was on her mind. The way he stood there without a worry infuriated her. She had to talk herself out of approaching him and putting her gun to his throat.

"I'll be back." Craig pulled out his nine and walked off.

"Craig, don't do that." Willow grabbed his shirt, but he pulled away.

Willow's eyes followed Craig's every move as he walked to the group of goons where Talvin was standing. Although what he was about to do was for her, Willow prayed he didn't start anything. Her prayers were in vain as Craig removed his gun and pointed it at Talvin before he walked away to continue his conversation with his homeboys.

Willow stole glances at Talvin to sketch his face into her mind, never wanting to forget how he looked. He glanced back at her, their eyes staring each other down before he looked in another direction. The fact that he didn't remember her face from the night of the shooting was a good thing to her.

As night came, the park became deserted. Everyone left, including Choice. Willow opened the door to Craig's car and found him smoking. She hopped inside, grabbed the blunt from his lips, and hit it until she couldn't hit it anymore.

"What did you say to Talvin?" Willow asked him, while passing the blunt back to him.

"The truth." He started the car and drove off.

"What do you mean?"

"I told that nigga if we didn't have the same boss, I'd blow his fucking brains out," he said in a serious voice.

"I told you not to get in this shit. I don't need you handling shit for me."

"I don't give a fuck," he yelled, interrupting her. "You think they only made one gun when they made that nigga? Fuck that bitch-ass nigga."

"Okay, I fucking get it, nigga, so calm down," she told him and decided to change the subject. "So who do y'all work for? Is that the job you were telling me about back in Hawaii?"

"What's up with all these questions?"

"I'm just wondering." She handed the blunt back to him.

"Some nigga named Rock. He the head nigga around here, and he got some crazy-ass loot. I'm tryna get like that one day."

"He ain't shit."

"How you know dude?"

"He's my father," she answered in an annoyed tone.

"Stop fucking with me." He stared at her, now understanding the resemblance between her and Melee.

"I'm serious."

"Why you ain't tell me?"

"It's not something that I brag about."

"Man, if niggas knew that was yo' pops, nobody in their right mind would fuck with you. That nigga Rock is ill. I should have known that nigga was yo' pops."

Craig continued to show homage to Rock and all Willow could do was sit there. She wondered if her father was really that nigga like everybody made him out to be. She wondered if she would have it easier if she would actually acknowledge the fact.

Willow debated asking Craig what he knew about Rock. She needed to pay him a visit, even though she hadn't seen him since the day at the hospital. She could have asked Junior, but she wanted to go see him on her own.

"Craig, do you know where Rock rests his head?" she asked while she closed his door after they arrived at the condo.

"He stays in the suburbs in the south."

"You know a street name?"

"Pinewood," he said while puffing on the blunt.

"Thanks," she told him as she gave him a kiss and waved good-bye.

"Wait." He got out of the car. "That wasn't a real kiss."

"That's the kind of kiss I give my girl's man," Willow said with her back on the door.

"You know what," Craig put his face close to hers, "you not even supposed to be kissing yo' girl's man at all. So, if you gon' do sum-thin', do it right."

They were alone there in the moonlight. He held her close, and she was protected within the circle of his arms. He didn't think about the next time they would kiss; he had dreamed about it. Her lips looked so inviting, yet he didn't want to invade them. First, he kissed her cheek, and moved slowly closer to the sweetness of her lips. He remembered that her lips were at first moist, and cool. She slightly parted her lips, and he did the same. Such sweetness he had never imagined.

"I love you," Craig said, looking into her eyes.

Willow stood there in shock for a moment, his statement catching her off-guard. Before she could even say anything, his strong arms were around her, holding her as close as possible while he bent down and kissed her gently. The soft kiss gradually turned into a deep, passionate one.

All of a sudden, she stopped and pulled away instantly. Alarmed, he looked down to her. "What's wrong?" Craig asked.

"Uh...Nothing. Sorry." She turned around. He scratched the back of his head nervously.

She smiled back at him as she walked in the door. After entering the condo, she made it to the living room and Junior and Kail looked at her like they had just seen a ghost. They both stood and if looks could kill, Willow would have been dead.

"Yo, where the fuck you been?" Junior asked.

"Your ass went to the park," Kail said as she hung up the phone with Choice. "You think that shit was smart?"

"I had Craig with me, so I was okay."

"Craig?" Junior's voice rose. "Don't ever trust that nigga to look after you, because the next thing you know, your ass will come up missing," he said, referring to Melee. "Don't leave until we figure this shit out, Willow."

"I got it," she said as she went into her room, "calm down."

She thought about she and Craig kissing, but Talvin was also on her mind. She wasn't a female bitch, but it was something about Craig that she couldn't shake. She blamed her actions on the fact that Duke was dead, and she was mourning, but even with that truth, she knew it was more than that. That day on the plane, she had felt something special with Craig. She only hoped that it didn't blow up in her face.

Nineteen

Willow walked down the stairs of her condo as the sun's rays glowed from the clear sky, melting the little ice that was left on the ground. With her Michael Kors purse hanging from her hand, she crossed the street, ignoring the calls from security.

She got inside her car, putting her purse in the passenger seat before accelerating down the road. Countless vibrations jiggled throughout her purse from her cell phone as Kail and Junior called nonstop, but she ignored every call.

Willow wasn't ignorant to nice things, but the houses on the street where Rock lived were not houses in her eyes; they were mansions. She eased through the neighborhood to look for signs of which would be his house. When she saw guards standing at attention, she knew she had found the right house.

She parked across the street, got out of the car, and crossed the street. Before her feet could even touch the lawn, the men guarding the entrance of the house started to walk her way when they noticed her.

"You got some business here, young lady?" one of the two men asked her as they stood in front of her, blocking her from going any farther.

They were wearing all black and pistols sat on their waistbands.

They had to be over six feet tall and they were buff. Willow looked at them sideways immediately. For some reason, she didn't feel a bit of intimidation from them. She had been in scarier situations.

"I'm here to see Rock." Willow tried to pass them.

"Rock doesn't see just anybody. Do you have an appointment?" the guard asked.

"I'm his daughter, nigga. I shouldn't need an appointment."

"It's cool," Junior said while making his way toward them as he waved them off.

Junior's pulse sped up and he was breathing very shallow once he made it in front of Willow. His muscles grew tense. He felt his temperature rise. He could almost feel his blood boiling in his veins. He smiled on the inside; Willow's action reminded him of Melee's attempts to get away from his watch.

"I'm sorry." Willow looked at him. "I just wanted to do this on my own."

"Let's go inside."

Willow followed Junior as she listened to him talk. She gave him fake grins as they approached the front door before he opened it. Darkness hit their eyes as she followed him inside the house. He hit a switch and the whole house lit up and she was able to see.

The inside was beautiful. There were murals painted on the walls, marble floors, and there was a beautiful chandelier hanging from the ceiling. Willow took her eyes off the beauty of the room to get a glimpse of her surroundings. She noticed more buff men standing at different positions; she knew they all had a certain job.

"Come on," Junior said, walking down a hallway.

They entered a room and it looked as if they were in the living room. The room was just as beautiful as the previous one. The furniture looked as though it was imported. The rugs were so fancy that Willow had to second-guess if she should stand on them.

Junior told her to take a seat before leaving her alone in the room. She nearly dozed off from how comfortable the couch felt to her body. It would have succeeded in its purpose had she not been so filled with mixed emotions.

The whole experience was bittersweet and Willow could taste it in her mouth. She heard talking and laughter. She was aware that people were approaching the room she occupied.

Willow blinked and before she knew it, two men were standing in front of her. One was Junior, her brother, and the other was none other than Rock, her estranged father. She stared at him as if she had never seen him in her life; it was how she felt.

Rock told Junior to leave and he obliged, closing the door behind him. He stared at Willow as if she were going to run into his arms. The only thing on Willow's mind was how to break the ice. Although she shared his DNA, he was a complete stranger to her.

"What's up, Rock?" she asked nervously, her palms sweating like a fat kid after gym class.

He kept staring at her with that look that she had seen on Junior's face countless times. He didn't say anything; he kept staring and it was starting to irritate her to the core.

"So you can't use words? Do I need to do sign language or something?" she asked while cutting her eyes at him.

He smiled at her in a sly manner as he adjusted his posture. He unbuttoned the silky shirt he had on, exposing the shirt underneath. He made his way over to the couch where she was sitting and words ejected themselves from his mouth.

"You call your pops by his first name? I see Anoki didn't teach you any manners. I see she taught you how to have that fly-ass mouth, though." He pulled a joint out of his pocket and lit it. "I knew you would come by one day like your sister did, but I just didn't know when. I'm not good at expressing emotions or no shit like that, but a nigga is happy to see his baby girl in the flesh." He puffed on whatever brand of weed that was rolled inside of the Bugler paper.

"Kail came to see you?" Willow asked in total shock.

"Yeah, she stopped by. She told me a lot about you. I haven't talked to her since then, though, but I'm more interested about why you stopped by." He continued to indulge in his substance through his lips.

"What all she tell you?" she asked out of curiosity.

"You think you the first to wear pink lipstick? I knew what it meant when I met your mother; she just didn't know that I knew." His facial expression changed.

"Yeah, I wear it." She crossed her legs. "That sort of thing tends to happen when you grow up without a father figure."

"Follow me and tell me the real reason why you came." He turned around and started walking. Willow didn't say a word as her feet slowly but surely followed him. Rock started going up the spiral staircase and she did the same. The second floor of the house had a lot more security; there were men in black everywhere.

Willow continued to follow him as they made their way to the end of the hallway. He turned the knob to a set of double doors and they walked inside. He cut on a light revealing the massive size of the room. There were security videos on every wall so Rock could see all movements in the house at all times. He made his way to a desk in the room and ordered Willow to take a seat.

"So, what's the real reason you came all this way to see me?" He lit another blunt.

"I can't just come see my father?" Willow asked as she took a seat.

He looked her up and down as he puffed. "I don't know; you tell me. How you liking the east side of town?"

"How you know where I stay, Rock?"

"I know every move you make, Willow. Who do you think ordered security for you? You think I would have little girls that came from my nut sac running around and not keep an eye on them? I know about you and Craig. I even know about you and Duke."

"So, you know about me getting shot and yet you've done nothing about it?"

"No," he responded calmly.

"If you ran the city like everybody say, then you should have known." She stood up.

"Sit yo ass down," he demanded while pointing to the chair underneath where she stood.

Willow continued to stand with her arms crossed.

"You definitely got my blood in you, kid." He finished the last piece of blunt he was smoking. "So, what do you want me to do about you getting shot at?"

"I don't know. What can you do?" She sat back down in the chair.

"Tell me what *you* want me to do. This is your request, right?" he asked while leaning back in his chair.

"What do you want me to say?" She looked straight into his eyes.

He put his hands down and got up from his seat. He walked over behind her and hunched over so his mouth was directly next to her ear. "Go home, baby girl," he whispered as the heat from his mouth gave her hives, "this road ain't one you wanna go down; trust me."

She turned around. "I'm already halfway down that road."

He stood back up and glared at her, giving her a look that was all so familiar. He walked over to the door that blocked them off from everyone else in the house. "Junior," he yelled as he opened up the double doors.

Willow heard a lot of noise and she could see him talking to someone. It must have been Junior. He closed the door and made his way back over to the seat opposite where she was sitting. He put his hands together as he started to speak again.

"I guess since you don't have an answer for me, there's nothing I can do." He pulled out another blunt.

"You smoke too much." She tried to change the subject.

"I got some business to attend to, Willow. I got Junior making a run down to the warehouse to bring you some things."

"Things like what?" she asked in a low voice.

"Well, I know times must be hard, so I'm giving you some dough. He gon' bring you something so you can protect yourself; is that cool?" he asked while puffing on his third blunt.

"I didn't come here for your money." She stood. "If you had been watching me, you would know I have a lot of guns, and money has never been an issue."

"It ain't about that," he said as a fist hit the door with a knock. He got up and started walking toward the door. "One day, you gon' have to accept the fact that I am your pops, and I got you on whatever you need. I got a lot of years to make up for and I know that." He opened the door and Junior walked in with a duffel bag.

Junior put the bag on the desk in front of Willow and started emptying it to show her the contents. He pulled out three guns and two stacks of money.

"Here." Junior pointed at them. Willow looked at him and then Rock.

"I have money and guns."

"Just pick one and take it just in case. This is three hundred thousand; if you need more, let me know. There is no limit to what I can get. If you ever want to retire that color on your lips, let me know." Rock handed her the smallest gun.

The gun felt good to the touch as she picked it up. She didn't want to put it down. She wanted to shoot it just for the hell of it. The cold titanium metal chilled her hand and sat so perfectly in it. She didn't want to let it go.

"Do you like that one?" Junior asked while leaning back on the desk.

Willow nodded her head yes and she started to rub it. She saw Rock snap and Junior ran over to the closet. He got Rock a coat and held it out so he could put it on. He brought shoes and jewelry out as Rock started picking through what he wanted.

"Willow, I have to bounce, baby girl. Take that gun, them stacks, and come by tomorrow. I guess I can teach you how to work it properly." He adjusted the coat on his body.

"I gave myself lessons a long time ago." Willow pointed the gun at him. "I'm very skilled."

"I'm sure you are," he said, walking toward the door. "Junior will see you out, and it was good seeing you."

"He's not as bad as you might think," Junior said as Willow walked around the desk; her father's scent present in every spot in the room. "Pops is cool. He just gotta lot of business to take care of since they found his business partner, Tony, killed in his apartment."

"That's fucked up," Willow said, not realizing that she was the reason for Tony's death.

Willow sat in the seat behind her father's desk. She got up swiftly, knocking a picture off the desk with her hand. She picked it up and her eyes popped out of her head. In the photo was Evelyn from the nightclub and the girl from Hawaii who had walked in on them killing Gino, Mahina, and the other Pink Lip Bandits that Kail had shot and killed in cold blood.

"Who are these two to Rock?" she asked as she faced the picture around so Junior could see.

"That's Evelyn, my moms, and that's Melee, my sister," he said as he pointed.

"Your sister as in my sister, too?" Willow asked as she set the picture down.

"Yes," he said, his response sounding slow. "She's been missing for a while now."

"I have to get out of here." Willow dashed for the door.

"Wait, you going to my homeboy Talvin's party tonight?" Junior asked, stopping her in her tracks. "He throws a bash every year and it's gon' be a lot of people there."

"Yes, I'm in that thing." Willow went out the door.

Willow's stomach turned flips like a gymnast as pictures of Melee constantly stared at her on every wall that she passed. She couldn't believe that they were responsible for her sister's death. She left the mansion as the brisk air hit her, cooling off her body's rising temperature.

She left to go find something to wear to Talvin's bash. She couldn't do anything about Melee; it was already done. And no matter how much she wished she could go back to that day and change what had happened, she couldn't. It was something she was going to have to learn to live with. The only thing on her mind now was getting revenge on Talvin.

Willow sat across the room; the picture of beauty. Beautiful mahogany hair ran down her back like rivers. Her skin was fairer than the goddess Athena. Her eyes twinkled like pure emerald ice when she was happy, but when she was angry, they became poisonous daggers; befitting an evil ice princess. Her lips were as full as a pink rose as she bent down and slipped her feet into her heels.

"Why are we going to this party again?" Kail asked, turning sideways to check out her figure in the dress that was hugging her body.

"Because, everybody gon' be there." Choice stood next to her fixing her lipstick.

"I don't give a fuck about everybody." Kail put her diamond earrings in her ear.

"Look, we all going and that's it." Willow entered the bedroom from the hallway. "So get the fuck dressed and hurry up."

Willow joined Choice in the mirror to check out her ensemble. She had to be the baddest bitch at the party if she wanted to get Talvin's full attention, and the small black number she chose to rock with her canary yellow heels was a sure way to have him drooling.

All eyes were on them once they made it into the party. The rest of the women there could have left. Everyone wanted to know the mystery behind the beautiful women with the pink lips. They all had different agendas. Willow was looking for Talvin, Kail was checking for potential clients, and Choice was there to keep an eye on Craig.

Willow walked around; her eyes cutting sharp as she looked for her target. She passed the open bar twice before she spotted Talvin in his one-of-a-kind tailored suit. Their eyes locked just like at the park, but this time, he smiled as he made his way toward her.

"Damn," a voice said from behind, "you wearing the shit outta that dress."

"Thank you." Willow engaged in conversation with the stranger.

"Go away," Talvin said as he approached them. Willow's eyes still focused on his.

The man scurried away as Willow glared at Talvin with her insides boiling. She touched her throat remembering what he had done to her. Visions of Duke lying in ICU hijacked her thoughts and made it difficult for her not to kill him right there in front of everyone.

"I want you," Talvin whispered in her ear.

"You don't even know me."

"We have all of the time in the world." Talvin faced her and grabbed her hand; his eyes told her to follow him.

She agreed as they brushed through the crowd; his hands massaging her along the journey. Men of all calibers tried to stop him to talk, but Talvin only had one thing on his mind: getting to know the beautiful woman he was holding on to.

They came to a room which was dark until Talvin hit a light switch brightening the room fully. It was quiet and as the door closed, the music from the outside vanished. He held her hand escorting her to a table draped in white lace cloth. He pulled the chair out for her as he watched her sit down properly, bending her knees while hiding her treasures like a real woman was supposed to.

"I'm Talvin." He held his hand out.

"Willow," she said as she did the same; his lips kissing her hand to say hello.

"Are you from Philly?"

"You can say that." She eyed the empty room.

"So, Willow," he said as he sexually harassed her with his voice, "do you have a man?"

"If I had a man," she said seductively, "I wouldn't be here with you."

"I respect that." Knocks interrupted their conversation. "Come in," he screamed and the narrow tan door opened.

Willow nearly swallowed her tongue when Craig entered the room. His black tuxedo complemented his dark complexion. The watch on his wrist could blind a man quicker than the sun. His facial expression changed as he got closer and realized that it was Willow that Talvin was serenading.

"What's up?" Talvin asked him as he kept his eyes on Willow.

"It's business." Craig signaled for Willow to leave.

"You can talk to me in front of my new woman."

"Yo' new woman." Craig cut his eyes toward Willow. "Yo, are you serious?"

"Do I know you?" she asked, playing dumb.

"So, you gon' do me like that?" Craig walked off. "I'll get at you when you don't have yo' new woman around."

Willow watched as Craig's nose flared up and down with anger. He opened the door and left the room. She could tell that his blood was boiling from hearing that she and Talvin were a couple. She wasn't trying to embarrass him; she was simply trying to keep him out of her scheme.

Willow and Talvin talked alone for the majority of the night inside the room until the party was almost over. They made their way back to the crowd toward the end. Eyes were in shock as Talvin introduced Willow as his girl. She smiled and played along; all of it a part of her sadistic plan.

"I have to go," Willow whispered in his ear as she leaned back, showing him Kail and Choice were waiting for her.

"Okay, that's cool, baby. I'll get at you first thing tomorrow." Talvin kissed her passionately as the women standing around threw daggers into her with their eyes.

Willow, Kail, and Choice walked toward the door to leave; all eyes still on them as if they were actresses. They exited the venue as a valet brought the car around to the front.

"Shit, I gotta' piss," Choice said suddenly, then made her way back into the building.

"Me too." Kail followed behind her.

"Can I take you home?" Craig appeared at Willow's side.

"Why would I even want you to?" She looked back, making sure Choice and Kail weren't nearby.

"Willow, if I ever meant anything to you, then you would let me take you home. No tricks or funny shit, just conversation."

"What about Choice?" she asked.

"Ditch her."

He disappeared into the night and Willow could see Kail and Choice coming out of the building. She fed them a weak excuse about how she wanted to feel the night air and they bought it. She walked toward the direction she saw Craig go while Choice and Kail drove off into the busy streets passing her.

Willow could see the lights from Craig's car in the alley as the hungry cats ran for their life fearing the smoke coming from his exhaust. She opened the door as the smooth sounds of jazz entered her ears. She sat down as her bright yellow heels dug into the carpet before she closed the door.

"The jazz type?" she asked as he pulled off. "I never took you for that type of man." She smiled.

"Never judge the book, right?"

"Right," she said as goose bumps filled her arm.

"So, you gon' tell me what you doing with Talvin?" he asked, the street light ricocheting off of the stop sign next to him and onto his face.

"It's business."

"You know he's the go-to guy when yo' pops need someone to disappear."

"People depend on me for the same thing."

"You expect me to believe you a killa?" He pulled in front of her condo.

"How many guns do you think I have on me?" She looked at him and smiled.

"One," he answered.

"Three," she said as she touched the spots where they were. "Don't underestimate what I'm capable of."

"The cover," he said, looking at her.

"The cover." She got out of the car.

"I gotta ask you something." Craig rolled the window down. "That day in Hawaii at that reception," he said as he leaned over so she could see his face and he could see hers, "did you and yo' sister do that shooting?"

Willow's head hung low as she gathered her thoughts. She could still see Melee lying there dead as the day came back to her. Her neck grew stiff as Craig looked at her for an answer. He positioned himself back in the driver seat; her eyes telling him everything he wanted to know.

"I didn't know she was my sister," Willow defended as she stuck her head inside the car.

"I understand." Craig looked at her before driving off. "The cover, right?"

Craig went into the night as he wondered what Willow was really capable of. He hadn't even committed a massacre of that magnitude. His mind ran a marathon as he dug deep within his skull trying to find a reason to stop feeling what he was feeling for her. It was too late; the love bug had bit him a long time ago, and no matter what Willow told him about herself, nothing would change how he felt.

Evelyn walked into the venue of the bash with her clutch at her side, dangling along with her arm. She was late and the party was over, but she still wanted to see Talvin. She walked throughout the building until she spotted him at the bar alone sipping on a drink. He saw her; his eyes telling her to sit down.

"I heard you made a new friend tonight." She grabbed his glass and started drinking.

"You have a husband," he said in a defensive tone. "You could never be mine, so I have to find someone that can be."

"So, you choose my stepchild?" she asked as his facial expression changed. "She is Rock's daughter, you know."

"I didn't know that." He grabbed his drink back from her; his words slurring.

"You know what he'll do to you if he found out?" she threatened.

"I'm interested in her, Evelyn, so whatever you're trying to do to scare that out of me, stop. I don't fear much." He stood. "It was fun while it lasted." He grabbed her face and kissed her lips one last time that night.

Evelyn finished the drink before walking out of the venue. She couldn't believe that Talvin had chosen Willow over her, especially after all they had been through. She was hurt. She couldn't believe it as she pinched herself, hoping it was all a dream. Talvin was the only thing that made her feel anything, and without him, she was numb and alone.

Twenty

"What if they don't like me?" Willow squeezed Talvin's hand.

"They are going to love you just like I do," he promised as he leaned over and kissed her cheek.

Willow watched as many golden hues from the color of the leaves lay scattered all around. The sound of children laughing and galloping rung out as they jumped on a heaped pile of discarded leaves. Lovers walked hand in hand to the sound of crunching under their feet as they walked a well-trodden path.

A slight breeze whispered along the trees and teased more leaves into releasing their tentative hold. Deeply engrossed in the message he was texting on his mobile, a young man sitting on a park bench, didn't notice when a wayward leaf landed on his head, but Willow watched closely; her heart beating with anticipation.

It had been a full month since her charade with Talvin had started. They were an item and everyone who was anyone knew it. They were joined at the hip and wherever you saw one, you saw the other. Willow was enjoying the idea of having someone, even if it was pretend. She had to remind herself of that, once she started having feelings for him.

Talvin was saying those famous three words in hopes that she would say them in return. He got her name tatted on him, he dropped dough on her, and he couldn't tell her no, despite what she asked for. To him, he had found The One. To Willow, this was a game of chess and he was merely a pawn.

Everything was going smoothly with Willow's plan for revenge. He was falling deeper and deeper for her. She learned everything she needed to know about him since the day of his bash. All of his secrets had surfaced and she planned to use everything she could to ruin his life.

She couldn't believe as the smell of barbecue hit her nose that she had let Talvin talk her into going to his family reunion. When she saw a group of loud black folks, she knew that they had arrived. The moment she had been dreading for a week had finally come.

Old school music played as picnic tables lined the center of the park. Lawn chairs were present along with coolers full of beer and soda. There were elderly men attending to meat in their pit and arguing about whose recipe was the best. Everyone was wearing the same family reunion shirt; everyone but Willow.

"Grandson," an old man said as he approached Willow and Talvin. "Who is this fine young tender thang?" He started sucking his teeth.

"This is my girl, Willow." Talvin laughed at his grandfather.

"You a fine young thang, Willow," he said, reaching out his hand. "I'm Paw Paw Wilson, and while you're here, you're family. You can have whatever you like." He smiled; his tonsils present through his cave-like mouth.

"Paw Paw, are you flirting with my woman?" Talvin asked, shoving his grandfather in a playful matter.

"She eyeing me," he said, winking at Willow.

Willow smiled at the old man's enthusiasm. She laughed as she looked at the blue jean overalls he was wearing. His white beard was braided and long. She looked at Talvin and then Paw Paw Wilson, noticing how much they resembled each other.

"Is that my baby boy?" a woman screamed approaching them. Willow turned around.

"Hey, Ma," he said as he hugged the woman and kissed her on the cheek.

"I'm Mrs. Wilson," she said as she looked at Willow. "And, you must be the woman who has my son's nose wide open."

"Ma," Talvin said, shaking his head.

"Shut up, Talvin," she said and started to laugh. "He always gets embarrassed if I talk too much. Come over here and meet everybody else. We all have heard so much about you."

Willow looked back at Talvin as his mother forcefully dragged her to a table with the aunts and great-aunts. Willow basked in her surroundings, never attending a function like this for her own family. She appreciated seeing a family together without the drama that hers consisted of.

After the food was served, Willow sat in Talvin's lap, as they watched the sun set. Everyone was packing up to leave but not them. They sat enjoying each other as the stars filled the sky.

"I got someone I want you to meet," Talvin whispered, gently raising Willow off of him as he stood.

Willow remained standing as the night air attacked her like a girl slicing open a face with a razor blade. She looked up at the stars as she constantly told herself this was for Duke. The feeling of enjoyment that she was feeling was real. The masquerade had faded a long time ago and she hated herself for having a good time and catching feelings for the man whom she considered the enemy.

The sound of the grass crackling under a pair of shoes hit Willow as she spun around to see Talvin holding a little boy. He appeared to be six or seven. Willow smiled at him. His small family reunion

204 ANDRE D. JONES

shirt overlapped his knees and Talvin's hands. His facial features looked as if Talvin had spat him out; his genes were strong.

"This is my son." Talvin smiled. "This was the only thing in my life that made sense to me before you came into the picture."

Willow played with the little boy under the stars as Talvin watched them run around in the dark. Willow never saw herself in a park with a child, running and playing. It made her feel unusual but good at the same time.

Night fell as Talvin gave his son to his moms to take home and watch. He held Willow's hand as they walked the path back to his truck and got inside. They cruised down the streets until they arrived at an abandoned warehouse.

Talvin guided her into the old building; the sheer darkness stripping them of the ability to see. They entered an old elevator and Willow's legs grew weak as they made their way to the third floor. The elevator doors opened as the smell of freshly picked roses filled the small elevator.

He grabbed her hand as the light from a hundred burning candles lit the room. He forced her to the ground onto a blanket as their bodies nearly knocked over the bottle of Moët that was chilling on ice waiting for them to indulge in.

"What is this?" Willow asked.

"My secret spot for when I want to just get away from it all."

"What's so special about it?" She grabbed the bottle from the floor and poured the Moët into two champagne glasses.

"My father use to run this place when I was a kid. I used to live here, basically. Whenever I want to think of him or just come back to the place in my life where I was the happiest, I come here." He handed her the glass of champagne.

"So, how many women have you brought here?" Willow asked

as she took a sip; her hair's shininess played off the light from the moon.

"None," he said as he looked into her bashful eyes. "No other woman but his moms has met my son, either."

"I'm honored." She leaned back and placed the champagne glass down.

"You should be." He looked at her thighs; the blood rushing to his manhood causing him to stand at attention like he was in the army. "I really love you."

"Show me," Willow said as she opened and closed her legs.

She had avoided having sex with Talvin until that moment. She couldn't resist. She had never had a man think so highly of her, and she had allowed the gesture to make her weak, telling herself it was only for that one night. She promised herself that when she woke up the next morning, the hatred that she felt for him would be back in her heart, and her plan would be back in action.

"The warehouse is off the highway before you get out of the city limits," Willow said as she described the details to Craig. "I'm not for sure, but I know there's a stash there. Find it and get it for me," she said, walking inside of Rock's house.

She eyed security as she made her way to his home office. She knew the way and an introduction was no longer needed in order for her to roam the estate freely. She knocked on the large door before she entered, never waiting for an okay to do so.

Willow focused on the room as she saw three figures upon first glance. The first was her father. The second was Evelyn, his wife, and the woman she'd met at the strip club, and the last was a girl she'd never seen. She walked toward them, their eyes following her.

"If it isn't the stripper." Evelyn grinned.

"Evelyn." Rock gave her a hand gesture and she left the room.

"Why did you call me here?" Willow asked as she took a seat.

"I wanted you to meet your sister." He got up from the desk and stood next to the girl. "This is Elysia."

Willow looked her up and down, her fashion on par with her own. Her face was as beautiful as Willow's and her skin tone matched hers perfectly. Elysia looked at her as her bright orange heels crossed from how she was standing. Her facial expression was coy and she had wondered how many other siblings she had; the same thoughts as Willow.

"This is my last child," Rock said as he read their minds. "I promise, no other kids will come out of the woodwork." He went to the door and left. "I'll let you two get to know each other."

"Nice to meet you," Elysia said, reaching her hand down and shaking Willow's.

"You too," Willow said as she stood up. "So, tell me about yourself. Was Rock a part of your life or was he a bastard to you, too?"

"My mom was, well, she still is, his accountant, so he's always been around. He told me I had another sister named Kail. Can I meet her, too?" she asked with open eyes.

"Maybe." Willow leaned on the desk. "Kail isn't as open to things as I am."

"Excuse me for being so pushy." She joined Willow and leaned on the desk. "I just lost my brother so siblings is what I need right now."

"I just lost my boyfriend so I know how you feel." Willow pulled out her cell phone. "Give me a minute," she told Elysia as she walked away and answered a call. "Hello."

"I found it and you were right," Craig said.

"How much?" She looked back at Elysia, who was ear hustling.

"Four hundred thousand and I have it all."

"Meet me at my condo in thirty minutes." Willow hung up the phone.

"Business?" Elysia asked as she stood up straight.

"Something like that." Willow walked back toward her. "I have to go, but get my number from Rock, and we should get together sometime." Willow rushed out of the room.

"Will do." Elysia waved good-bye.

Willow walked down the staircase moving as fast as her feet would allow. She had to take something from Talvin; she had to convince herself that she hated him. Stealing from him would shake up his world. He may even suspect her, but that was a risk she was willing to take.

"You look like your mother." Evelyn walked up to the staircase as Willow's heel touched the beautiful granite leading to the front door.

"So I've been told." Willow stood in front of her. "What is your problem with me?"

"I don't know, but I don't like you." Evelyn leaned closer so only Willow could hear. "I will get rid of you like I failed to do your mother. But, at the end of the day, the bitch met her end anyway."

"Just like your daughter," Willow whispered, playing her game. "But, I didn't fail with that one. The bullet went right through her and she was dead in less than a minute."

Evelyn pulled back as she looked in Willow's eyes searching for the truth. She could tell from the way her eyes stared back that she was telling the truth. Evelyn hated her, from the hair on her head down to the lipstick that colored her lips perfectly. She wanted her dead.

"Touché," Evelyn said as she walked up the stairs, "touché, bitch."

Twenty-one

"Just tell me you ain't have shit to do with it, baby." Talvin grilled Willow as she opened up the door to her condo after he awakened her from his knocks. He walked in.

"What are you talking about?" She yawned, holding her mouth because she hadn't yet brushed her teeth.

"The warehouse that I took you to was robbed." He fixed the fitted cap on his head.

"Baby, I don't have anything to do with that." She saw the briefcase from where she stood that held his four hundred thousand.

"You promise?" He kissed her forehead.

"I promise," she lied.

"I'll get at you later." He kissed her lips and left out of the door.

Willow locked the door as she leaned against it. Kail entered the room as she walked to the refrigerator and poured her a glass of orange juice. She looked at Willow, then at the briefcase, immediately knowing something was up.

"You did a job without me?" she asked, sipping the cold juice.

"You know better than that," Willow walked to the couch, "this is personal business."

"You should just kill that nigga while you can." Kail joined her on the couch. "Shit gon' get sticky; trust me."

"I got this," Willow said as she reached over and grabbed the briefcase and slid it underneath the couch. She didn't want to risk anyone else seeing it and she planned to stash it as soon as possible. "Oh, I met a sister of ours."

"A sister?" Kail asked surprised.

"Well, you know that girl that you shot after walking in on us at the reception?"

"Yes," Kail said, taking another sip of the juice.

"She was our sister."

Kail held the juice in her mouth as she gulped it all down in one swallow. She thought back to the day as she got a good image of the girl's face in her mind. She could see a small resemblance; *it was possible*, she thought to herself as she shook it off.

"She was in the wrong place at the wrong time."

"I know." Willow walked over to the hallway. "Rock has another daughter that's gorgeous. I think she would make a good fourth member for The Pink Lip Bandits."

"You thought the same thing about Choice."

"She's proven herself."

"Well, I need to meet her." Kail stood up. "We can't just have anybody in this shit. They have to be about money. They have to be ready to eat." She passed Willow to go in her room. "'Cause I stay starving."

The rain poured on endlessly, pounding on the rooftops and turning the sidewalks and roads into vast lakes of dull, muddy water. Dark gray clouds covered the sky, only letting a few rays of feeble sun slip past the barrier. The monotonous sound of raindrops beating on the sidewalk blended in with the occasional whoosh of the breeze through the treetops. Everything was bleak, gray, and dreary—even the atmosphere as Willow, Kail, and Choice, all wearing raincoats, approached the modest-sized home that Elysia lived in.

Willow approached the door as she knocked softly, letting the roof of the home be their shield. She knocked again as the door opened and Duke's mother answered. They all looked at each other in confusion as Mrs. Williams stood in the doorway glaring at them.

"Is that Duke's mom?" Choice whispered to Kail softly so only she could hear.

"Yes," Kail said as she looked on.

"Willow, it's good to see you." Mrs. Williams grabbed and hugged her. "How have you been?"

"I've been good." Willow looked around the inside of the home. "Is Elysia here?"

"Yes, she's here," she moved to the side so they could pass, "come on in."

They went into the living room as they looked around. The television sitting from one end of the wall to the next was like a movie theater screen. The smell of mint and tea leaves filled the room. The oversized brown furniture sat diagonally to the door and from the stitching that was barely visible, they could tell it was imported.

Willow looked on the walls as pictures of Duke, Elysia, and Mrs. Williams filled it. Traces of Duke were everywhere and she could even smell him as if he had been there within the past hour. She kept analyzing the situation as Kail and Choice took a seat while she stayed standing.

"It's funny how things work." Mrs. Williams fixed the long eyelashes that were put perfectly on her eyes. "Who would have known that you and Duke had the same sister?"

"What?" Willow asked as her ears started to pop.

"Duke is my son, and Elysia is my daughter." Her voice sounded robotic and slow to Willow.

Willow couldn't believe what she heard. She looked at her sister and Choice for direction, but their eyes told her that they couldn't help. Elysia came out of a room as if the hallway were a runway. Her beauty lit up the room as her soft curls bounced in unison to her walk. The strapless Michael Kors top she had on hung off of her shoulder as the white shorts on her thighs hugged her as if they were conjoined with her skin.

"I'll be going now." Mrs. Williams hugged Elysia, then Willow, and left out of the door as the rain fell and poured onto the patio window.

"How come you didn't tell me you were Duke's sister?" Willow asked as they sat down on the couch.

"I didn't know you were his girl until my moms told me." She looked at Kail. "You have to be my sister, too. I see my face in yours."

"That's kind of you, but this kind of beauty is rare." Kail leaned in. "Now, I don't know why these other bitches came," she said as she pointed at them, "but, I came here for business. We're a part of this organization called The Pink Lip Bandits and we want you to join."

"The Pink Lip Bandits?" She looked at their lips, all colored in pink.

"It's a lot of money to be made." Choice leaned in as if ears were listening outside the door.

"If it's about money, then I'm in." Elysia leaned in also.

"That's cool and all." Kail pulled a lipstick tube out of her raincoat pocket. "But, how do you look with pink lipstick on?"

Twenty-two

hoice wiped her mouth after she closed the lid to the toilet. She had been throwing up for three days straight, and the thought of her being pregnant stained her mind like a red drink falling onto a white shirt. She turned on the cold water as she ran her fingers underneath the faucet, softly splashing light trickles of water on her face to cool her off.

"Choice, come on," Kail screamed as she banged on the door with their next job in her hand. "We gotta' go, bitch."

Choice opened the door as the feeling of nausea took over her again. She closed the door as she ran over to the toilet, emptying the rest of her insides. She sat there with her hair in her hand as she wiped her mouth off before flushing the toilet.

"Choice?" Willow opened the door and entered the bathroom. "You okay?"

"No," she said as tears formed in her eyes, "I'm pregnant."

"You're pregnant?" Willow tried to process the thought in her mind. "Are you for sure?" She sat down next to her on the bathroom floor.

"I'm late, I'm throwing up, and my titties been sore as fuck." She put her face into her hands. "I don't know what I'm gon' do. Craig doesn't want any kids and neither do I."

Willow sat quiet as she tried to put her thoughts together. She didn't want to say the wrong thing even though she had feelings for Craig. She was slightly happy for them. Now it was her job to be a supportive friend and nothing else.

"You would be a good mom," Willow said as she helped her up off the floor. "Talk to Craig, tell him, and let him know. He might want the baby. Some people don't know what they want until it's presented to them."

"You think so?" Choice asked.

"I know so."

"Thank you, girl," Choice said, hugging her.

"Okay, enough of this Maury Povich shit." Kail burst into the door. "Choice, congratulations and all that good shit, but can we focus on this?" She held up the job printed on the piece of paper.

They all met in the living room to discuss the job, the biggest Vinny had ever given them. He knew it wouldn't be easy for Kail to kill Rock while his subordinates were all around, so he wanted them to kill them and rob their biggest stash house. He told them a king was nothing without his minions.

Willow, Kail, Choice, and their new member, Elysia, sat for a couple of hours until their plan was foolproof. The men they were going after weren't just any dudes. They were members of the mafia and they were trained to kill. Once they got their weapons and ammo together, they left and drove off into the night.

"You sure you don't want to sit this one out?" Willow asked Choice.

"Her ass wants to get paid, so she better work for this money." Kail parked a couple of blocks away from the stash house.

"I'm good." Choice cocked her gun. "Let's make this money."

"You good?" Willow asked Elysia as she looked back into her eyes. She knew Elysia wasn't made for this life, but she wasn't either. It was something she was going to have to get used to. She was her and Duke's sister, so she promised to watch her back.

"I'm a little nervous, but I'm ready to make some money," Elysia said, the pink lipstick adding to her beauty.

"Let's go." Kail opened the door and got out with the others following behind her.

They all walked down the dark street, their faces flashing in and out from the broken street light that was flickering on and off. All of them had their guns ready. They didn't plan to talk; they just wanted to get the job over.

After they arrived, Kail approached the door as she signaled for them to wait. She could hear voices laughing through the door, and the smell of cheap cigars ushered their way out of the cracks, hitting her nose. She gave Willow the okay to kick the door in as she moved out of the way.

Willow got close to the door as she stretched her leg muscles. She aimed her gun at the door as she lunged forward on one leg as her heel connected with the door. The door went off the hinges before they all rushed inside shooting any and everything that moved.

"Check the back," Willow screamed as she guarded the door, making sure no one would leave.

Kail, Choice and Elysia went in different directions as the sounds of guns blazing filled the house. Willow left her position at the door, barging in the room after them when the bullets stopped flying.

"Where is the fucking money?" Kail asked as she sat on top of one of the Italian men as she hit him in the face with the butt of her gun. "Answer me, motherfucker," she warned.

He didn't say a word which aggravated Kail. She held the gun directly in the center of his forehead and she asked him one more time. Before he could blink, Kail shot him, and his brains scattered underneath them on the carpet.

"Look for the money." Willow ran to check on the other girls.

"Get the fuck off of me," Elysia screamed as she was held from behind as Willow entered the room. "Get him the fuck off of me."

"Let her go," Willow yelled as she pointed her gun at the man. She wanted to shoot, but her aim wasn't as good as Kail's. She didn't want to risk shooting Elysia.

"Yous bitches think you can come in here and steal from us?" he spat. "Fuck yous."

Kail entered the room, pointing the gun and aiming at the man's head. Within seconds, his grip on Elysia was let go as his body became heavy. He fell onto the floor from a hole through his head. She walked over and shot him repeatedly until she was satisfied.

"Don't negotiate with killers." Kail knocked over packages of exposed cocaine. "I told you to leave her ass at home because I'm not saving her again."

"Thank you." Elysia picked up the gun.

"Don't thank me," Kail said as she left out of the room with Willow and Elysia following behind her. "It won't happen again; trust me."

They met Choice in the hallway with two silver briefcases in her hand. Kail grabbed them as she fell onto the floor and opened them. Dead presidents filled the briefcases to their capacity. Kail closed them as she stood up with a briefcase in each hand.

"Let's bounce." Kail headed for the door.

"Wait," Willow said as she walked to look throughout the house. "We need to check and make sure everyone is dead. You know how we do, Kail. This shit is sloppy."

"You check. I'll be in the car." She headed outside.

Willow, Choice, and Elysia all went throughout the stash house to check their work. There was no one breathing so they left and Choice and Elysia got in the car. Willow knocked at the driver side door before opening it up. She grabbed Kail by the shirt and pulled her out of the car.

"Kail, I'm so fucking tired of your shit," Willow said, clenching her teeth. "Who the fuck do you think you are?"

"Willow, let go of me." Kail pulled away from her. "You got all these other pink lips here; I ain't think you wanted my help." She got back inside of the car. "Quit recruiting bitches that ain't about that life." Kail smiled. "This is our life, not theirs," she said as she pointed to Choice and Elysia.

"Bitch, you been tripping lately and I'm sick of your shit." Willow walked down the street.

"I'm leaving your ass." Kail started the car. "If y'all ass want to walk down this dark-ass street, then go ahead," she warned as they got inside the car. "That's what the fuck I thought," she said as she burned off.

Willow kept walking into the night after she saw Kail and the other girls drive past her. She was annoyed and the only way she knew she wouldn't slap Kail across her face was to get away from her altogether. She didn't know what was going on with her, but she couldn't deal with her like she used to.

Willow walked down the street as silence was present. The wind gently blew the sickly smell of rotted garbage from the pitch-black alleys that even junkies were afraid to go into. Silence continued as the occasional shadow of a person leaked across the roadway.

There was a faint, tiny sound of a nightclub up at the end of the dimly lit block, under Halloween-orange streetlights, and the hiss of the music faded into a kind of grainy wash that filled the street, seeping into the darkness between the pools of light on the dirty sidewalk.

Willow was glad she heard something because absolute silence would be too frightening. Metal shutters, caked with graffiti, were strapped like plasters over the reinforced windows, and they softly rattled. There weren't any businesses there anymore, and the doorways were all locked and barred, and the only things that stood sentinel were the poles and posts carrying electricity, like the skeletons of trees.

She saw old bars that still had their neon signs flickering and buzzing; a few letters burnt out for good measure. Some ragged flyers were posted to the peeling paint of sickly yellow walls, but there weren't many attractions on that side of town. It was the perfect place to put a stash house.

The place felt incomplete in its incompleteness; the gap in the row of buildings on one side felt like the hole in gums after a tooth's just come out. It sucked at Willow, the wilderness of an abandoned lot blooming with twisted crabapple, and rotted brush, and the litter of a thousand fast-food restaurants.

"You need a ride?" Craig asked as he pulled up beside her.

Willow stopped; her feet became frozen as her body jumped from the voice beside her. But once she realized it was Craig, she kept walking. She was reluctant at first to converse with him. All she could think about was Choice being pregnant as she looked at him. All she could think about were the murders she was just a part of. She wanted to stop, but being around him was a constant reminder to her that she would never have him, and after losing so much, she couldn't handle that.

"No," Willow said and then continued walking.

"I was just going to pick up something for Rock at one of his spots down the street," he said, driving along at her speed as her legs never stopped walking. "But, I can take you home first."

"You not going to let me walk, are you?" she stopped.

"I can't," he said as he hit the unlock button, "just get in."

Willow got inside of the car as she put her gun that she held while walking on the dashboard. She didn't say a word; she sat there as the buildings changed in her view. She was feeling a certain way about Craig and he could feel it.

"What did I do?" He turned away from the road for a second to look at her.

"Kail is annoying the fuck out of me," Willow said.

"That's what little sisters do." He smiled. "I got one, so I feel you."

"Choice is pregnant," she blurted out.

Craig couldn't process what she had said quick enough. His mind didn't understand what she was saying; he never thought he would hear those words together in a sentence. When it finally hit him, out of shock, he swerved to the other side of the street.

"What the fuck are you doing?" Willow grabbed the wheel.

"She's pregnant?" he asked with a serious face as he swerved back into the correct lane.

"Yes, she's pregnant." She shook her head. "So, whatever we doing, that shit got to stop."

"Why?"

"It's bad enough I'm fucking you behind my home girl's back, but it's even worse if I fuck you while she's pregnant and carrying a child by you."

"It's the same." He pulled up in front of Willow's condo.

"No, it's not; trust me, it's not." She got out of the car. "I'll talk to you later."

Craig sat there for a minute as he watched Willow sway inside of her building. He never had a thought in his mind to be a father. He didn't think he could be one with the life that he lived. He shook off those thoughts as he headed to Rock's biggest stash spot to go pick up the two million dollars like he did every month. Little did he know the money was long gone.

Kail dropped Choice and Elysia off at their homes as the two briefcases full of money sat side by side on the floor of the passenger seat. She promised them she would give them their cut later that night but fot now, she had some unfinished business to handle. In the meantime, she would quickly stash the money at the condo.

She headed to the police station after leaving the condo to drop off the tape recorder that Vinny had given her personally. She was told to take it to the station and make sure someone named Detective Hall received it.

Kail pulled up in front and parked. She got out of the car as she took the tape recorder out of her pocket and walked inside of the public entrance through the double glass doors. To her left she saw the dispatcher room with a large glass sliding window.

She walked to the desk where a cop was sitting as she waited for him to acknowledge her. She stood there for five minutes, her blood boiling at the fact that she was being ignored. Already hating them, Kail slammed her hand down on the desk as he looked up at her from the paper that he was reading.

"May I help you?" he asked with a smirk.

"Of course you can, fat ass," she said as she folded her arms. "You think I like to just sit here and look at you, Mr. Three Hundred Pounds? Of course, I would be standing here for assistance."

"You better watch your mouth." The cop stood up.

"I don't gotta do shit but stay black and die." She leaned in closer to him. "Now, tell me where the hell Detective Hall is."

"Wait here." The cop sat down and got on the phone.

Kail stood there and watched the little hand on the clock pass the big one. It had only been a few minutes, but she was about to leave. Just as she was about to go, the sound of heels clicking behind her made her turn back around. A woman slowly approached her.

The woman had the kind of legs that needed stilettos, although any man worth his salt would have taken a second look. Her legs were long and lean and made a man want to rub his hands along them from bottom to top and back again. The two-inch heels were all she needed.

She was of mixed descent and her hair was in a short pixie cut. Her hair was long at one point and from how her head moved, you could tell she had recently gotten it cut off. Her eyes were the color of the sky at the peak of a Sunday morning.

"You got something for me?" she asked Kail as she stopped in front of her.

"Detective Hall?" Kail looked her up and down.

"Yeah, it's me, toots, Philly's finest. You can take a picture later and I'll even sign your shirt, but the only question I need you to answer is, do you have something for me?" She raised her voice.

"Here." Kail put the tape recorder in her hand.

"You can leave," she said as she started to walk off. "Oh, and Kail, the next time you show up at my precinct, you talk to my cops like you got some damn sense."

Kail walked out of the door of the precinct and got inside of her car. She started the car, pulled off, and rolled a window down to let the breeze cool off her face as she drove with a clear mind. She had no idea, but she had just given the cops something that could destroy not only Rock's life, but Willow's. She had just helped drop a dime on her family, and she didn't even know her involvement in it.

Twenty-three

Talvin sped down the dark Philly Street with malice in his heart. He hadn't slept since he'd seen Willow and Craig kissing. It had been three days and his eyes were the color of blood from the insomnia he was experiencing. The only thing on his mind was vengeance and he was about to serve it to Craig fully.

He fixed the fitted cap on his head as the hemi from his truck roared and vibrated the tar covering the street. He pulled in front of Craig's apartment as he cocked his gun. He hopped out of the car like a madman as he made his way into the building. He was going to end it once and for all. If he couldn't have Willow, no one could.

"May I help you, sir?" the door attendant asked as Talvin ignored him, passing through the tall glass double doors.

Talvin was prepared to die for his love for Willow. He couldn't help but feel disrespected by Craig, and one of them had to die. He pushed the button for the elevator and as the lights above flashed the number one and opened, his whole plan changed in his mind as Choice stood before him.

"Where's yo' nigga, bitch?" he asked her as she entered the elevator and stood behind her. He raised his shirt and took out his gun.

"I don't know," Choice said as the elevator closed behind her with Talvin's gun pressed against her head.

"We gon' wait for him together." Talvin grabbed her face. "Now, what fucking floor is it?"

Choice pushed the button to the floor that she and Craig now shared and called home. She regretted moving in with Craig earlier that day. Had she known that a gun would be against her face when she woke up and packed her clothes, she would have stayed asleep.

"Where is he?" Talvin asked as the elevator doors opened.

"I'm pregnant." Choice's eyes started to water. "So, whatever beef you have with Craig is between you and him."

"It's between me, him, and Willow," Talvin said while Choice pulled out her keys and walked to a door, the gun still pressed against her body.

"Willow?" she asked, opening the door.

"Yes, Willow." They walked into the apartment. "You didn't know Craig and Willow was creeping behind yo' back?"

"Do you fucking think I knew something like that and I just moved in here with this nigga?" Choice said, plopping down on the couch.

Choice wiped the pink lipstick off of her lips as she sat wondering if there were any truth to what Talvin was saying. She wasn't naïve, she knew Craig and Willow were cool, but she never thought that they would hurt her like that. She felt like an idiot for putting her trust in them. If she made it out alive, she promised herself that she would have nothing to do with either one of them again.

"Call him," Talvin said as he pushed his gun into her. "Tell him to come home now."

"He doesn't listen to me." Choice put her hand on her stomach.

"You better make him," Talvin said with conviction.

Choice pulled out her cell phone as her hands started to tremble.

She dialed Craig's number in hopes that he would pick up the phone. She could see in Talvin's eyes that he would kill her if he had to. She just hoped that Craig would care enough to come save her.

"This isn't right," Willow moaned, looking down at the top of Craig's head as he slurped up her wetness from her pudding cup.

"Just lay back." Craig flicked his tongue in a snake-like motion, making Willow lose control of her senses.

Willow knew what she was doing was wrong. She would have killed someone for doing the exact same thing to her. She felt trifling for sneaking with Craig at the presidential suite that had become their hiding spot. But, as the orgasms continued to take over her body, she let go of those thoughts.

Craig continued to lick as Willow dug her nails into his scalp from the pure pleasure. Her legs shook like she was having a seizure after someone flashed electronic lights in her face. She fed Craig every drop of her ecstasy as she came repeatedly.

"I love you," Craig said, looking up at her; the juices from her clitoris dripping from his goatee.

"I love you, too," Willow said with honesty.

Craig's lips met hers as he entered inside of her. They slowly kissed as he went in and out, touching the bottom of her opening with each stroke. He continued to stroke as he kissed her neck, then her chest while he kissed and bit at her light-brown areolas.

Willow was at heaven's door from the way she was feeling. Her body moved back and forth as the tension between her thighs built up, sending a tingling sensation all over her. She moved her hips in a circular motion as Craig picked up his speed. They moved off of each other as their hearts beat together and made music.

"I'm about to cum," Willow moaned as she came on Craig's pole as he continued to stroke.

"Cum again," he whispered, biting her ear as he felt the warm cum that had just escaped her run down his legs. "Cum again for me."

They could feel their body heat from how close they were to each other as Craig went deep in her. He gazed into her eyes, as he kissed her nose and then her lips. His hands wandered down until they met hers, and he held her hand while he continued to make love to her.

They sunk down into the cool sheets of the king-size bed, and Willow waited for the sensuous storm to envelop her, and teased out every little corner of passion from her secret places. When she saw Craig's face glow and his body tighten, she knew he had found the map and her passion had been found.

"I haven't been fucked like that ever," Willow said as she basked in the silk sheets.

"That's because I didn't fuck you." Craig rolled over next to her and kissed her cheek. "I made love to you."

Willow couldn't deny it; she was in love with Craig. No matter how many different ways she tried to slice it, there was no other way to explain it. There was no excuse for her actions. She was in love with her best friend's man.

"Your phone is ringing," Willow said as she saw it vibrating on the television mount.

He got up and walked over. "It's Choice," he said and put the phone back down, "she doesn't want anything."

"Answer it," Willow said as she put on her best friend hat. "It could be about the baby."

Craig didn't feel the same way he felt about Choice as he did Willow. If it weren't for Choice being pregnant, he would have ended things the minute he touched down from Hawaii after meeting Willow. Willow was everything he wanted in a woman. She was beautiful, independent, and could take care of herself. She was everything he had ever searched for.

He got back up and looked at it. "It's too late. She hung up."

Thirty seconds later, Willow's phone started to vibrate. She got up and as she looked down and saw that Choice was calling, she felt something wasn't right. She looked at Craig as she answered the phone with questions running through her head like a last leg at a relay race.

"Hello," she said as she leaned on the mount naked.

"Can you give the phone to Craig, please?" Choice asked as Willow's fingers grew numb.

"What?" she asked as if she didn't hear her.

"Willow, please, stop playing dumb. I know you and Craig together because he's not answering his phone and I can put two and two together."

"Why would you think that?" Willow grilled.

"I don't know," Choice said with an attitude, "it may have something to do with your boyfriend Talvin standing here with a gun to my head because he saw you and Craig kissing the other night."

Willow didn't respond as Craig stood asking her with his mouth and hands what was going on. Their secret was out and as strong as Choice's tone was, Willow knew it was no convincing her otherwise. She passed the phone to Craig as she went and collected her clothes.

"I'm on my way," Craig said through the phone and slammed it down.

"Fuck." Willow tore the sheets off of the bed. "Where is my bra?"

"Here," he said as he threw it her way after finding it under his pants.

They both got dressed in silence without saying a word. Guilt ate at both of their consciences and by the time they made it to the car, the feeling was so thick and opaque, it could have been cut with a knife.

"This is our fault," Willow said.

"It will be okay." Craig tightened his hand around the steering wheel.

"I would never forgive myself if Talvin did something to her."

"He won't," he said, looking forward.

Willow looked up at the inky blackness of the night sky as they got out of the car at Craig's apartment. She saw it was deep and pristine, ice cold, and the sense of eternity that looked over her mind was spiritual, like a rare rapture that few people experienced as she prayed that Choice was okay.

The beeping of the elevator brought Willow's mind out of the blank state that it was in. The closer they got to the apartment, a bad feeling took over her. She looked at Craig as his hand clenched around the gun he was carrying. His facial expression was serious with a hint of worry.

Craig didn't try his key as he approached the door; he kicked it in, the frustration he had built up releasing in the heel of his Timberland boot. They entered the apartment as Talvin sat next to Choice on the couch; the gun still pressed against her in the same position.

"They look good together, huh?" he asked Choice in a sarcastic tone.

Choice looked at Willow with distant eyes. Willow knew from the glare she was receiving that they were no longer friends. The Pink Lip Bandits had lost another member. She would no longer be the child's godmother that Choice was carrying. Willow was aware there was no mending the friendship, so she didn't care to explain.

"This is a bitch-ass move even for you," Craig said as he pointed the gun at Talvin. "If you had a problem with me, you should have come to me. Don't get my bitch involved."

"You got my bitch involved." Talvin stood up.

"She chose, my nigga," Craig said with a smirk. "It ain't my fault she chose me."

The room filled with tension as the gun moved, its weight becoming a part of Talvin's. In his sight, quickly, he aligned his fingers into position. The world filled his sight as he glared into the expanse of the void he was hoping to create. That space and moment filled and flooded his arms.

Recoiling with a sense of dread and stopping from the refrain, he pulled the trigger and his ears filled with the explosive crack, sending mixed messages everywhere. His eyes widened to take in the echo of the hollow tunnel he was trying to create with his bullet.

Craig shot back instantly. Willow ran to Choice and they ducked behind the couch as the room filled with an angry swooshing sound. The shooters were hitting everything but each other, trying to dodge the women they loved. The bullets stopped as the sound of guns dropping to the ground boomed in the air. Willow looked over the couch to see Talvin and Craig going blow for blow, their fists meeting each other's flesh.

"Where's your gun?" Willow asked Choice as she shoved her.

"I thought we were girls, Willow." Choice started crying.

"Choice, you need to stop crying and think." Willow looked at her. "Where's the gun that I gave you?"

"Not here," she responded as tears fell from her eyes. "How long have you been fucking him?"

"I met him in Hawaii before I even came back to Philly. It started there and I didn't even know he was your nigga until the day at the hospital. I promise."

"Bitch-ass nigga," Craig yelled as he and Talvin continued fighting.

Willow ran over as she tried to break it up, but her efforts were in vain. She was like a Chihuahua trying to break up two pit-bulls. They separated on their own and Talvin ran toward the door with Willow close behind him.

"Talvin," she yelled as he stopped.

"Bitch, I swear I'm gonna kill you," he said with a smile. "I trusted you and this how you do me?"

"I never trusted you. You killed Duke and I was in the car." She pointed to the small scar on her neck. "This was from you, so fuck you. You better hope you kill me before I kill you."

She watched him go down the emergency stairs as she made her way back inside the apartment. Choice was hitting Craig at the top of the head when she entered. The sounds of the open palms connecting with the core of his head echoed throughout the apartment.

Choice stopped hitting him as she grabbed her stomach. Blood started flowing down her legs as she kneeled down. She started screaming to herself as she cringed up, never releasing her grip on her stomach. Craig ran to her side as he grabbed her, but she started pushing him away.

"She's having a miscarriage," Willow said as she remembered Kail on the ground with the same look on her face when they were teenagers.

"I'm losing our baby." She looked at Craig. "I'm losing the baby," she cried in between grunts.

"We have to get her to the hospital." Craig picked her up gently.

Willow's heart spiraled into a deep abyss as she turned around to leave. Shattering the warmth and confidence from within, quickly the feeling of security diminished, letting shame and confusion fill in their absence. She didn't know where she was supposed to be, but in the middle of a love triangle was not where she belonged, so she walked away without looking back.

"I'm on it," Kail said as she entered the house across the street from Rock's estate with her cell phone in her hand. "I'm on the job now," she told Vinny before hanging up.

She had been staking out the neighborhood for the past week so she knew everyone's schedules. Kail needed the house directly across the street from Rock's, and when the opening came, she grabbed it.

Kail went up to the highest level of the house with the sniper, half the length of her body in her hand. It dragged on the stairs as she went up bumping it against each step. The tribal-print tank top she had on snugged her body as she looked out the window across the street at Rock's house.

Vinny was on her case about the job not being done. She had been laying low waiting for the perfect opportunity to do the job. All of her efforts had been in vain; Rock wasn't an easy man to touch, and she was learning that more each day.

She put the tactical weapon up to her eye as she increased the view. Going from one window to the next, she searched every room in the house so she could put a red mark on Rock, but he was nowhere to be found.

"Fuck." She kept searching for him through the tall windows.

Her heart settled when she spotted him in his office. She could see his coffee cup and the morning paper in front of him. A glass rose was next to the newspaper, ready to fill his next appetite for a high. A cigar was burning in his mouth as her finger slid up and down the trigger with excitement.

The sound of a gun being cocked took the excitement out of Kail's mind and made her focus. She glanced behind her as the sound of shallow footsteps got closer to where she stood. She could smell the gun powder from the gun behind her as she put the sniper down at her feet. She turned around as Junior put the gun against her forehead.

Kail looked at him, no fear in her heart as he murdered her with his eyes and clenched teeth. She smiled at him as she pushed the gun with her forehead daring him to do something that she knew deep down he couldn't. She looked him dead in the eyes as she lowered his gun with her grass-green-colored finger.

"Go home." Kail picked the sniper up and aimed it at Rock.

"You think I won't kill you?" Junior asked as he shot beside Kail, making her flinch.

They both looked at each other; their eyes met with a fury and hate so strong like a furious storm was raging inside both of them. With their weapons ready to draw blood to end this battle, they held strong.

"I'll shoot you quicker than you would shoot me." Kail pointed the gun at him; her jaw clenched.

"You'll be on the ground before the bullet can even reach me."

Kail looked at him as she lowered her gun. She was there to take a life, not lose her own. She passed by him, her shoulder shoving into his body as she walked out of the room. She didn't want to play Russian roulette; that was no fun for her and she left knowing that she would kill Rock one day if it were the last thing she'd ever do.

Twenty-four

The sky was gray and musk filled the cold night air. Evelyn stared up trying to look for the moon, but its face was nowhere to be seen. Dark clouds filled the night and all she could see was a bird fly by, adding to the eeriness of the night.

The stars in the sky were nonexistent; between them arose puffs of gray. Those balls of cotton seen during the day shifted into streams of gray, the color of ash and soot. They blanketed the sky, hiding the full moon in its full glory behind them. But the moon started to fight to shine its light on the earth, and as Evelyn leaned on her car, the light rested on her face, adding a glow to her already tanned skin.

The moon hung high in the sky, a perfect silver disk, bleaching the land into a ghost-like replica of daytime. Evelyn smiled as she looked at the stars passing by her up above. She knew one of them was Melee, high in the sky with no worries. She smiled as her deceased daughter's face entered her mind.

The thundering noise of the hemi echoed through the darkness; the cacophonous sound of a ton of steel and screeching tires made Evelyn realize that she was no longer alone. She looked behind her as the red truck parked and Talvin appeared at her side.

"You have five minutes." Evelyn started to count down.

"You were right about Willow." He used his hands to talk. "I hate that bitch. I want her dead."

"She killed my daughter," Evelyn said as a tear fell from her icy-cold stare. "I want her dead also." She wiped her eyes in fear of showing emotion in front of anyone. "She's just more skilled than you. She's smart and she thinks more ahead than you."

"Then we need to put our heads together to end this bitch."

"I'm ahead of you." Evelyn opened the door and grabbed something from her car.

"What is this?" Talvin asked.

"Security," Evelyn said and kissed his lips. "Something tells me this is our security. As long as we have this, I'm sure Willow will play by our rules."

Willow thought it was unusually quiet for a Saturday night. Usually there were taxis and pedestrians, but today there was only a bored-looking crossing guard sitting against a giant potted plant in the middle of a two-way intersection.

She walked deep into the alley, and then turned left at the trash heap past the tramp finding her high. There beyond the puddles and shattered street lights was a door. "Virgin Mary," she whispered, as the door slid open. How could she forget the password? She saw this alley, that tramp, that debris in every nightmare since she'd last seen her father. And here she returned to see him again.

The doorman pulled his shirt over the pistol wedged deep behind his belt. It was the only sign of sincerity toward the girl he remembered as an infant, always happy and crying in her mother's arms. He remembered her at her beginning, smiling and laughing. Yet her mother always had her arms wrapped around her. Willow noticed, but only glared at this sign of weakness; he would be the next one killed. In this world, only the fiercest survived.

Willow was inside the place her father called his private office. Time had dismantled the crispness of the wall paper; cigar smoke stained the ceilings. Chairs were withered down to their foam stuffing, and plywood held up the bar. Her father once poured liquor in crystal glasses to men in tailored attire. Where were they now? Shattered and forgotten, just like those prized glasses.

It was slightly past 2 a.m.: Rock would be arriving soon. She looked around for the portrait of Bonnie and Clyde that hung above his favorite chair, the one where her pops always sat. It, too, had aged and hung slanted, its clean imprint among the wall behind it. She sat at the small table for two and peered out into the hazy crowd waiting anxiously. Women rubbed at the thighs of married men. They were all part of the business.

Willow's life was a cycle. Men entered, made money, and left. Either they found another girl to fondle their legs, or were slaughtered. No one who entered left an impact. The only person she had was her sister, Kail. She never left, at least Willow thought.

The doorman sprang up, as someone beat on the door. His hand fell to his pistol; Willow's heart to the floor. She swallowed her nerves. Was she ready to see this man again so soon, twenty-odd years after the failed attempt to assassinate her mother in front of her timid eyes? The doorman pulled the pistol out; the steel collided with the dim lights, shining a glare in Willow's direction. To her relief, it was only a base head, begging for more medicine from his suppliers.

"Will?" a muffled voice came from behind. The voice she knew too well, a familiar nickname only to the ones before the attack. It was Rock. Her father had been in the back room, feeding his very own cravings. The medicine was too strong. He stood in the shadows of his office behind a daughter he once knew.

"Willow?"

This time she turned around, solid in the face. Weakness led to death, even in her father's arms. Rock knew the rules of this life, and corrected himself. Willow had died with her mother; now only a Teflon shell remained.

Rock sat down at the chair across from her. It wobbled as his weight hit it, and he, too, swayed deliriously. His hair had an aging tint, the only precious feature. The rest of his face cracked in a mixture of smooth skin and residue. He always had trouble wiping the white medicine from his nose. With him was a bottle of brew and his trusty Bible. Willow wondered if he ever even read it, or was it just entertainment for his busy hands. As he tweaked, he could run his fingers through the pages, imagining a story of his own creation.

"So, you're here for closure, huh?" Rock muttered. He fumbled over his words in the beginning, but eventually found his route.

"Yes," Willow whispered, ready to hear the story of her parents.

"Your mother was a beautiful woman. Yeah, she was something sweet… She had to die. Either that or it would have been all of us, including Junior. You hear me?" He then described to Willow everything, as if she weren't there to see it all already. The way she screamed when she was shot, the way the house looked after it was shot. Then, without hesitation, he told Willow that it had to be done.

"I mean, it was my fault." Rock wiped at his nose, licking the white smear off his fingers. His teeth were like an animal's, overlapping and menacing. This was no man that sat in front of her this night, but an animal itself. Willow sat silent. She never believed she would hear this expression of guilt.

Rock smiled. "I'm happy you're alive."

Willow jolted up, knocking the Bonnie and Clyde portrait to the floor. Her ears rang at the senseless words that foamed from Rock's mouth: a bark he unleashed at the worst moment. No amount of training from the streets could have prepared Willow for the moment.

Tears blurred her vision, as the crowd all turned to watch her as she ran out of the establishment. Weakness meant death, and the tears that began to fall were welcoming trouble. She ran past the doorman, as he once again hid his pistol under his shirt. Down the alley she ran, past the tramps and trash, back to her car.

"I'm happy you know the truth," she heard her father yell from his office.

Willow got inside her car and sped through the clear streets with tears running down her face. She took her gun out of the compartment where she'd hidden it and questioned if she should go back and shoot up Rock's office. Her heart was beating so loud that the radio's volume at its highest level couldn't compete.

She parked and walked into her condo as Kail stopped her at the door. She glared at her for a moment; the same look she had given her right before she had shot her. Willow, aware of the look, held her hands on her gun ready for whatever that was about to happen. That night she would have killed Kail with no thought behind it.

"We have a job," Kail said as Willow walked by, never acknowledging her presence.

"Then do it."

"No, bitch," Kail pointed to herself and then Willow, "we gon' do it."

"Kail, you can't make me do shit that I don't wanna do, and tonight I'm not doin' nothin'."

"I knew them niggas would make you soft." Kail shook her head.

"You done forgot about this money. You let love cloud your fuckin' judgment."

"Don't be bitter at me because you didn't find love."

"I found love, bitch," Kail said as she beat on her chest. "But, I had to give it up for the organization, remember?"

Willow looked at Kail with sympathy. She remembered the day Kail's boyfriend was shot and killed in front of her. She remembered the stress being too much for Kail and it causing her to have a miscarriage. Memories from that day played in her mind.

"Yeah, I remember."

"Good." Kail handed her the job. "Then if I had to give it up, so can you."

"I'm not you, Kail." Willow tossed the job to the floor.

"You not gon' grind with me?" Kail asked as she grabbed Willow's collar.

Willow didn't say anything; she didn't even try to move away from Kail's grip. She stood there, looking at her sister who was on the verge of a breakdown. She wanted to fix her, but too many pieces had fallen and cracked, and no amount of glue could put Kail back together again.

"If you won't grind with me, then I can't rest my head here." Kail released her grip on Willow and walked into the hallway; her lipstick the color of fresh cotton candy.

"What?" Willow walked behind her.

"I'm leaving, Willow." Kail searched her closets for luggage. "It's obvious we don't trust each other, so let's stop faking the shit."

"You shot me, Kail," Willow snapped.

"And, you will never get past it. You only want to sulk behind these niggas when there's money to be made. I'm about my money. That love shit don't do anything for you. You will realize that one day."

"So you just going to bounce like that?"

"Just like that." Kail picked through her clothes.

Willow watched Kail pack two suitcases full of clothes. She took everything that had any value related to it and before Willow could decide if she wanted to convince her, Kail was gone. The front door of the upscale condo was left open, swinging back and forth as the lights in the hallway flickered softly inside of the house.

Twenty-five

"Willow," Elysia screamed as she banged on the door. "Willow, open the fucking door."

Willow sluggishly walked to the door; the house shoes on her feet sliding due to her not picking up her feet. She peeked through the small hole in the door as if she didn't hear her sister's voice on the other side. She unlocked the locks one by one before she made her way to the couch which had been her safe haven since Kail had left.

"Damn." Elysia walked through the door. "This place is a fucking mess."

Elysia looked around as the remains of Chinese food, pizza, and other delivery containers filled the room. She walked toward the couch as she nearly fell from her heel getting caught in the center of an empty pint of ice cream. She sat down next to Willow who was covered up in a cheetah throw blanket with her head facing the inside of the couch.

"What the fuck is going on with you?" Elysia pulled the blanket off of her. "You think 'cause Kail left, you supposed to sit in here and die?"

"Go home." Willow hid her face with a pillow.

"Get up, Willow," she said, grabbing her and standing her to her feet.

Elysia walked over to the floor windows and opened the blinds. Willow squinted her eyes at the unforgiving rays that shot throughout the living room. She sighed as she leaned on the couch as she stretched her limbs, which had been still for days. Her hair was wild and big, like a lion that had just competed for the role as king of the jungle.

"What about The Pink Lip Bandits?" Elysia asked as she looked at Willow from the window. "What about Choice and Craig?"

"I don't know."

"So, you just gon' let life pass you by. Huh? You want to rot in here?"

Willow looked at her; her face was naked and dry, and screamed for a facial. Her clothes were basic as the sweat pants and wife beater hugged her frame. She looked around at her condo; her first time seeing it since she had isolated herself from civilization. Her eyes widened at the mess it had become.

"You see?" Elysia asked. "Bitch, shake this shit off."

"Look at me." Willow saw herself from the reflection of the flat-screen television. "I'm atrocious."

"Go shower, change into something decent, and let's make our move."

"Our move?"

"You want Talvin?" She sat on the couch. "Let's get him."

"Why would you help me?"

"You're my sister." Elysia smiled. "Now, go shower and get ready."

Willow walked into the bathroom and let everything that she was feeling drain away with the water after softly hitting her skin. Feeling exhilarated, she got dressed and realized it was time to stop sitting around.

Willow couldn't help but to feel some kind of piece of her was gone. She wasn't used to not seeing Kail every day. They had been like conjoined twins constantly at each other's side through anything. She pushed the thought of her sister in the back of her mind while she walked back into the living room.

"You ready?" Elysia she stood up.

"I don't even have a plan," Willow admitted.

"I do," Elysia walked toward the door, "now, let's go."

Willow wasn't herself as they pulled into the parking lot of the hospital that brought so many bad memories in her mind. She didn't ask questions; she just let Elysia be the lead as they walked into the hospital and got onto an elevator.

"Where are we going?" Willow asked as the elevator jerked as it started going up.

"To go see Choice," she said.

"No, I'm good." Willow said as she hit the button pad on the elevator to try to make it go down.

"Look, we gon' need her," Elysia said as she hit Willow's hand. "It's only me and you now, so we gon' at least need her for all of the jobs that's at your house waiting to be worked."

Willow knew she was telling the truth as the doors to the elevator opened. She had looked over the requests from several clients, and all of the jobs required a three-person squad. She had to make things right with Choice because Kail was long gone.

Craig was coming out of the room as they approached the door. Craig and Willow immediately saw nothing in their path but each other. Willow felt as if it took her an hour to get to the door because his eyes were stuck on her like super glue. She waved with a sway of her hand as they stood face to face.

"I'll be inside." Elysia walked into Choice's room.

This is yo' girl's man, Willow kept thinking to herself as her heart did the two-step in her chest. She couldn't help but get weak at his presence. She was madly in love with him and as she smelled his alluring scent, it calmed her mind down. She wanted to run into his arms, but she couldn't.

He looked back at her, the same thing running through his mind. Willow was now the forbidden fruit. No matter how bad he wanted to bite it, he was going to have to resist temptation. He stole a peek at her body as they went into a weird hugging moment.

"Craig." Willow closed her eyes.

"Don't," he said as if he knew what she was going to say. "I understand and you don't owe me an explanation or anyone else."

"But, I'm—"

"It's cool," he said softly as he grabbed her hand. "I don't know how, but we have to stop this."

"I know." She took her own hand back after so willingly giving it to him. "I don't know how either."

"We have to figure it out." He kissed her forehead and left. "We have to."

Willow watched Craig get onto the elevator as she cried eternally. She felt sad knowing that she would never taste his lips again. She felt nervous at the thought of not ever being able to wake up to his face again. She felt like the last piece of her heart had just shattered and fallen to her stomach into the pit of acid that lay there.

She entered the room after a soft knock to alert them that she was coming in. It had been days, and she couldn't believe Choice was still in the hospital. She walked in the room as the television flashed pictures of old westerns. She could smell death, a familiar one that all hospitals reeked of.

"I can't even trust that bitch with my man," Choice was saying as Willow entered. "How am I going to trust her with my fucking life?"

"That shit with Craig is nipped in the bud," Willow said as she got deeper inside, making it possible for them to see her.

"You see?" Elysia walked over to Willow. "She ended that shit."

"It should have ended way before that." Choice crossed her arms.

Choice was on edge after losing her baby. She had to stay in the hospital because the amount of blood that she had lost was more than a normal miscarriage. She had caught an infection during the transport from Craig's apartment to the hospital, and once it was cleared out of her system, she could leave. She had been getting poked with needles for days and she was highly frustrated.

"Choice, it's over with," Willow said honestly.

"I don't like second chances." Choice rose. "Giving someone a second chance is like giving them an extra bullet for their gun because they missed you the first time."

"Trust me." Willow walked closer. "I have enough bullets and none of them are for you. I just need to get back to the money, Choice. I don't give a fuck if we kick it or not. It could be strictly business. Just be real enough to have my back and I'll do the same."

Choice thought hard. "I'll think about it," she finally said but rolled her eyes. "Did you get that nigga Talvin yet?"

"No, I'm about to work on that now." Willow grabbed the keys from Elysia's hand. "I'll be back in thirty."

The smell of fresh orange peels and pencil shavings welcomed Willow as she walked into the private school on the outskirts of town. She walked into the front office as her heels made music on the soft granite with each step that she took. She rang the little bell on top of the counter for assistance as she stood straight up waiting to be helped.

"May I help you?" the administrative assistant asked as she came from a side room.

"I'm here to pick up my stepson." Willow pointed at the clock on the wall. "He has a doctor's appointment in an hour and I wanted to get him there a little early."

"May I have his name?" she asked as she walked to the counter.

"Tyron Wilson," Willow answered with a grin.

"Are you on the list that can pick him up?" the assistant asked.

"I sure am." Willow handed her identification.

"Thank you so much for that," she said as she handed Willow back her driver's license. "I'll be right back with him."

Willow walked outside of the office knowing that Talvin's only weakness was his son. He had fallen off the face of the earth and no one had heard from him. If she had his son, she would have him where she wanted him. He would crawl out of whatever Rock he was hiding under and meet her anywhere she wanted.

Willow stood outside of the glass office as she watched the woman walk through the doors to the main entrance of the classrooms. She saw her return with Tyron running toward Willow with open arms. Willow bent down to grab him and picked him up. She squeezed him tight as she gave him a kiss on his forehead.

"Willow, Willow, Willow," Tyron repeated as he smiled.

"Tyron, Tyron, Tyron," Willow said, copying him. "Let's go, kiddo."

After walking outside to the car, Willow put Tyron in the backseat and closed the door. She got in the driver's seat, started the car and drove off as she dialed a number on her cell phone. She promised herself that she wouldn't hurt Tyron; no matter how it ended. Even if she became desperate for revenge, she wouldn't let it consume her enough to hurt a child.

"You got some nerve calling me, bitch," Talvin said as he answered the phone.

"Say hi to Daddy." Willow leaned in the backseat while at a stoplight, then put the phone up to Tyron's ear.

"Hi, Daddy," Tyron said with a smile. Willow put the phone back to her ear.

"So, now can you take some of the bass out of your voice?" Willow asked as she turned and pulled into an arcade.

"I'll kill you."

"Before or after I kill him?" she whispered softly enough so Tyron couldn't hear.

"Before," Talvin said loudly. "You've changed everything now, Willow."

"Meet me at the warehouse."

"The one where you had somebody steal my dough?"

"Yes, that one," Willow said as she pulled the phone away from her ear and held it to her mouth. "I'll be there sometime today, so make sure you're there."

"Don't hurt my son," Talvin said before Willow pressed the end button.

"You want to go play some games?" Willow asked Tyron as she pointed to the arcade.

He nodded, unaware that he was being held hostage, and that's exactly how Willow wanted it. She planned to tire him out, pick up Elysia, and continue her mission.

Twenty-six

K ail walked down the beaten path, the night air whipping her hair as if she were in a photo shoot. Her legs moved a little faster once she heard the humming sound of the neon lights from afar. She entered the empty building with one objective on her mind.

She eased down the walkway, never letting her guard down; her hand always on her pistol that was hidden on her. She hadn't been in Sweet Lips since the day she and Willow had reconnected with Choice, and surely the owner wouldn't have wanted to see her again after putting a red dot on her.

She sat at a table, placing her gun down on a coaster before she pulled out a freshly rolled blunt and lit it. She knew they were there and she was aware they could see her. She sat puffing, letting the extensive feeling from the marijuana give her patience. The last thing she wanted to do was grow impatient and start shooting to make someone appear.

"I'm glad that you could come," Vinny said as he appeared through a door with Evelyn at his side.

Kail looked at her; immediately recognizing her from the day she had put the scope on her. Evelyn stared at her, their eyes paying attention to nothing but each other. The tension was so thick in the room it could choke them by draining every ounce of oxygen from their lungs.

"I don't think we've been properly introduced," Evelyn said as she and Vinny took a seat at Kail's table. "I'm Evelyn, your father's wife."

"My sperm donor," Kail said as she tossed the blunt, which was at its end, on the floor before putting it out with her heel. "No need for labels. I'm here, so what's up?"

"What's up is that my Poppa," Evelyn looked at Vinny, "paid you a hefty amount to make Rock disappear."

"I can't get close to him with Junior around," Kail defended.

"Excuses are like assholes," Vinny pointed at her, "everybody fuckin' got one."

"That's true," Kail shrugged her shoulders, "but, everyone's asshole isn't as pretty as mine. Now, we can talk business, figure out how to take over this city, and become bosses, or we can talk about what I didn't do and waste time."

"I agree." Evelyn crossed her legs and leaned back. "Willow," she said softly.

"What about her?" Kail asked. She, too, crossed her legs as they shined under the mercury lights.

"What if she needs to be disposed of?" Vinny interrupted.

"That could happen," Kail said with a grin. "I'm not opposed to the idea at all."

"You mean you could kill your sister?" Evelyn asked out of curiosity.

"Wouldn't you if you had to?" Kail picked up her gun that was on the table and pointed it toward Vinny. "You're no saint when it comes to siblings. You think I don't know what happened to Uncle Gino?"

"I never said I was." Vinny grinned. "I'm a businessman and that means that sometimes family is expendable."

"Agreed," Kail said.

"You remember that job I gave you with Detective Hall?" Vinny asked as Kail batted her long eyelashes, saying yes with them. "Well, on that tape is something that will bury Rock under the jail. The problem is your sister and your brother. Neither one of them will sit back and not do anything. Get them to leave town or kill them."

Kail sat there as she remembered she and Willow as little girls running across the shoreline. Back then, she never thought it would come to this. It was them against the world. But as they matured, she always figured she would have to repeat history and kill her sister like Mahina had done her mother.

She sat there for a moment, pondering on if she could actually go into it with the frame of mind to kill Willow. She didn't want to, but it wasn't about that; she had to. She locked that inside of her head as she thought about what power she could have in Philly with all of them out of the way.

"I'm in." Kail stood up. "I'll be in touch," she said before she left.

"Do you think she could do it?" Evelyn looked at her Poppa.

"She's a beast, a savage." Vinny stood up without a doubt in his head. "She is about money. She would commit suicide if offered enough money."

"Do we really want somebody like that around, especially in our circle?"

"Don't worry," he said while walking to the bar. "People like that always self-destruct. Give it some time and she will go boom all on her own."

It was a beautiful sight; the house was built nicely with a Victorian edge to it. Under the sun, it beamed a deep blue, with pale ivory running along the edges outlining the house. In general, it gave a feeling of calmness to all who passed by. But Willow wasn't passing; she and Elysia were watching it in hopes of seeing Talvin, so they could make their move.

It had two floors total; windows popped out of every direction, but didn't amazingly make it look overrun with windows. Indentations of small figures were carved into a line outside the attic window. In all truth, the house reminded Willow of the mansions the South used to have before the Civil War.

"Is he here?" Elysia asked.

"I don't know." Willow fixed herself in her seat. "But, he knows we have his son." Willow looked in the backseat at the sleeping boy.

"You think he would show up here before he is supposed to meet you?"

"I hope so," Willow said.

They sat there for another hour in vain. Countless cars passed, but none of them were Talvin's. Tired of waiting, she started the car and just when she was about to pull off, the door to the house opened wide.

"Is that Junior?" Elysia asked as she got closer to the dashboard in hopes of confirming who she saw.

"What the fuck is he doing here?" Willow asked.

"Yo, who is that?" Elysia asked, referring to the chick on his arm.

"Talvin's sister." Willow shook her head. "They came to my house to tell me that Duke had died. She's the chick who was with Junior that day."

"You never met her while you went to them family functions with him?"

"No, but, he always said he had a sister. But, she was never around."

Willow sped by without them seeing her. She eased through the red light and never looked back. The situation she was in was getting stickier than a piece of gum that had sat in a mouth overnight. She knew that this thing with Talvin would be a domino effect; when she killed him, it would involve other people's lives and not just her own. She was ready for the consequences from her actions.

he old dilapidated warehouse encased Talvin as he stepped onto the cracked linoleum. The distinctive odor of rats and rusty nails filled the room as Talvin stepped, ever so cautiously, to the other end, where he saw an elevator. When he was at the elevator, he saw the two floors that he would be traveling up. He saw nothing of importance on them, but he received an eerie feeling from looking at them; a shudder and a chill that went from his feet up to his head. He turned around and pressed the barely intact button to call for the elevator.

As soon as he stepped into the elevator, he knew that he shouldn't have agreed to meet Willow there. However, he was going to go through with it. He saw a mahogany handrail that was ripped out at one end, and the doors were covered in rust. The tile he stood on was the color of the night sky, but Talvin didn't look down too long to care. He looked at the four buttons that were next to the dented and rusted metal door. *B, 1, 2, 3.* He pressed *3* and waited for the elevator to start. He saw the up arrow flash red and when the door stopped and opened, his eyes met Willow's.

"You remember this place?" Willow walked up on him, her gun out in front of her, pointing at him.

"I do." He stepped off of the elevator; his eyes searching for his son. "Where's my shorty?"

"Somewhere safe." She looked at him. "This conversation is for grown folks."

"Willow, do you know what you doing?" he asked as a rat crawled past his foot.

"I'm ending this relationship permanently."

"I loved you."

"I never said that you didn't, Talvin," Willow said as she got within arm's reach of him. "The problem is I don't love you."

"Yes you do," Talvin looked at her. "You just can't admit it to yourself."

Willow stood there as her lungs went into overdrive. There was some truth to what he was saying. She couldn't deny it, no matter what words came out of her mouth. She cared for him and the way her heart still fluttered in his presence, she couldn't deny it.

"You're right," Willow said as her heart grew heavy. "But, Talvin, you can't just do what you want when you want. You took something from me."

"But, I replaced it." He walked up on her. "I replaced it with me."

"That's not good enough for me. You think I don't know that you and Evelyn are in cahoots. If I don't kill you and her, I will never have a normal life. I will always be looking over my fucking shoulders." A tear fell from her eye. "No," she screamed. "I do enough of that with the kind of work that I do."

"I don't care about Evelyn like I care about you."

"You don't get it." Willow pressed the gun against his heart. "It's not about who you love more or less. It's about me."

"Let me take care of you."

"Talvin, you can't even take care of yourself. I'm all I got at the end of the day."

Talvin grabbed her hand as he pressed the gun against his chest harder, leaving a mark that could be seen if he were shirtless. His eyes swam inside of hers as he waited to be drowned by his fate. He could see the hurt inside of her caused by him. His mind was open to his end by the woman that he loved.

"Do it," Talvin said as he closed his eyes. "I have no regrets."

"That's unfortunate." Willow pulled the trigger. "I have tons."

Talvin's eyes bulged out of his head as the pieces of fragment exploded through his chest wall. He leaned into Willow, his eyes never leaving hers. The smell of the perfume she always wore helped him leave this world and enter the next, and before his body hit the weak boards lining the floor, he was dead.

"Damn, Talvin," Willow said as tears started rolling down her face. "Why did you make me do this?"

She leaned down and kissed him on the lips, staining his lips with her pink essence. She went to the elevator; her heart weeping more and more with each floor she went down. She left out of the building, tossing the gun she had just used into the creek on the side. The gun started to flow with the water into the darkness that was the middle of nowhere as a piece of her heart went with it.

She walked back to her car praying that Talvin's son would be asleep. She opened the door, stepped in slowly and laid her head on the steering wheel. She started crying hysterically. There were tears of joy, pain, and sorrow. She couldn't hold it in; she had to let it out.

"You okay?" Elysia put her hand on her back.

"No, I'm not okay, Elysia," she said, leaving her head on the steering wheel. "Should I call an ambulance or something?" she asked, letting her heart cloud her judgment.

"No, let Rock clean everything up." She pulled out her cell phone.

Willow opened up the door to the car and threw up. She wiped her mouth off and drove off as the expression on Talvin's lifeless body tattooed her brain.

"He said he's going to get someone to clean it up." Elysia looked at her. "It's okay, Willow; it had to be done."

She nodded her head and gave her a little smile while tears still accompanied her face. She cut the music off and tried to enjoy the ride. She couldn't help but keep her eyes on Tyron through the rearview mirror while driving. He didn't realize it, but because of her, he would never be raised by his father. Someone had put her through the same pain, and she empathized for the way that he would feel one day.

Willow drove in silence as she dropped Talvin's son off at the porch of his home and Elysia back at her house. She wanted to pay Evelyn a visit to see if she couldn't get some understanding from her. She had a bullet in the chamber with her name on it, and hand-delivering it was the only way she knew how to give it to her.

Evelyn's feet swished in the warm water as the Chinese woman massaged them. She soaked her feet, exfoliated them with a pumice cream, scrubbed off the dead skin and dry spots with a foot file, and then she filled her nails with a clear coat.

Unaware of her surroundings from the sliced and peeled cucumbers on her eyes, Evelyn never paid attention to the little sound of the bell that hung on the top of the door, alerting everyone that someone had entered the salon.

"Do you have an appointment?" the clerk asked.

"No." Willow spotted Evelyn. "I'm a walk-in."

"Right this way." The clerk showed her to the seat next to Evelyn. Willow looked at her as she relaxed, her hair overlapping the back of the massaging chair that she sat in. The clock on the wall whistled with each flicker of the hand. The smell of acrylic filled the air as the water in the tub at Willow's feet started to bubble.

"You know," Willow said, alarming Evelyn of her presence, "I've never had one of these mother-daughter spa days before."

"That's sad." Evelyn removed the cucumbers from her eyes. "Me and Melee came here once a week, sometimes twice a week depending on our moods."

Willow put her feet into the water as her heels stood straight up next to her chair. Another Chinese woman started massaging her feet as she pressed the button on the chair to level one, letting the vibrations work out some of the tension in her spine.

"I never had that chance with my mother."

"I'll never have that again with my daughter." Evelyn leaned up. "So, we're even."

"We are far from even, Evelyn." Willow reached over and put her hand on her thigh. "I still owe you one."

"So, you came all of this way to threaten me knowing that you can't touch me in a place of business. You may be bold, my dear, but you're not dumb. You know you can't do anything in a place like this." Evelyn put the cucumbers back onto her eyes and lay back.

The sound of the bullets hitting the ceiling made Evelyn's body rock. Her face immediately grew red from fear as the workers ran for their lives. Willow held the ice-cold gun in her hands. Evelyn jolted up as her heart sat next to her tonsils, making it hard for her to speak.

"Sit back down," Willow instructed. Pieces of the ceiling fell down into the water at her feet.

Evelyn obliged as the blood in her veins went away, leaving her body numb and cold. Her eyes followed Willow's gun as she sat back in the chair in shock at Willow releasing fire in a business. She had misjudged her and she hoped it didn't cost her her life.

"I have a few minutes until the cops arrive." Willow pointed to the cucumber slices sitting on a table inside of a bowl next to Evelyn. "Get back comfortable; put those back on your eyes."

"I'd rather not." Evelyn inhaled.

"I think you better because I'm not asking you again."

Evelyn was hesitant, but she grabbed two fresh slices of cucumber. She could smell their natural oils mix in with the smell of the soap bubbling at her feet. She placed the cucumbers on her eyes and leaned back as she was told.

"I'm not going to kill you here." Willow grabbed a towel to dry her feet off. "But, I am going to kill you. That is a promise."

"Why not here and now?" Evelyn asked out of curiosity.

"Because, the Bible says death comes like a thief in the night." Willow put on her heels. "I want you to be unaware of it all."

"Who's to say I won't kill you first."

"That's a possibility," Willow said as the sounds of sirens filled her ears. "But, I highly doubt that. I'm going to let you get back to your spa day. I hope I didn't ruin it."

She heard the noise. Faint at first, but then, as it got closer, Willow heard the deafening screech. She covered her ears from the pounding as she fled out the back of the building. If she had to compare it to something, she'd compare it to an animal, crying out in death.

Evelyn jumped up at the sound of feet running into the building. The first thing her eyes saw were police uniforms when she removed the cucumbers. Guns were pointed at her while officers asked her to get on the floor. She looked around as she kneeled, trying to find Willow, but she was long gone.

"Not she," a Chinese woman said as she entered the building, "it was anoda one."

Evelyn got off the ground as the cops helped her. She yanked away, grabbing her purse as she headed for the door. Refusing to talk, she left out of the building; the sun shining on her as she removed the sunglasses from her purse and placed them on her eyes.

She hit the alarm to her car and got in as the sounds of ambulances and fire trucks grew nearer. She started her car and pulled out in front of oncoming traffic. She felt like somebody was watching her as she stopped at a light. She could feel their eyes looking at her, piercing through her being. Willow would keep her promise; she just didn't know when or where.

Twenty-eight

"One, two, three." A man with a navy blue jacket with *DEA* in gold letters on the back of it screamed as he banged the battering ram against the door.

A group of men rushed in with all-black attire as their guns pointed at anything suspicious. They worked their way inside the estate as some went into the bottom level of the house and others rushed up the stairs.

Detective Hall stood at the front door and smiled. She had finally received enough evidence to take down the notorious leader of the mafia, Rock Evans, and today was like Christmas for her. She eased up the stairs as the badge hanging on her belt loop shined under the lights.

"Get the fuck down," a cop screamed as Detective Hall entered the room.

"Ernest Rock Evans." She walked over to where he was lying face-down. "I dare you to make the wrong move because I'll put a bullet right through your head."

"Sandy, it's nice to see you." Rock looked up at his old friend.

"It's Detective Hall to you now, Rock," she said, putting her knee in his back.

"Isn't this police brutality or some shit?" he asked while never showing signs of discomfort.

"No, brutality is your organization." She pushed her knee deeper into his back. "I knew it would be a matter of time before you slipped up."

"There's no banana peels at my feet, baby," Rock said as the cops pinning him down stood him up.

"I see one right there." Detective Hall pointed a few steps in front of him and got close to his ear. "You're not as put together as you may think. I have a voice that ten of the best analysts in this state can match to yours on the tape that we have," she said, referring to the delivery Kail made to her.

"That's interesting," Rock said as they pulled him away. "It was a pleasure seeing you again, Sandy."

"Arrogant bastard," she yelled as she kicked his desk. "Take everything that may be incriminating. Look for everything the tip gave us."

Detective Hall tore the room apart as she remembered her and Rock from back in the day. She couldn't believe how they had gone down two different paths. It pained her to have to lock up her old friend, but as she smashed through the desk drawers, she found comfort in knowing that now, he would be off the streets and safe.

Willow walked into her condo as darkness hit her eyes. Shadows seemed to swirl around at her feet, sucking her in. In a burst of panic, she fumbled for a light switch. She flipped it up and down frantically, but the room remained immersed in darkness.

Fear settled in and deep down, she knew she was not alone in the dark. Something brushed her back. She turned, but there was nothing. Nothing she could see, that is. The room was dark, so dark. She made sure her eyes were open, fearing she had gone blind.

She couldn't see her hand, even though it was literally an inch from her face. She gathered her courage to call out a hello, hoping against hope that someone would answer as she removed her gun from her waist and pointed it wildly in the air. Nobody did.

Outside she could hear the autumn wind howling, and it almost sounded like laughter to her panicked mind. A low chuckle broke her thought process, directly in front of her. She screamed, but heard nothing in the overwhelming blackness.

The lights flickered, then came back on as Willow eyed around. Her eyes stopped when she noticed Kail sitting on the ottoman that went with the imported living room set. Her heart slowed down a little, just a little, as she remembered what her sister was capable of.

Kail smiled as the lipstick on her lips, as red as the blood pumping through her veins, shined with the light that hung directly in the middle of the room. Her all-black attire, skin-tight jeans, a tank top, and heels, hugged her as if they were painted on. Her hair hung forward over her breasts, and her hand, with a gun closed inside of it, rested at her mouth.

"What are you doing here?" Willow asked as she took a step forward.

"Visiting." Kail stood up. "I'm here on business, sis."

"We don't have any kind of business to talk about." Willow pointed her gun at Kail. "This looks like a job to me."

"It is," Kail said as she pointed her gun at Willow.

Willow felt like she could pick up a building and break it over her knee as the adrenaline rushing through her intensified. She moved around behind the counter in the kitchen fearing shots would be fired. Her face was serious and her hands were steady as Kail looked at her with empty eyes.

"Just leave, Kail," Willow begged.

"I was going to tell you the same thing." Kail pointed toward the front door that had luggage leaning near it. "I've already packed your bags for you. There's a first-class ticket to Hawaii inside. Take those bags and go, Willow. I won't ask you again."

"What happened to you?"

"I'm trying to spare you and give you a way out. Take it," Kail screamed.

"I'm not leaving, Kail," Willow said and then snarled.

"Don't make me kill you, Willow." Kail's lips trembled. "Please, Willow, I'm begging you. I honestly don't want to hurt you, but I will. Don't make me do this."

"You've been my sister all my life," Willow said as her eyes closed a little from the water forming inside of them. "I don't know life without you. We've been through everything together Kail, and you trying to end it for what? For money and power?"

"I guess you're about to find out what life is like without me." Kail pulled the trigger and opened fire.

Willow released the contents of her gun as the sound of glass breaking and bullets hitting different objects filled the air. The sound of a bond breaking could be heard from a mile away as they ducked and covered and released a bullet when the opportunity presented itself. To anyone who was passing, they would have sworn they were at the bridge watching the once-in-a-year fireworks show that the city put on in July.

Willow heard the bullets stop flying from Kail as she counted how many shots she heard. She knew Kail was reloading her gun, so she took the opening and fled for the door. Bullets chased after her as she dodged down the hallway, her heels turned sideways on her feet from how fast she was running.

She headed down the stairs, skipping a couple as she held the rail. She burst through the entrance of the building as she ran into traffic, stopping cars from their destinations. Honks from both sides of the road warned her to get out of the street, and drivers hung their heads out of the window cursing her out.

She made it to her car, getting inside as she checked behind her to make sure Kail wasn't following close behind. She put her hand underneath the seat, breaking three of her five manicured fingernails to find her spare key. She started the car and drove off, running over any curb in her path.

Willow felt like she was trapped alone in the darkest abyss with a sword pierced through her heart. Her broken heart was silent; it couldn't be seen, but she bled inside. It was still and for a moment, she only felt numbness. Anger and sadness surged through her with so much power, she knew what she had to do. Her heart stopped beating, for it had only beaten for her. Her mind went black, as did her heart.

Her hands tightened around the wheel, and her fingers dug into her palms until she felt them bleed from her kung fu grip. But this pain was nothing compared to how she felt thinking about the relationship she and Kail had once had. She stopped at a light as she felt lost, not knowing which way to go.

"You look as pretty as always, Willow," a voice that sounded so familiar bellowed out from the backseat of the car.

Willow looked through the rearview mirror as the light turned green. Her eyes grew to the size of golf balls, and she pulled over on the side of the road. She didn't understand, as if her brain short-circuited and needed to be rebooted. Around her, everything was in fast-forward while she was motionless in the middle of it all. *How could this happen*, she thought to herself as she tried to collect her thoughts.

She pressed the heels of her hands into her eyes until she saw nothing but sparkle. She tried to turn around, but it was more like a stumble and fall that left her in a trembling heap in the driver's seat.

"Duke, is that really you?" Her lips started to tremble. "I thought you were dead," she whimpered.

"It's really me, shorty." He leaned in the front seat and placed a towel over her nose from behind. "Go to sleep, and when you wake up, I'll explain everything."

Willow looked around the car, and everything was suddenly fading to gray. Her heart sped up so fast, it almost hurt. She slowly tried moving around, but she couldn't. She felt like a ribbon slowly falling to the ground. She didn't feel a hit; it felt like falling in a black hole, and all she saw was darkness.

About the Author

Andre D. Jones, a Texas native, is an up-and-coming author with stories as blazing as the heat his state is known for. Penning tales in an incomparable manner, he tends to leave the mind stimulated once his work has been read in its entirety. With a love and passion so strong for writing, Andre writes as much as he can, anywhere he can, on anything that he can. Juggling being a full-time student with a major in English and working full time, he is busy working on his next novel in his small hometown of Waco, TX.

BY S.K. COLLINS
AVAILABLE FROM STREBOR BOOKS

CHAPTER ONE

Early Spring 2004

"Damn! I can't be late for work again!" Zeek cried as he slammed the door behind him and sped off down the street. He had only two minutes to catch the 8:35 a.m. bus, so he ran desperately to the bus stop. His heart raced as he broke out into a heavy sweat, praying he would reach his destination in time. His red Staples shirt blew in the wind as he forced himself to run faster knowing his job was on the line. He made a sharp left and took a shortcut through a vacant park. He knew taking the detour would give him the best chance at making the bus. He tucked the back of his shirt in so he wouldn't get it snagged on the fence he had to get over. He jumped the fence, but he somehow managed to bang his knee on one of the raised rusted posts. He ignored the pain and rushed and made it to the corner.

Zeek's pupils enlarged as his eyes zoomed in on the last passenger stepping onto the bus. He knew he only had seconds to make it there before the bus pulled off. "Hold the bus, please! Miss, can you please hold the bus?" he yelled as he ran desperately.

The woman rolled her eyes and let the doors close behind her. "Yo, driver! Hold the bus!" He immediately started to wave his hands in the air, hoping to obtain the driver's attention.

Unfortunately, the driver never checked his rearview mirror, so the bus proceeded to pull off, leaving Zeek utterly down and out. While holding his knees in an attempt to catch his breath, Zeek hopelessly yelled, "Aww, come on, man! Come on! Damn…I know you seen me… How the hell could he not see me?"

Now with the bus gone, he had to think fast. He knew he could either wait for another bus or run another twenty blocks to Brookline Metro Station and catch a train. Right then a bus that ran a different route pulled up in front of him. He knew it wouldn't take him to his job, but he would be close, at least in running distance. Without a second thought, he ran up the steps and sat as close to the front as possible. He wiped his clammy hands off on his shirt as he thought about being late.

"I hope there ain't no traffic," he said nervously to himself as the bus pulled off.

The twenty-minute ride into town felt more like hours as Zeek sighed heavily. Before the doors of the bus were fully open, he squeezed out of the tight space and took off running. He dodged and weaved through crowds of people who were on their way to work as well.

"Sorry!" he yelled as he ran out in front of a taxi as the driver smashed down on his horn in anger.

He checked the time on his phone and became even more nervous as Staples was now only a short distance away. *What the hell am I going to say this time?* he thought hopelessly. He'd pretty much run out of excuses for being late.

Zeek quickly entered the store and tensely peered around for his manager. "He must be in the back." He sighed in relief as he headed for his register.

His co-worker, Tara, was finishing up with a customer when she looked up and saw Zeek trying to creep in. She shook her head and waited for the customer to be out of earshot before she spoke. "Boy, why you late again? You know Dan gonna go off on you, right?"

"Dan can kiss my ass," he said in a hushed tone as he tried to clock into the register.

"If he can kiss ya ass, then why you whisperin'?" she said after sucking her teeth.

"I ain't whisperin' shit. Dan's tight shirt-wearin' ass know what it is. Fuck...why can't I clock in?"

"Boy, you always be fakin'. You are such a bama." Tara quickly cut her eyes to the back of the store and happened to see Dan making his way to the front. She smiled and looked back over at Zeek. "Here come Dan. Let's see you talk that shit now."

Zeek's eyes widened as Dan made his way over to his register. Dan's yellow, overly round frame walked tall in his snug-fitting shirt as he had Zeek in his focus. Zeek's lips started to quiver as he thought about what excuse to use. All he could do was tap his shaky fingers on the cash register keys as Dan moved closer.

Zeek swallowed hard and said the first thing that came to his mind. "Hey, what's up, Dan? I've been trying to clock in for the longest time, but it's not working. Is there a problem with the system?"

"Nope. Ain't no problem with the system. The problem is you," Dan said as he stared at Zeek with his hands placed firmly on his hips.

Zeek swallowed hard as the realization of what was happening started to set in.

"I decided to let you go."

"Come on, Dan. I need this job. Just give me another chance." Zeek begged.

"I'm sorry, Zeek, but you brought this on yourself. I can't give you any more chances," Dan said, standing his ground.

Zeek knew Dan was overly tired of his call-offs and late-to-work routine. It was clear to him after being late this morning that it was his fault that he was fired. He looked over at Tara and became even more embarrassed after he saw that she had been laughing at him. With nothing else to be said, Zeek lowered his head and slowly walked toward the door. He looked back at Dan one last time to see if there was any slight chance he could salvage his job, but Dan had already walked off. He shook his head in disappointment that he had to move on.

Zeek forcefully pushed through the doors and started to walk fast down the busy street. He tightened his lips and balled up his fists as he thought about what had happened. "Damn, I shouldn't have been late! I can't do shit right!" He cursed himself after failing to try to be more responsible.

He'd intended to stretch his twenty-first birthday weekend until the crack of dawn and still get up for work on time. He had hoped this morning would have been the start of a more mature Ezeekiel Harris, but yet again, he was dead wrong. "What the fuck am I going to do now?" Zeek said as he wiped his eyes.

His mind was racing a mile a minute and he couldn't help but feel worthless. He headed back to the bus stop and looked enviously at everyone who drove past him. The summer hadn't even begun and with the money he would've made working, his mind was set on buying a car in September. Now losing his job had ruined his plan. Zeek needed to come up with another way to get a car, but for now, he wanted to go home and sulk in his sorrow.

Once the bus arrived, Zeek stepped up on the bus and took the first available window seat. He still couldn't believe he'd been fired. He shook off the thought as his eyes started to water again.

"Damn, I'm such an asshole," he said as he thumped his head against the glass.

He peered dejectedly out of the window as the bus left downtown and headed back to his neighborhood. His surroundings altered drastically as the business buildings turned into rundown row houses, and the professional working class shifted to corner boys and drug addicts. Zeek shook his head as the U.S. Capitol came into view. The immaculate structure represented a country that attracted millions of tourists from around the world. It also symbolized the power and security that every country respected.

Damn, there's such a thin line between wealth and poverty. I gotta find a way to get in between, Zeek thought as the bus moved deeper into the hood.

Zeek arrived back at his house but didn't bother to go in. He sat down on the porch steps and tried to clear his head. He was so distressed from losing his job that he didn't want to make it worse by sitting in an empty house. All Zeek's friends were at work so it made him feel even worse about being unemployed again. Zeek decided to call his girlfriend and tell her the bad news. He knew she would understand. Zeek needed someone to talk to, someone who could console him.

Zeek pulled out his cell phone and was about to dial her number until he saw his best friend, Lonzo, walking toward him. Zeek forgot Lonzo went to work around this time of morning, and was caught off-guard as Lonzo quickly approached. He pushed his phone back into his pocket and decided to wait until Lonzo was gone before he called his girlfriend. *I can't let him know that we're back together yet*, Zeek said to himself as Lonzo crossed the street.

"Zeek, what are you doin' here, man?" Lonzo asked as he approached the walkway.

"Young, I got fired," Zeek said, giving him a defeated look.

"What you get fired for?" Lonzo asked with slight irritation in his voice.

Zeek started to shake his head out of disappointment as he waited for the words to leave his mouth. "I was late for work again. I missed the damn bus. I tried to hurry up and clock in, but fat ass Dan caught me. I was only like five minutes late. I don't think he should have fired me over that, though."

Lonzo shook his head in amazement that Zeek didn't see his job termination coming. "Come on, Slim. You know you was fakin' wit' that job. You were always late or not showin' up. People see that as being irresponsible."

Zeek knew what Lonzo had said was right, and that was his whole reason for wanting to make a change. Zeek wished he could be more like Lonzo; he always had it together. He'd had the same job for over five years and never missed work. Even though Lonzo had been Zeek's best friend, they were totally different when it came to their work ethic. Zeek could have easily admitted he deserved what he got, but he didn't.

"I ain't sweatin' it," he said, shrugging his shoulders. "I can always get another job. That place wasn't for me anyway," he assured Lonzo.

"Man, you know how hard it is to find a job right now? It took you months to get the one you had."

"True, but what 'bout ya spot? Ain't they hirin'?" he asked curiously.

"Yeah they hirin', but I'm not tellin' them about yo' ass. You ain't gonna have me lookin' bad. Shit…you need to see if you can get your job back at the copy center."

"Come on, man. I knew you since kindergarten and you won't stick ya neck out for me?" Zeek asked as he held his arms out wide, completely stunned by Lonzo's disposition.

"Nope. The way you carried every job in the past gives me enough reason not to. So if I was you, I'd try to get back in that rental office you used to work for."

Even though Zeek badly needed a job, he knew for certain that going back to the rental office wasn't an option. "Naw, I'm good off that. There was nothin' but bamas in that place. Those people got on my damn nerves."

"Well, any job beats sittin' on this hot-ass porch for the summer. If I was you, I'd get off my ass and make it happen. Ya dig?" Lonzo rebutted.

Instead of Zeek taking heed to what his boy was saying, he decided to blow him off. "Yeah, whatever," Zeek said as he waved Lonzo off and looked away.

"Maybe you should look into doing some modeling or acting. You already got the body for it and the ladies think you're cute. Shit, if anything, you can at least be able to work with beautiful-ass women. What man wouldn't want that perk?"

Zeek did have that butter-brown skin and muscular physique that the ladies appreciated. His only drawback was that he never had any money.

Zeek looked up at Lonzo and shook his head. "Me be a model? Man, that's the dumbest shit you ever came up with."

"Yeah, whatever," Lonzo said as he checked his watch. "I'll get up wit' you later. I got to get to work before I'm late my damn self."

Lonzo gave him dap and made his way down the street, while Zeek stayed on the porch with plenty to think about. Zeek then bent over, placed his hands on his face, and sighed. "What the hell am I going to do?"

Printed in the United States
By Bookmasters